KEEP

C000178668

THERESA TALL
freelance producer. A former radio news editor,
she also hosted The Beechgrove Potting Shed on
BBC Radio Scotland, but for many she will be
most familiar as the voice of the station's Traffic
& Travel. Late 2014 saw the publication of her
first book, *This Is What I Look Like*, a
humorous memoir covering everything from
working with Andy Williams to rescuing chickens
and discovering nuns hidden in gardens. She's
much in demand at book festivals, both as an
author and as a chairperson.

KEEP HER SILENT

Theresa Talbot

First published in the United Kingdom in 2018 by Aria, an imprint of
Head of Zeus Ltd

Copyright © Theresa Talbot, 2018

The moral right of Theresa Talbot to be identified as the author of this
work has been asserted in accordance with the Copyright, Designs and
Patents Act of 1988.

All rights reserved. No part of this publication may be reproduced,
stored in a retrieval system, or transmitted, in any form or by any
means, electronic, mechanical, photocopying, recording, or otherwise,
without the prior permission of both the copyright owner and the
above publisher of this book.

This is a work of fiction. All characters, organizations, and events
portrayed in this novel are either products of the author's imagination
or are used fictitiously.

9 7 5 3 1 2 4 6 8

A CIP catalogue record for this book is available from the British
Library.

ISBN 9781788545334

Aria
an imprint of Head of Zeus
First Floor East
5–8 Hardwick Street
London EC1R 4RG

Also by Theresa Talbot

The Lost Children

About *Keep Her Silent*

'Do that which is good and no evil shall touch you'

That was the note the so-called Raphael killer left on each of his victims. Everyone in Glasgow – investigative journalist Oonagh O'Neil included – remember the murder of three women in Glasgow which sent a wave of terror through the city. They also remember that he is still at large...

When the police investigation into the Raphael killings reopens, Oonagh is given a tip off that leads her straight to the heart of a complex and deadly cover-up. When history starts to repeat itself, it seems the killer is closer than she thinks. Could Oonagh be the next target...?

For Bruce Norval, and all those fighting for
justice

Prologue

Cartland 1975

There was no colour in this place. The white walls bled into themselves and the ceiling met the floor, suffocating Dorothy trapped in between. She ran her finger along the side of the bed, picking off the white paint from the metal frame, letting the sharp flecks embed themselves under her fingernails, enjoying seeing the blood-red bruise spider outwards.

At first she'd tried to keep the date in her head by the numbers of days that had passed, counting them out by the daylight shining through the tiny opaque window behind the metal grid. But she had no way of knowing how long she'd been awake – or how long she had slept – and like the white walls the days and nights bled into themselves and became just one long stretch in purgatory.

The small metal shutter on the door slid open, and Dorothy felt the now familiar sickness rise in her stomach. A fat face filled the hole.

See that mad cow that chopped up her husband? That crazy bitch that drowned her own wean. That was what they said outside her door when they thought she couldn't hear. Or maybe they knew she could hear and that was why they said it.

'Oi, you awake?'

Dorothy lifted her eyes to the door but didn't answer. 'Oi. Are you fucking deef or what? I asked if you were awake.' She still didn't answer and Fat-face opened the door.

'Watch her – she's bloody mental.'

A woman shot Fat-face a look. 'Please close the door and leave us alone, will you?' She walked over to Dorothy. 'May I?' She gestured to the empty stool. It seemed like a long time since anyone had been nice to her. Offered her the common courtesies afforded to decent folk.

'I'm Dr Skelton. Can I speak with you for a few moments?'

Dorothy nodded her head and Dr Skelton sat down. Dorothy took in her good leather shoes and dark tan nylons. She wasn't wearing any jewellery, but her nails were perfect little pink shells. Underneath her white coat she wore a dark camel skirt and cream sweater. Dorothy longed for her own things. Her own jewellery. Her wardrobe full of expensive clothes.

'Dorothy, do you know why I'm here?'

She shook her head.

'Dorothy—' she used her name at the beginning of each sentence as though Dorothy would forget who she was otherwise '—we're trying to work out why you did what you did.' Dorothy shot her a blank look. 'You know your husband and son are dead, Dorothy, don't you?'

Dorothy didn't answer. Instead she glanced at the hemline of Dr Skelton's skirt. 'Is that Italian?'

A hint of confusion worried her forehead before she answered, 'Oh, the skirt? Well, yes, it is, but that's not what I'm here to discuss.' She smoothed her skirt over her knees and continued. 'Dorothy, why did you try to cut out Andrew's heart and wrap it in the pages of the bible?'

The sickness rose in Dorothy's chest and spasms tugged the back of her throat as she began to throw up.

'Dorothy, if you won't talk to me I can't help you. Please, just let me help you. Did Andrew beat you, Dorothy?'

'No.' Her voice was little more than a whisper.

'What about Robbie? Did he harm your son?'

Her throat ached at the memory of her family and the pain seared through her body as she tried to claw back what had happened.

'Did he ever abuse Robbie?' Dr Skelton caught her eye and Dorothy couldn't fathom the meaning behind the look. 'Did Andrew interfere with Robbie...' a beat '... *sexually*?'

The words swam in Dorothy's head, and she gagged at the very thought of it. 'No!'

'It's more common than you think.'

Dorothy was glad she lived in a world where she was blind to such horrors.

'Why did you drown Robbie?'

The sound of Robbie's heels banging against the bottom of the bath pounded her head. The image of his bulging eyes as his lungs filled with water. His tiny limp body. 'I loved my boy; I loved Robbie.' Dorothy repeated the words over and over until they lost meaning and became a jumble of random noise.

Dr Skelton stayed for a bit longer. She went on to explain to Dorothy that she wouldn't be going on trial for killing Andrew and Robbie. She'd been declared insane and therefore not fit to plead.

'But I want to stand trial.' Dorothy forced the sharp flecks of paint under her nails. 'I want to go to court.'

1

Glasgow 2002

Oonagh O'Neil removed the dust mask from her face as she opened the front door. 'Welcome to paradise.'

Would it not be easier just to move?' Alec Davies picked his way through the rubble and followed Oonagh into the kitchen.

'No. I like it here. I just need to make a few minor adjustments, that's all.' Oonagh picked up the sledgehammer and swung it full force into the wall. It hardly made a dent, but bounced back and sent a shudder up her arm, which quivered through her entire body, jerking her head back. She swung it above her head again but Alec leapt across and grabbed it before she made the second blow.

'Are you mental?'

'What?'

'That's a supporting wall, Oonagh.' He eased the hammer out of her hand.

'Is that like... important?' She bit her lip and pretended to laugh, but was mortified. She looked around. Her home was a war zone. Dust lingered in the air and metal props were in place where solid walls had been only a few days before. Tools lay abandoned against the back door and there was a cement mixer slap bang in the middle of her kitchen.

'When are the builders coming back?'

She sat down on the floor and looked at the clock, forgetting it was no longer there, just cracked plaster. 'Dunno, an hour or something.' Without her mask the thick air caught the back of her throat, making her breathless. 'They're away for materials.'

'Well, d'you want to leave the demolition work to the experts?' Alec reached out his hand and pulled her back onto her feet. 'Come on, why don't we go out? Where are you staying?'

She looked at him, didn't quite understand the question. 'Well, here.'

'Are you ment...?' He stopped himself mid-sentence. 'I thought maybe you were staying at your mum's... or had checked into a hotel.'

She shook her head. 'It's fine. Upstairs won't get started until next month.'

'Oonagh, behave yourself. This place is like Beirut.'

She shook the dust from her jeans and sweatshirt. After the attack she'd considered moving; wanted to sell the house, which no longer felt like home. But that would be admitting defeat. So instead she'd had the hall floor sanded and stained to ensure every last trace of blood from the bottom of the stairs was gone, but it wasn't enough. She'd almost been able to smell the attack. Had felt the danger brush her flesh as she'd walked from room to room. Next she'd set about a few minor renovations in an attempt to change the look and the feel of the place, but within a few weeks her home had resembled a builder's yard.

Oonagh looked around at the mess as though she was taking it in for the first time and stroked the small scar on her neck with her thumb. The mark from the heel of his shoe was still faintly visible on her shoulder, but the doctors assured her that would disappear – in time. The small scar from the blade would always be there, along with, she guessed, the dull ache of fear in the pit of her stomach.

'Come on.' Alec draped his arm over her shoulder. 'Pack a few things and I'll take you round to your mum's.' He glanced at the cement mixer. 'You can't stay here, Oonagh.'

The dust caught the back of her throat once more and made her cough.

'I mean, this must be playing havoc with your asthma.'

'Right, OK!' She ran her fingers through her hair. It was coarse and gritty. She knew he was right. 'Can we

17

go for a drink first?' She knew it wasn't yet lunchtime and was glad he didn't give her a lecture.

'D'you want to get changed or anything?'

She looked at him and shrugged. Desperate to get that first drink of the day to take the edge off.

'I mean, you look great,' he added. 'You always look great. But...'

All the mirrors downstairs had been put in storage along with the rest of her furniture. She took her mobile from her back pocket and looked at the camera. 'Oh, Jesus, Mary and Joseph!' Her chestnut bob was grey and coarse. The same dust had also left a deathly pallor on her skin.

'How much did that set you back?' Davies nodded his head towards her new mobile. Oonagh mumbled something under her breath. Truth was, she wasn't sure.

'May I?' He reached out and she handed it over.

'I know it seems a bit gimmicky having a camera,' she said, 'but...' She wasn't sure quite how to justify her latest toy and made her way to the stairs by way of changing the subject. 'Give me five minutes and I'll make myself presentable.' She looked back at Alec, but he clearly wasn't listening and instead was engrossed by the new gadget. 'Actually, make that six,' she said, picking a piece of dried cement from her hair.

*

18

It was mid-afternoon but the bar was dark and cosy. Alec sat across from her. She'd begun to depend on him more and more since the attack. He was the nearest thing she had to a big brother and she always wondered what her life would have been like had she not been an only child.

'Can I tell you a secret?'

Oonagh felt a slight tingle of excitement prick her skin. DI Alec Davies didn't do secrets. 'Yes, please.' She took a large gulp of red wine and settled back in her chair.

'This is strictly off the record.'

She held up two fingers, the opposite of her Girl-Guide promise, and gave him the V sign. 'You have my word as a tabloid journalist.'

'I'm serious, Oon.'

'C'mon, you wouldn't even bring it up if you thought I'd blab.'

He took a long sip of his pint, not taking his eyes off her. They went back a long way; she trusted him implicitly. She guessed it wasn't quite a two-way street.

'We're resurrecting a cold case from 1975.'

Oonagh slid forward on her seat. Alec dropped his voice.

'D'you remember the Raphael killings? You'd maybe be too young to remember.'

Oonagh settled her empty glass on the table and nodded; didn't want to break the flow of the conversation. She remembered Raphael; he'd killed three women in Glasgow, which had sent a wave of terror through the city. He'd never been caught and people still talked about him to this day. She'd only been a kid when he'd carried out his crimes but he'd become so much part of Glasgow folklore that she was sure she remembered. He'd earned his nickname because of the biblical quote he left on each victim: *'Do that which is good and no evil shall touch you,'* a quote attributed to the Archangel Raphael. The women had been killed with one clean wound to the throat, sliced with a scalpel. The killings had stopped as abruptly as they'd started and as far as anyone knew Raphael was still at large.

The waitress put two fresh drinks on the table, causing Oonagh to jump. 'Couple in the corner sent them over.' She tipped her head to the seat at the window where two middle-aged men raised their glasses and nodded. 'It's OK, they're regulars. Not nutters.'

Oonagh smiled and mouthed an exaggerated thank you.

'Does that happen a lot?' Alec pulled the fresh pint towards him, giving a brief nod in the direction of the window without turning his head.

'From time to time. More so recently, since…'

'Quite the people's champion, eh?'

'Yes, quite, anyway, enough of this boring guff, can we get back to the conversation in hand?'

'We think we may have a new lead.'

'In the Raphael killings? Bloody hell. What?'

'I can't go into details at the moment, but there's enough evidence to suggest that we may have DNA from the killer.' Oonagh took in the enormity of what Alec was saying. She reached out to touch his hand. 'And we think we can match it with a known suspect.' He responded by giving hers a little squeeze.

The news made Oonagh's heart beat faster and she drew her hand away. She'd been looking for a decent story to get her teeth into for eighteen months now. 'So who is he? Or can't you give names at the moment?'

'No names, no pack drill, all I can say is that our prime suspect has been dead for the past ten years.'

Oonagh sat back on her seat, obviously deflated. 'Oh, shite.'

'And I've got an exhumation order from the Scottish Office.'

2

Glasgow 2002

Oonagh stared at the screen, which was threatening to give her snow blindness.

Three months into her six-months deadline and her book still hadn't materialised. She'd written every day of her professional life for the past twenty years, yet she was struggling when it came to this.

The building work would be finished shortly and then there would be really nothing else to occupy her. She wandered from room to room and wondered if this place would ever feel like home again.

Writing a crime novel had seemed like the natural thing to do. Of course, she'd got an agent and a publishing deal within days. She wasn't vain enough to believe it was her writing prowess that clinched the deal. Oonagh knew she was a marketable commodity. Her name would guarantee free publicity with press interviews and put bums on seats at book festivals. Even if her book was shite, it would sell enough copies in the first run to make it worthwhile for the publishers. But her book wasn't shite. It just wasn't there at all.

She opened up her emails. Upsetting as they were, they provided an almost welcome relief from her deadline. Just a few had trickled in at first, then they'd gained momentum until there were a dozen or so each week. People from all over the world contacted her detailing the abuse they'd suffered, some as kids, but not all. Some at the hands of the church, but again not all.

> I was given up for adoption when I was just three days old. Your programme brought home the horrors of thousands of families torn apart by the Magdalene institutes...

> My mother was born in a Magdalene laundry. She never spoke of her past, or her experience, but I now feel I have a better understanding of the pain she felt...

> I was fourteen when my scout leader first abused me... I'm a grandfather now and have never told a living soul what happened. But I'm slowly realising that it wasn't all my fault...

She slammed the lid closed. 'Damn.' Of all the stories she'd covered in her career, the abuse that went on behind the doors of Glasgow's Magdalene Laundry had opened up the floodgates and provoked a bigger response than she could ever have imagined. Normally Oonagh would have been chuffed to bits, but there was just too much shit in the world, too much unhappiness to deal with.

She sat on the top step, hugging her knees to her chest.

Outside was threatening rain, so fairly decent weather for Glasgow. Cat head-butted her leg. She'd considered getting rid of him after her attack. But found that, despite the fact he'd tried to eat her face to finish her off, she'd grown quite fond of him. She had little memory of the attack itself, just a vague fuzzy recollection of lying at the bottom of the stairs and Cat lapping the blood that had gathered in a pool by her head. That memory gap should have been a good thing, blotted everything out, but instead she filled the gaps herself, each image more gruesome and horrific than the last.

She grabbed her jacket from behind the door and checked her car keys were in her bag. 'Mind the house whilst I'm out and don't open the door to any strangers.' Cat glanced at her for a moment, sniffed the bottom of the stairs then darted out of the front door.

The traffic was fairly light and she made her way along Byres Road to the studio. She pulled into a parking space just as Ross was pulling out. He gave her an exaggerated wave and a smile that she didn't trust; Oonagh noticed the baby seat was missing from the back and guessed he'd be off on a hot date.

She had a few minutes to spare and nipped into Make-up. 'Oh, Oonagh, I wasn't expecting you here.' Abby looked at the clock and Oonagh touched her arm.

'No. It's OK, I'm not booked in.' She slipped the square silk scarf from her neck. 'Can you just do me a quick repair job?'

Abby was the make-up of make-up artists. A genius who could obliterate hangovers, forty-eight-hour drug binges and the red-eyed evidence of a broken romance with a wave of her magic brushes. She examined Oonagh's neck with apparent impartiality. 'You know, hon, you can hardly see it; it's really faded.'

'Mm... maybe, but can you just dab a bit of powder and paint on it anyway?' Abby complied and in less than ninety seconds all trace of Oonagh's scar was gone. She examined herself in the mirror. 'Thanks, Abby.' She reached over and kissed her before heading off to Alan's office.

The door was slightly ajar and she rapped it with her knuckles and let herself in before he had a chance to answer.

'Ah, speak of the devil.' Alan gestured for her to sit down as he cradled a phone on his left shoulder, held a mobile in his right hand and tried to type with his spare fingers. 'We were just talking about you.'

'We?'

'Yes, myself and Ross.'

Her back stiffened, 'I'm all ears.'

'He has some ideas for *The Other Side*.' Oonagh sat back in her chair and let Alan do the talking. 'Thought it would be a good idea if the programme was a double header. Get a co-presenter. He's thrown a few names into the hat and—'

Oonagh cut him off before he went any further. 'I don't think so!'

Alan shrugged and held his hands wide, inviting Oonagh to explain. The initial series of *The Other Side* had been her idea and examined the underbelly of Scotland. She'd managed to get commissioned for a six-part series, then the network had bought the rights and it had gone national. But series two needed to have a different angle to stop it being formulaic. 'This is my baby and I'm not letting that wee shite get within spitting distance of it.'

Alan stood up and closed the door. 'Listen to me, Oonagh, you're lucky you're still here after that stunt you pulled.'

Oonagh's stomach shifted; she wasn't quite prepared for this. 'Are you kidding? That shower deserved everything they got.' Clearly not everyone thought uncovering historic abuse in the Catholic church was Oonagh's finest hour.

'You still don't get it. You were a fucking liability. You broke every rule in the book and could have had us sued.'

Oonagh elected not to tell Alan of emails and support she'd had in the wake of the programme. This wasn't the time for petty point-scoring. Her investigative techniques had fallen way short of legal and she knew it. The station had only managed to wriggle out of a court case when the church had feared even more dirt would come out in that particular wash.

'You need to go with a double header on this one.' Alan had calmed down slightly, but he was keeping her on a tight lead. 'Then when the dust settles...' Oonagh pinched the end of her nose to stop her nostrils flaring.

Alan sat back down. His voice softened slightly. 'You just seem to have a knack for rattling cages, Oonagh.'

'Really?' She swallowed hard. 'Well, I'd rather rattle a few cages than rattle my jewellery like the rest of the twats in here!' She jabbed her thumb behind her in the direction of the production office.

'Why are you so... so angry?'

'I'm not angry.' It was only a half-lie; she was more furious than angry.

'Oonagh, forget that I'm your boss for a moment.' Alan's choice of weapon when he needed to remind Oonagh who was in charge. Her back stiffened again but she gave him a weak smile. 'Can I talk to you as a friend?' Clearly he really meant business. 'How's the love life?' That came from left field and threw her off guard.

'Good job you're asking as a friend and not as my boss, Alan. I'm sure you've just broken at least three employment laws right there.'

He ignored the jibe. 'You're a lovely-looking girl, Oonagh.' He was really putting the boot in now. 'It's a shame to see you on your own.'

'I know. Sad, isn't it? I've got a T-shirt with *Great Looks – Shite Personality* on the front.' Oonagh sat back and crossed her legs. 'Are we here to talk about when I was last laid or why that little prick Ross isn't getting anywhere near my programme?'

Alan ignored her. 'He thought one of the *Big Brother* team would be perfect. Really appeal to the—'

'Big Brother? What the fuck's that about?'

'Oonagh, it's one of the biggest-rating shows on television. It'd be a real coup to have the winner co-present—'

She couldn't stomach this. 'Please tell me this is a joke. And a bad one at that.'

Alan put both phones down, a sure sign he meant business. 'You're a bit out of touch, Oonagh. If we've a hope in hell's chance of getting sponsors we need to widen our demographic.'

Oonagh realised she was losing this particular battle and changed tactics. 'Alan, you're right, you've got a knack of knowing what works on screen. No, I'm not against the idea in principle. It's just, well, I'm not sure, Alan, I just feel…' She wasn't sure how to get out of this one and had to think on her feet. 'Right. OK, I'll come clean. We're too far into this series to make any vital changes.' She was furious but refused to let it show. She didn't even have a schedule together and was still mulling around ideas in her head. But she wasn't going to let that petty wee fat bastard Ross muscle in on her act.

'Oh?' Alan lit a cigarette and looked up with interest. 'I hadn't realised you'd got so far into it. What's the theme?'

Shit. Oonagh threaded a strand of hair behind her ear. *'Women Who Kill.'* The words were out of her mouth before she knew what she was saying.

Alan leaned forward, a hint of a smile playing on his lips. 'Carry on.'

Fuck. 'I can't tell you too much at this stage, Alan...' she dropped her voice to let him think this was confidential information '... but I've uncovered some great stories here. Women kill for many more different reasons than men do.' She didn't have a clue what she was talking about. 'There's a ton of research to show that...' she was already up to her ankles and the crap was now lapping around her shins '... women who've been incarcerated for murder... or indeed manslaughter – over 80%, would you believe? – have had previous history of...'

Alan held up a finger. She'd known that would do the trick. 'Oonagh, I don't want a whole load of facts and figures and mind-numbing stats.' She nodded, to show they were both on the same page. 'I want real people, relatives, eye witnesses, the killers themselves. I want good interviews, decent sound bites. Have you managed to speak to any of the killers themselves?'

Oonagh gave Alan a slightly disappointed glance. 'It's me you're talking to – d'you think I wouldn't already have had *that* in the bag? Oh and, Alan—' she leaned forward in her chair and tried to look as pious as possible '—I'd rather you didn't refer to them as killers. These women are human beings. They've paid their debt to society and have a right to move on.' Alan's face reddened slightly and Oonagh was starting to believe her own bullshit. 'That's OK, times are changing, Alan, and we all need to change with them.'

He nodded and looked for an excuse to change the subject. 'So, how's the book coming along?'

This time she was more truthful. 'Oh, don't, it's flipping hard work, you know!'

'You know what Ross said when he was in here?'

'What?' She tried not to grind her teeth.

'He said every journalist has a book inside them...' he let out a little snort '... and that's where it should remain!' He let out a belly laugh. Clearly he thought Ross was hilarious. Oonagh pretended to go along with the joke. He was probably right, but secretly she wanted to smash his face in. She made her excuse and left.

3

Arkansas 1975

Marjory Channing stepped into the white overalls and pulled them up over her shoulders.

'Put this on—' he shoved a white baseball cap towards her '—and take your make-up off.' He wagged his finger in front of her face. She did as he requested, wiping her lipstick off with a tissue from her pocket. He pinned a laminated ID badge to the front of her overall that confirmed she specialised in industrial cleaning. He patted his handiwork and let his fingers linger on her left breast just a little too long.

'Where did you get that?' Marjory removed his hand from her breast as she looked down at the badge, which bore her passport photograph.

'Lady, I can get you a Cuban passport, a new Social Security number and an access-all-areas pass to Disneyland.'

Despite her fear she tried to suppress a smile. 'You're good.'

'Not that fucking good, lady. I keep getting caught.'

He looked around; the corridor was empty. 'Right, come on.' She followed him up a narrow staircase, which led out to an atrium. The building was grey and industrial-looking but surprisingly clean. She wasn't really sure what to expect – she'd never been in a prison before. 'Here.' He moved some boxes that sat in front of a door and held it open for Marjory to go inside. She hesitated for a moment and he let out a sigh. 'I'm a forger, not a rapist; if I was going to hurt you, you'd be dead by now.'

'Thank you for those words of comfort.'

'That's British humour, right?'

'Sarcasm.' She nodded. 'It's my second language.' She followed him inside.

The room was filled with mops and buckets and boxes of disposable gloves. He took a set of keys, which hung from his belt, and opened a further door at the back. The strong smell of disinfectant coated her mouth. Her white plastic shoes were at least two sizes too big and squeaked on the metal floor. This room had a narrow window halfway up; she had to stand on tiptoe to get a proper view of the ward, which was thirty or so feet below them.

It wasn't quite as she'd expected. It looked more like a cafeteria and spanned the size of a school assembly hall. It was hard to count the amount of beds. A rough scan, she reckoned forty to a row, and three rows deep. The men lay supine but relaxed on the beds and chatted among themselves. The cots didn't look very comfortable, but they only offered respite for a short time, so comfort was not a main priority. Certainly not among prisoners. Each cot was occupied and Marjory could see a queue two deep had formed at the double swing doors. Prison officers kept them in line, but the atmosphere seemed relaxed and casual. Most of them had fat roll-ups perched between their fingers or wedged behind their ears.

'Is it always this busy?' The forger was sitting on the floor having a cigarette. He shrugged. 'Guess so.' Marjory dragged a box to the window and stood on it to get a better view.

Each man on the beds was hooked up to a needle leading to a clear plastic bag. Each bag slowly filled with the deep red liquid feeding from their arms. Guys with bandanas, white aprons and matching white plastic boots seemed to be drawing the blood. It was difficult from her position to see what other staff were in attendance. 'How many doctors, nurses are there?'

'Usually the doc comes in and out, make sure there's no bleeders.'

There were four would-be medics in total for the entire ward. Each tapped the crook of the prisoner's elbow before piercing his arm with the flat bore needle that linked up to the plastic bag. Each one looked experienced in raising a vein. Once the blood began to flow they were onto the next guy. Marjory had to admit, it was a pretty efficient operation. They had it running like clockwork. Each medic looked after his own row and the plastic bags filled with blood at varying levels. Once filled the needle would be removed and the donor ushered to the double swing doors at the back of the hall, presumably to some sort of recovery area. By that time the next guy was lying on the cot waiting to be hooked up.

'These guys?' She gestured to the nurses. 'They're wardens, nurses...?'

'Cons.' He attempted to blow smoke rings, but failed.

'Yeah, but are they trained... to...?' She struggled to keep the anxiety out of her voice. He just shrugged again. 'Don't take much training to stick a needle in your arm. That's what most of them are in here for in the first place.'

Marjory tried to find a retort as to what was wrong with this, but decided to shut up. 'What's the incentive?' She couldn't help notice her accomplice had needle marks on both arms.

'Seven dollars a pint.'

Cigarettes, porn mags and toilet paper were all valuable currency inside prisons. Seven dollars could go a long way.

'No shit.' She tried to sound tough and vaguely American, but guessed she came over as a stuck-up British twat. Her Glaswegian accent held little truck here. No wonder there was a queue at the door. It was like a production line. She found it strangely hypnotic. There was only one problem. 'That guy?' She pointed to the con-cum-medic. 'He's using the same needle for each donor.'

'Mm?' The forger had given up trying to blow smoke rings. Marjory repeated herself. 'He's not changing the needle.'

He stood up and eased his hand on the window ledge and peered over the side. 'You know how much needles go for in here?'

Marjory didn't know. She realised she didn't have a fucking clue about life in general.

But it was slowly dawning on her.

'Ain't no problem, lady – they're all used to sharing needles. They ain't complaining.'

'But the blood.' She struggled to keep the urgency from her voice. 'There's an enormous risk of cross-contamination.'

'Fifty bucks.' He held out his hand.

'Who the hell's in charge of this?'

'I want my fucking fifty bucks.'

She stuffed the dollar bills into his hand. Her legs were shaking and she felt sick. He walked away and she followed him back downstairs to the outside yard.

'That'll take you back outside.' He tipped his head towards a utility truck. The driver was drumming his fingers on the steering wheel.

'My clothes?'

He shrugged his shoulders.

'My stuff? I had a handbag, shoes...' Her voice trailed off as the forger walked away and left her to the mercy of the guy in the truck.

4

Glasgow 2002

Oonagh scanned the faces but couldn't pick out Alec. If she were on an identity parade she'd be snookered by now. All the men looked the same; some had kilts, others wore black tie, but they all had regulation copper haircuts and seemed to morph into each other. The women were more easily defined.

Oonagh was glad she'd plumped for the long sleeveless black dress, cut away at the shoulders with a mother-of-pearl choker-style collar, which hid her scar. It was a good choice for the event, and the only decent one she'd had which wasn't in storage or at the cleaners.

At last she saw a face she recognised. DS McVeigh was waving frantically as he squeezed his way towards her. He looked as though he'd had his hair cut that very afternoon, but still it stuck out in wiry ginger tufts from his head. And he'd grown a moustache. Oonagh stretched out her arms. 'Jim.' She hugged him and kissed him on both cheeks, leaving a slight smudge of lipstick. 'You scrub up well.'

He tugged at the cuffs of his white shirt, James Bond style. 'D'you think?'

She stood back slightly. 'You're actually bordering on handsome.'

He blushed and laughed. 'You looking for the boss?' Jim McVeigh never referred to his superior officer by his first name, even when he was out of earshot.

'Either that or a drink.' A waiter passed and slowed down enough for them to each take a glass from his tray.

'Quite an event.'

Jim looked around and sort of tipped his head in agreement. These charity balls were getting more and more lavish each year. 'So tell me, Jim...' Oonagh took a sip, looking over the top of her glass '... is it true Glasgow coppers have the most impressive balls in Scotland?' They both burst out laughing. She liked Jim. He was a good laugh. He suddenly straightened his face and smoothed down his jacket; Oonagh turned round to see Alec negotiate his way through the crowd towards them. 'His bark's worse than his bite, Jim.'

He raised his eyebrows. 'Really? His bite's pretty bloody lethal, believe me.'

'I've been looking everywhere for you.' Alec bent to kiss her cheek and she stood on tippy-toe to meet his embrace. 'This guy bothering you?' He tipped his head in McVeigh's direction. Oonagh knew he was just teasing, but she also knew he was still easily irritated by his partner that he'd been assigned over two years ago.

'He's looking after me, now leave him alone.' She slapped Davies affectionately on the shoulder. 'You're both off duty.'

Alec did a slight double take. 'What the hell's that on your top lip?'

McVeigh shuffled slightly. 'It's a moustache.'

'I can see that, but have we not already had this conversation?'

'I grew it on holiday. I can do what I like on holiday.' He looked to Oonagh for backup. 'Within reason.'

'Get rid of it – you look like a twat.'

'I think it makes you look distinguished.' Oonagh brushed an imaginary piece of fluff from McVeigh's shoulder; she caught Davies watching and wiped the smear of lipstick off his cheek with her thumb.

Davies raised one eyebrow and McVeigh picked up the cue, made his excuse and left.

'Why d'you do that with him?'

She linked his arm. 'Do what?'

'The Doris Day routine.'

'Oh, behave. You need the love of a good woman, Alec. You're too flipping grumpy.'

'Can I start with a few bad ones first, then move on to the good ones when I'm a bit older?' Someone in the distance suddenly caught his eye. 'Here...' he guided

Oonagh through the crowd '... there's someone I want you to meet.'

He was the only man in the room in full uniform. A row of medals decorated his left breast, scrambled-egg braiding adorned his hat, which he held tucked under his arm. She recognised Gordon Threadgold immediately – Chief Constable of Strathclyde Police. Oonagh had had cause to interview him enough times when she was a reporter; he was a high-profile public figure. Alec reached out his hand as they drew near. 'Sir,' was all he said as the men shook hands. His face beamed. It was the first time Oonagh had heard him address anyone as sir; she'd never seen him be subservient to anyone in fact. 'May I introduce you to—?'

'Oonagh O'Neil.' Threadgold clasped Oonagh's hand and held it in both of his. 'What a pleasure to meet you.'

Oonagh didn't have the heart to tell him they'd met several times in the past fifteen years, but long before she was a well-known face on the box every night. 'Pleasure's all mine, Chief Constable.'

'Only for another,' he made a big deal of looking at his watch, 'twenty seven days, then I'll be picking up my gold clock.

'I thought it was a bit like being the president...' Oonagh looked him in the eye to see how far she could take this '... or the Pope – they could never take the title away from you.' Alec looked mortified then instantly relieved when Threadgold threw his head back and laughed at Oonagh's quip.

The older man placed his hand on Oonagh's shoulder. 'Can you excuse us for a few moments?' he said. 'I just need a quick word with this fellow.'

Oonagh nodded and the men snaked their way through the crowd to a clearing near the door.

Jim sidled back up to her, a fresh drink in each hand. 'Davies seems very…' she pondered on the words '… smitten with Threadgold.'

For the second time that night she made Jim McVeigh laugh; this time he almost spilt his drink. 'He'd belt me if I'd said that to him.'

'What's the story, then?' She'd never heard Alec mention Threadgold before.

Jim just shrugged and carried on drinking.

*

Davies looked at the older man's eyes. They were slightly cloudy, and creased at the edges, but he held himself as tall and as straight as a man half his age. Davies always looked up to him. Admired him.

'You've won a watch there, son.' Threadgold nodded in the direction of Oonagh.

Alec laughed. 'I wish! We're not a couple, sir. Just friends.'

41

Threadgold raised a single eyebrow, then changed the subject. 'Alec, it was me who suggested you for the Raphael cold case review.' Davies nodded. Threadgold pressed his lips together. 'I want this closed before I die, Alec; Malloy put his heart and soul into that case.' He breathed deeply through his nostrils at the memory of his friend.

'I'll do my best.' Davies's heart sank. Malloy had been Threadgold's best friend as well as police coroner. The murder of him and his son had sent shock waves across the entire force. Everyone had liked him. Everyone, it would seem, but his wife, who had killed him right in the middle of the investigation.

'We'll do everything we can, sir. You can count on that.' Davies meant what he said, but held out little hope. The so-called fresh evidence amounted to little more than a letter from the suspect's daughter implicating him in the killings. Even if they could link the DNA, cracking a twenty seven year-old case was almost impossible. And with the key suspect six feet under he would need a modern-day miracle.

'I'm relying on you, Davies.' And with that he was gone, leaving Alec Davies with the need for a very strong drink.

5

Glasgow 1975

Dorothy looked at the clock, then the telephone. He was late more often this weather, but rarely called. Robbie was tucked up in bed and the wind gathered outside making the windows rattle. She'd loved this old house when they'd first come to see it and together they'd turned it into a home. But lately, inch by inch, the loneliness had begun to crush her.

The plate of food on the table had long spoiled, but she picked it up and placed it in the oven. It didn't seem right to let it go to waste. The telly was on in the background, and provided some much-needed company. Next door's dog yelped from the garden and she turned the dial to increase the volume, just enough to drown out the constant yelping without the danger of waking Robbie. The newspaper lay folded on the table; she scrunched it into balls and threw them onto the open fire.

Filling the void each day was becoming increasingly difficult. She knew she should be grateful, but it was hard. Her mum told her how lucky she was. Everyone told her how lucky she was; it was every girl's dream to marry a doctor. That was what they said, so it must be true.

The nursery door was closed, but she eased it open, taking just a peek. They'd decorated it in yellow and lime green. It was perfect. So still. Not even a breath of wind. Not even a breath. She wrapped her arms around her waist. It felt empty. *You can always try again soon.* They meant well. They all did. But losing a baby at eight months. The chord still had to be cut. The labour pains endured. Clinging onto that dead child she knew they'd take away and act as if it had never been there. Had it been six weeks later Dorothy would have been afforded all the sympathy of a grieving mother. But this. This. Nothing. A miscarriage apparently was God's way of telling you the baby was too weak for this world. Too ill. Not right. So she just had to get on with it.

She had no idea where the scissors had come from. But she clasped them in the palm of her hand. They were too small to do any real damage, but looking down she saw she'd worried a small hole in her skirt. Her beautiful Italian wool skirt. The point of the blade had worked its way into the flesh in her thigh. The release was almost ecstasy. The pressure in her chest eased with every tiny drop of blood that escaped from that wound. Leaning back against the door, she allowed a long deep sigh. A tiny groan of pleasure escaped from her mouth. Dorothy took just a few moments to compose herself, then looked in on Robbie before heading back downstairs.

The phone rang and she picked up the heavy black receiver, holding it to her ear. They'd had a new trim phone in the bedroom, but she rather liked the old Bakelite model that had already been installed in the hall and they'd decided to keep it.

'D'you know where your husband is tonight?'

She instinctively stepped back. 'Sorry?' she said, her heart missing a beat.

'Ask your husband what he's been up to tonight.'

'Who is this?' The line went dead. Her stomach displaced slightly as she heard Andrew's key turn in the lock.

6

Ayrshire 2002

Oonagh drove north along the coast road, the same one her dad took her on as a kid. Maidens beach stretched out to her left, white horses crashing against the shore; the silhouette of Culzean Castle perched on the hilltop contrasted against the early evening sunlight. She turned left onto a single-track road and eased her car through the woodland area until she got to the clearing. It didn't matter how many times she'd visited, the sight of the castle always made her catch her breath. Nestled in the crook of the Ayrshire coastline, the gardens enjoyed an almost tropical micro-climate from the Gulf Stream.

She'd arranged to meet Maura Rowinson at seven. The estate was part of a National Trust property, but Maura had assured Oonagh she could access the castle after closing as she had rented an apartment.

Oonagh followed the road round to the right of the main castle to the luxury holiday apartments and parked in the courtyard. There was only one other car there, an

MG, British racing green. Oonagh parked alongside and switched off the engine. She caught a brief glimpse of someone at the window, but her arrival would have been obvious for several minutes given the length of the drive. As she got out of the car a slight flutter of nerves played on her chest, but she'd left Gerry, her production assistant, in a pub less than three miles away with a mobile phone, access to a landline and instructions to call the cops if she didn't check in within the hour.

A middle-aged woman with blonde hair tied back in a ponytail came out to greet her. She looked familiar, but Oonagh couldn't place her. 'Oonagh.' She stretched out her hand; Oonagh smiled.

'Maura? Good to meet you. In person,' she added and allowed herself to be led inside and through to the main room, which looked out onto the Firth of Clyde. There wasn't much that still impressed Oonagh, but this view did. She stood at the window. 'Wow, this is magnificent.'

'Not bad, is it?'

'Long-term let or...?'

'I'm here for the summer.'

A slight finger of anxiety stroked her chest and Oonagh wanted the small talk over. The view impressive and the house designed to within an inch of its life, but that wasn't why she was here. She'd found Maura online. Or rather Maura had found her. It wasn't uncommon for people to contact Oonagh with the promise of a story. The next big scoop. More often than not they were nutters, but occasionally there was a story worth following. It had taken several emails and a few furtive telephone conversations before Maura had finally opened up enough to tell her it was a story connected to the tainted blood scandal. Oonagh's first instinct had been to pass it on to the health correspondent. She had little interest in the saga. Haemophiliacs infected with hep C – or was it hep B she could never remember? – from contaminated blood products. They'd been campaigning for years for compensation and there was little more that could be told on the story. But Maura had convinced Oonagh that her take was different. Said she had a human interest story that would be wasted on the health corr. It had been a while since Oonagh'd been to Culzean so she'd agreed to meet her.

'Tea?'

There was a current trend for people to have 'do not resuscitate' cards on them. Oonagh wondered if there were similar ones with 'no more tea'.

'No, I'm good, thanks.'

'So, shall we get down to business?'

Oonagh was a bit surprised, she hadn't expected her to be quite so direct, but since she was: 'Yip, fine by me. So, what's the new angle on this?'

'I'm not quite sure where to begin.'

Oonagh decided against saying the obvious and just let Maura continue at her own pace.

'I need you to know that the world was a different place then. No Internet, no email – we didn't even have mobile phones.'

Oonagh fingered her own mobile in her pocket.

'Oonagh, what d'you know about the tainted blood scandal?' Maura cut in and interrupted herself before Oonagh had a chance to answer. 'Of course, you're completely across it – you're a journalist.'

Oonagh felt a wee bit stung, and slightly embarrassed. Yes, she knew the basic details but couldn't recite it chapter and verse. Medical negligence stories were ten a penny. 'I'm... *familiar* with it.' She hoped Maura would fill in the gaps. She took her hand-held recorder from her bag and placed it on the coffee table.

'I'd rather you didn't.'

Oonagh glanced at the machine and toyed with the idea of switching it on regardless, but didn't.

'We stumbled across it by accident.'

'We?'

'That doesn't really matter at this stage, but we had no idea people would get killed.'

'OK, hold on. Can we start at the beginning?' Oonagh began to feel slightly uneasy. She glanced at her phone. One bar; shite signal.

'Please, just hear me out. It's not easy to get this all in chronological order.' Maura was drumming her fingernails on the coffee table. Her nerves were rubbing off on Oonagh, and irritated the hell out of her.

'You seem a little... anxious, Maura.'

'Really?' She didn't even try to disguise the sarcasm in her voice. Instead she gave a quick smile and crossed her legs, tucking her hands underneath. Fingers interlocked.

Oonagh gave a weak smile. 'What is it you want to talk to me about? It's not just the tainted blood scandal, is it? That story's years old.'

'I was a chemist. I worked in the pharmaceutical industry once I'd graduated.'

Oonagh feared this was going to be a long story, and she had no idea where it was going. But her gut instinct told her to stay put. She guessed she'd need to keep Maura on track.

'I thought I was on top of the world. The pharmaceutical industry had money to burn. It still does. I was going off to conferences in the Bahamas, Bermuda, Virgin Islands, you name it. Unlimited expense accounts. It was unreal. It's bad now, but back then it was a licence to print money.'

Oonagh wasn't sure Maura's back-story would gain her much public sympathy. But she wanted her to continue. 'What's this got to do with...?' She wasn't quite sure how to finish that sentence.

'I worked for a Canadian company, Merk-San UN. You've heard of them?'

It was a rhetorical question. Oonagh thought she vaguely recognised the name but nodded anyway. 'It was the early seventies, and they were among the first to develop a way of extracting plasma from blood products, which could then be used to treat haemophiliacs.'

Oonagh continued to nod sagely, hoping Maura's story would soon start to unfold.

'Factor VIII; the vital clotting agent missing in haemophiliacs. It was billed as being revolutionary. The answer to everyone's prayers.'

Maura walked over to the dresser and opened her briefcase, which was tucked under the chair. She took out a floppy disk. 'It's all in the public domain now, so here.' She passed the disk to Oonagh.

'What's on it?' What she really meant was, *Will I need a chemistry degree to understand it?*

Maura seemed to guess what she meant. 'It states quite clearly that the risks of contamination were known as early as the 1940s.'

'Hang on. You said they'd only discovered the procedure in the seventies.'

Maura slipped the disk into the PC and the electronic whir sounded as the tiny on-lights flashed on the monitor. She opened a folder, which contained a list of files. 'Look.' She sat on the hard-backed chair and leaned to one side, allowing Oonagh to view the screen over her shoulder. A copy of a handwritten note had been scanned onto the file.

Experiments with human volunteers from the military, prisons and state hospitals were abandoned in 1947 when it became clear that plasma induced hepatitis...

Oonagh's eyes quickly scanned the details. She stopped at the last line.

... carried a high risk of mortality...

'Bloody hell!' Oonagh let out a long sigh. 'So why did they start using the plasma products in the seventies?'

'This report had been lost, or deliberately hidden. Whatever the reason blood products were big business in the seventies and eighties. Merk-San UN couldn't keep up with the worldwide demand.'

Oonagh's mind was racing.

'It was worth millions.'

'Maura, I'm sorry but I need to get this on tape.'

Maura bit the inside of her cheek.

'Please?' Maura said nothing, so Oonagh leaned over and switched the machine to record. The buzz of her phone made her jump. It was a text from Gerry.

R U OK?

She was shocked to realise the hour had come and gone. Through the picture window the sun had dipped into the sea and the Ayrshire sky had turned red. Maura switched on the lamp. Oonagh let Gerry know she was fine, otherwise she imagined he'd be at the door with a SWAT team circling the area.

'There was a programme in Arkansas whereby they harvested the blood from state prisoners.'

'Harvested?'

Maura nodded. 'It was like a production line. Most of the inmates were serious drug abusers, and as a result had a high risk of hep C. And as it turned out HIV, but that wasn't known about at the time.'

'I'm still not getting why they had to use blood from prisoners.'

Maura pushed her glasses up onto her head and rubbed her eyes.

'It takes thousands of donations to extract the plasma for each patient. We couldn't keep up with the demand. It's hard enough getting enough donors for ordinary transfusions. This was off the scale. Haemophiliacs needed the plasma products as part of their everyday treatment. The prisoners were an unlimited supply. They were paid for each donation. Seven dollars a pint. They queued up like it was the January sales. It was gruesome. Like a production line. There were no proper hygiene rules followed – they used needles several times over causing contamination before the blood was even in the bag.'

She explained that skid-row donors – prisoners, prostitutes, drug addicts and the like – meant a constant, cheap supply and no one bothered to check the source.

'Oh, God, I feel sick.'

'You haven't heard the half of it.'

Oonagh wasn't sure she could stomach any more.

'The Arkansas operation could only cover part of the demand. The world was opening up and Taiwan was one of the major customers. So Merk-San moved to Europe and struck deals to ensure the supply continued.'

'So prisoners across Europe were being paid to donate blood?'

'Europe proved a tougher nut to crack, so instead the company struck a deal with the USSR as it was at the time.'

Oonagh could almost see the can of worms open up in front of her. The Soviet bloc wasn't known for its human rights records; she dreaded to hear what was coming next. People selling their blood to buy bread? Nothing prepared her for what Maura told her.

'There's a paper trail which leads to the source of the Russian blood products.' She pronounced Russian as Rush-ee-ahn.

'Go on.'

'Skid-row donations, as cheap as it was, still had an element of cost and had its limitations.'

'I'm not sure I want to hear this.' A million horrific images flooded Oonagh's head.

'Why pay for one pint of blood when you can get eight pints free?' Maura paused before delivering the killer punch. 'That's right, they took the blood from corpses.'

'What?'

'Thousands of them. Maybe even tens of thousands. The Soviet morgues provided more blood than anywhere else in the world. Apart from the ethical implication, there were never any checks on the standard of the blood, the risk factors, what the deceased died of. Nothing. This blood was given to NHS patients across the UK. Across the world, in fact.'

Oonagh struggled to find the words. She was about to ask why this hadn't been in the news. Why it hadn't been widely reported. She worked for the very same media who treated this as a second, third, even forth item news story. 'I'm assuming you can back all this up?'

Maura nodded. 'Sadly yes. Although some of it you'll have to take on trust for now.'

Oonagh wasn't sure what to do with this information. 'I'm not known for my trusting nature, but carry on.' She was trying to lighten the mood, but Maura didn't return her smile.

'There's more, a whole lot more. But for now, take the disk.' She caught the look on Oonagh's face and gave a half-smile. 'Yes, of course I have a copy.'

Oonagh slipped the disk into the side pocket of her handbag. 'There's a lot to digest here, Maura. You've sat on this for years. Why are you coming out with it now?'

'The shit's about to hit the fan, Oonagh.'

'This stuff already looks pretty brown and smelly to me.'

'This is just the tip of the iceberg. As I said, times were different then. Maybe I could have done more, maybe we both could have, but—'

Maura faltered. Her eyes were tired and red. She looked as though she was no stranger to a night-cap or three to help her sleep 'A friend of mine, she continued, 'Forensic pathologist. He'd worked out something was far from right.'

'Why didn't he do anything about it?'

'He tried but...' Maura pressed the back of her hand under her nose '... he was killed before he had a chance.' She looked down at the floor. 'He wasn't the only one. And I got scared and ran away.'

Oonagh had a million questions and knew she'd have to tread carefully.

'Maura, you need to go to the police with this. I have a friend who is quite high up and—'

Maura threw her head back and laughed. Really laughed. 'The police? Honestly? They'd have this buried quicker than a mason's handshake.'

Time to change tactics. 'You prepared to go on camera?'

Maura hesitated.

'We could have you in silhouette. Disguise your voice.'

This was a story. A big story. But Oonagh knew she'd need concrete evidence, cold hard facts. 'Maura?'

'You know the biggest con act in the history of the world?'

Oonagh shook her head, but she realised it was a rhetorical question.

'The devil convincing the rest of the world that he doesn't exist.'

He came again tonight. Dear God, thank you. I need him more each day. He keeps me strong and shows me the way. I pray he'll keep Robbie safe too. My blood is bad, I can smell it through my skin. That's why the baby left before she was born. He told me that, but says it's not my fault. But I know it is. I must have done something to make it go sour. If only I could scratch through my skin and let it all drain away. Others can smell it too. I see them look at me when I'm outside. They can smell my rotten blood. I can hear them whisper, they think I can't hear them, but I can. I hear everything. There are so many sounds I can hardly bear it some days. The constant chatter from inside people's heads. Why don't they stop? Just for a second. If they stopped I could get some peace. His voice is the only thing that calms the noise. He'll keep me safe. He laid his hand on my shoulder; the smell from my putrid blood doesn't repulse him. Tonight he laid his

hand on my shoulder and told me his name.
Raphael.

7

Glasgow 2002

Alec Davies looked at the bulging case file on his desk. It stretched over twelve box-files, each one tattered and worn at the edges from the past three decades. He was almost afraid to make a start on it. He'd glanced at it before, and knew most of the key facts – there were few cops in Glasgow who didn't – but even before he read it he knew it would be stuffed full of inaccurate witness statements, contaminated crime scenes and a conspicuous absence of vital evidence. A bloody nightmare.

There seemed to be no connections between any of the victims. Davies sifted through the profile case of each of them. This was going to be a shitty job.

There was a rap on the door and McVeigh entered before he had a chance to say bugger off.

'Wee cup of tea?' McVeigh placed the china mug on the desk. 'It's infused with rose petals.'

'What is it with you and fucking tea?'

'I got it in Florence. They have the most spectacular tea houses.'

This was all Davies needed to convince him the whole world was going mad. He looked at McVeigh. 'And what the fuck is that on your top lip?'

'Nothing.' McVeigh ran his index finger under his nose to check there was nothing lurking there.

'Aye, I can see that, but... it looks weird.'

McVeigh's top lip had a strip of chalk-white flesh in the shape of a moustache. The rest of his face had the freckled sun-burned look that only the redhead could appreciate.

'Why is it a different colour from the rest of you?'

McVeigh craned his neck to catch his reflection on the mirror behind Davies. 'I grew a moustache on holiday.'

A feeling of déjà vu washed over him. 'Well, where is it?'

'What?'

'The fucking moustache.' Davies could feel his ulcer coming back.

'I shaved it off. You told me to!' He looked like a petulant teenager. 'You said I looked like a twat.'

'Aye and you look like an even bigger twat now!' He thought this day was never going to end. 'Grow it back again. Fuck's sake, is it too much to ask that I have an assistant whose face is all the same colour?' He looked at the china cup on his desk. 'And can you get me some... some Bovril for a change? I'm sick of tea.'

He felt a slight pang of guilt. McVeigh did his best and was shaping up to be a fairly decent detective. But he found it hard to be nice to him. He just couldn't put his finger on it: McVeigh got on his tits.

There was a rap on the door, which changed the subject away from tea and top lips. 'You seen this?' It was one of the desk sergeants, laughing as he pointed to two men guiding a huge machine on wheels through the office.

Davies stepped toward the door and craned his neck to get a better look, 'What the fuck is that?'

'Oh, it's arrived.' McVeigh eased past him and seemed to be the only one with a handle on what the hell was going on. 'It's a health monitor,' he said as he walked out giving the machine a loving stroke.'

'What's a health monitor?'

'It does everything, measures blood pressure, pulse, weight, you name it' By this time the two guys had negotiated the monstrosity through the double doors. 'It can even tell you your risk of having a heart attack.'

Davies felt his own heart sink and hoped to God there wasn't a breathalyser installed on it or he'd be snookered.

'Why is it here?'

McVeigh was now on a roll, clearly delighted at being in the vanguard of this brave new world. 'Part of the force initiative for us all to keep in shape.' He gave Davies the once-over and did a really annoying little nod-cum-wink thing, 'No excuses now,' then added a smirk to the ensemble. Davies could just tell there was a six-pack lurking under his M&S sweater mocking him with a whiter than white smile.

'Can we get back to work?' He jerked his thumb back towards his office, making sure McVeigh followed. 'You had a look at this?' He pointed to the box on his desk. McVeigh shook his head, but Davies knew like most of Glasgow he'd have a rough idea of the case. Everyone knew about Raphael. His killings were apparently random, with no obvious pattern, and made little sense. But every religious nut in the city was under suspicion.

He opened the lid of the first box and flicked the spring catch that kept the papers in place. There was a handwritten note signed by Dr Andrew Malloy. Davies held it between his thumb and forefinger. Poor Malloy.

He stood up and pulled on his jacket. 'Come on.'

'Where we going?'

'To do a bit of plod-work.' He barged out of the office, deliberately forcing the two delivery men to step aside as the rest of the office cooed over the new 'guilt-machine'. McVeigh scurried after him, pulling his jacket off the back of his chair on the way out, and fell into step beside him. He resisted saying, *'But you haven't finished your tea,'* and for that Alec Davies was truly grateful.

8

Glasgow 2002

Normally murder briefings had a sense of urgency, but not this one. The victims had been dead for almost thirty years and the only suspect wasn't going anywhere. The budget was tight; Davies guessed Threadgold had done his best to push the boat out, but they'd struggle to find enough man hours to do this case justice. There were only three people assigned to the case: himself, McVeigh and a new graduate, Toria Law. He didn't hold out much hope for a speedy resolution.

Toria caught Davies staring at her; she responded with a nervous smile.

'You any relation to Amy Law?' He'd worked with Amy on a case in the past. She was a good cop and had been transferred to Serious Crime in Edinburgh.

'Sister,' she said.

'You as gobby as she is?'

'Not really, but I can be if you think it'll help my career.'

He turned to the whiteboard, wiped his mouth with the back of his hand. Didn't want to let her see him smile.

'Right, here's the deal.' He went through the main details of the case, what they knew, which was surprisingly little.

Each murder had made headline news. There was nothing particularly gruesome or gory about them. And apparently nothing the police could find to link the victims. Nothing except the way that they died. But Davies knew that wasn't right. There were very few random serial killers. Some newspaper clippings sat on top of one of the files. Composite photofit pictures filled the pages of each story, which could have been any one of a thousand men in the city at that time. Grainy pictures of Glasgow closes and streets where the women's bodies had been discovered. It looked the grey and dreich place that he remembered so well from his childhood.

Each victim had had their throat slit and been left fully clothed. No sign of any sexual interference.

He pinned the pictures of the dead girls on the board. 'As far as we know there was nothing to link each of the victims—'

'They all look alike?' Toria phrased it as a question and held one finger up as she spoke.

'I was just coming to that, but thanks, Toria.' Oh, God, he thought, this is going to be tedious.

Toria held up a finger again. 'They were all killed on a Thursday night...?'

'Yes. But at this stage we can't assume this is significant—'

'But it might be,' added McVeigh, who looked a bit pissed off at being left out so far.

'Of course...' Davies rubbed the underside of his ribs; that ulcer was threatening to make a spectacular comeback '... but... oh, for fuck's sake can I just finish this without you two piping up every five minutes? It's like herding fucking cats,' he muttered before going back to the whiteboard.

Davies knew that often details that looked significant could lead an investigation down the wrong path completely, yet to ignore even the smallest detail could prove fatal. The Yorkshire Ripper proved to be a case in point. Peter Sutcliffe had been interviewed by the cops nine times during the investigation. He even matched the bite marks taken by forensics. But hoax tapes and letters profiled the Ripper as being from Wearside and were used to eliminate all other potential suspects – including Sutcliffe himself.

Davies knew that every detail had to be used as a line of inquiry and not as a point of elimination. He continued and outlined what they had.

'OK, no apparent link, they all look similar and were all killed on a Thursday evening as they walked home.

And, of course, the biblical quote left on each body. Which links the killer, not the victim.'

The case notes were a nightmare. Thousands of men had been interviewed but there had been very little to go on. Media reports had asked for the public's help in finding the killer, but all that had led to were thousands of phone calls to an already overstretched police force. Some of the calls had made no sense at all. But each one had had to be logged, wasting valuable time and resources. The murders pre-dated computers on the force and every statement had been stored on handwritten index cards, making it impossible to cross-reference. The key suspect at the time had been a petty thief, Willie Mack.

The pictures of the dead girls showed no sign of frenzied attack, no sign of a struggle. And according to the autopsy reports each one had died after a single slice to the carotid artery. Not the work of a small-time crook more used to grabbing videos and sovereign rings. But Mack had been seen prowling around the back courts of Glasgow tenements during the time of one of the murders. Davies reckoned he'd been more likely looking for an opportunistic open window than a potential victim. He'd been questioned several times, but let go when his wife and cronies had provided cast-iron alibis for each murder. Davies had never believed that Mack was the killer anyway, but now he was their best hope.

Toria held up her hand again. Davies let out an exaggerated sigh. 'You don't need to put your hand up every time you want to speak.' He wondered if she was taking the piss and struggled to remain patient, but he was still fresh from a one-day management training course, which had told him and a few other cops nearing retirement that they were no longer permitted to treat the rookies like shit. McVeigh didn't count. McVeigh wanted to be one of the big boys and if he was to survive then he'd need to take all the shit that got thrown at him. Otherwise he'd sink without a trace. With the others, though, Davies knew he couldn't risk it. They were too quick nowadays to file a complaint form with everything from racism to bullying to sexism. The only thing that was still permitted, according to employment law, was a bit of bigotry. So, by all accounts he'd get away with firing a few Orange and Fenian bastards about and all he'd get was a stern talking-to.

'Right, any questions?'

Toria was about to raise her hand then pulled it back down before she spoke. 'Just one.' Davies nodded to her to continue. 'Why has the case reopened? I mean, what's the new evidence?'

'Good question,' and it was. Had it been up to Davies the case would have remained where it was. Technically they didn't have enough to re-investigate it.

'Well, as you know we've received a letter from the daughter of our only suspect from the time. Apparently

67

she's now saying she knew all along her dad was the killer.'

This time it was McVeigh who butted in. 'But what actual evidence do we have?'

Davies was feeling weary. None of this was stacking up.

'I mean,' continued McVeigh, 'is there any actual evidence apart from this daughter who may or may not have a grudge against her dad?'

'Well, yeah and no.' Davies couldn't tell him he thought he was right. It wouldn't be the first time he'd seen this. Forensics had gone back over the evidence and managed to find a scrap of DNA picked up from the first of the victims, Janet Channing. Traces of saliva on the shoulder of her raincoat, which she could have picked up from the bus, from the supermarket, from anywhere in fact.

Didn't mean it belonged to the killer. But Threadgold was determined this case would be closed before he hung up his truncheon and that was about the size of it. He might be about to make way for fresh blood, but he still had a lot of clout in the force.

'And for that you got an exhumation order?' McVeigh didn't even try to keep the surprise out of his voice.

'So why are we re-investigating the case?' Toria was clearly comfortable enough now to speak without bobbing her hand up every few seconds. 'Surely it would be more prudent to wait and see if the DNA matched the suspect before going to all the trouble of tracking down witnesses and...' She let her voice trail off. She'd been seconded to the team, if you could call it a team, from another case. A gang of professional shoplifters was targeting the designer stores in the city centre. Blagging hundreds of thousands of pounds' worth of booty each day.

'Toria, love, if you want to go back to sitting in front of a screen analysing CCTV footage for eight hours at a time then be my guest. If not, then...'

'Shut it?' She finished his sentence for him.

'*Comprende.*'

They were both right, of course, but Davies had a horrible suspicion that somewhere along the line the DNA would miraculously fit their only known suspect, and if that was the case there wouldn't be too many questions asked and it would be a case of 'case closed'. But he'd never get the chance to reopen the investigation and he needed a motive to find out why these girls were killed. It just didn't fit.

'We're treating this as though the suspect were still alive. We're treating this as though the case were fresh. As though those poor women were killed yesterday. Is that clear?'

McVeigh and Law both nodded.

9

Glasgow 1975

He sliced through the skin, creating a Y-shaped incision through the torso; there wasn't much fat on this one. The cuts were clean. Tidy. He was always careful to ensure that. Normally he'd let his assistant do the initial incision, take out the vital organs, but he'd insisted on doing this one entirely alone. The only thing the mortician had to do was measure its height and weight.

The instruments had been laid out exactly as he'd instructed. The clear plastic safety glasses fitted neatly over his own, and he made sure the paper mask covered his nose and mouth. Carefully he peeled back the thick layer of skin that flanked the breastbone and braced himself for the smell. It was the one thing he never got used to; no one did. And once the smell of death touched you it never went away. A drop of blood spilled onto his blue scrubs, splashing down onto his white rubber boots. He was careful to wear two pairs of disposable gloves, with a Kevlar glove in between on his nondominant hand. There could be no room for mistakes here.

Next, he clamped the open torso at either side of the navel to reveal the organs. Bruising was evident along both arms and legs – that was to be expected – with further evidence of bleeding into the joints. The main organs would be removed and weighed. Tissue samples taken and, of course, the obligatory blood tests. Everything as it should be. The only thing missing was the consent form.

For Andrew Malloy being a surgeon was as much about working on dead people as the living. For as long as he could remember he'd wanted to be a doctor. As a kid he'd worked in his dad's butcher shop before getting a Saturday job in the local vet's.

'Any experience of working with animals?' they'd asked.

'Only dead ones' he'd replied without a trace of irony. He was sure he'd got the job for his cheek alone. Then at medical school slicing through bodies had come like second nature to him. He was mesmerised at how a cadaver was reduced to no more than a collection of blood, flesh and bone. Sinews and muscles. Meat and carcass. Yet still it had a soul. He never forgot that. And was forever grateful to the souls who'd donated their bodies to medical science in order that he and his pals could practise being grown-up doctors.

It was a twist of fate that determined the discipline of medicine each student fell into. And *fell* really was the operative word. Punishingly long hours as a hospital consultant meant few women opted for that. Constant overnights and being on call did not make for an easy motherhood. The nice guys went into paediatrics. Anaesthetists, well, they were the silent assassins. The good guys who made everyone laugh, but then would put you to sleep with a snap of their finger. In an instant the patient would be under. Every bodily function at the mercy of the one who wielded the God complex. It was they who had the power of life over death, not the surgeons. It was they who ensured that the patient could drift into slumber and feel no pain, or if they were so inclined ensure that the unlucky sod was paralysed yet was aware of each slice of the knife. There were enough rumours to claim that those with a marginally sadistic streak would gauge it just right, just enough for the tiny perception of pain and awareness throughout the operation. Enough to be aware but not enough to think it was real. They'd forever more have post-op trauma but think it was all a bad dream.

The psychopaths became surgeons. As simple as that. There had to be a sadistic streak to slice a person open without feeling a degree of panic. As far as Andrew was aware, there had been no studies to suggest such, but there was certainly enough evidence associated with the personality traits of a surgeon: the ability to remain calm under immense pressure; the indifference to human suffering when slicing someone open. For him, pathology was the perfect option. Never had to speak to a single patient, and he got to hose them down afterwards. The smell of death was bad, but the stench of the living could be a whole lot worse. The total nutters went into psychiatry, but that was a whole other story.

Andrew spoke into the Dictaphone. He'd recently got into the habit of keeping two sets of autopsy notes. One for the public record, for the death certificate, and one for himself.

He looked down to the body on the slab. Normally it was a foregone conclusion. The deceased had suffered from haemophilia and had died from internal bleeding.

Once the body was opened up Andrew could see at a glance the cause of death.

Taking tissue from the liver would be a mere formality. The grey, bloated organ was pocked with disease; typical of the damage caused by the cirrhosis. But still, the tissue had to be inspected. Analysed.

With such damage to a vital organ the most likely scenario was that the male on the slab in front of him was a chronic alcoholic with years of abuse behind him. He might even have been a drug abuser. No one could blame him. Haemophilia was a shitty condition, often with a poor prognosis for the future. Was it any wonder the poor sod turned to the booze? The only problem was, the male on the slab in front of him was nine years old.

10

Glasgow 2002

The cuff loosened from the top of her arm. 'Blood pressure's normal, Oonagh. How're the panic attacks?'

'Fine.' Oonagh O'Neil fished around in her bag for a tissue to avoid eye contact. 'Much better, thanks.' She was aware that her hands had a very slight but detectable tremor. Mags was clearly having none of it. She'd been her GP for over five years now, not that long really, but she was a good doctor and took the time with her patients. She had the bedside manner many others lacked. Oonagh liked to think they might have been friends had they met under different circumstances.

Mags sat back and crossed her legs, obviously couldn't be fobbed off. She was noticeably taller than Oonagh, and her blonde hair was cut short in an Italian-boy style that Oonagh had toyed with but never had the courage to see through. Oonagh didn't know that much about her, but imagined she pretty much had the perfect life Oonagh longed for. Her husband was most likely kind and supportive. They'd probably met at uni. He'd have put off studying for his PhD until after she'd finished med school. They'd have two immaculate blond children who took piano lessons every Thursday after school and would run into their parents' room on a Sunday morning, jumping on the bed and thwarting any plans for sleepy love-making. Her husband would scoop them up and go downstairs to start breakfast, leaving Mags to have a much-needed long lie in.

Oonagh suddenly felt lonelier than she had in years and was mortified to feel the telltale sting of sadness on the tip of her nose as her eyes filled with tears. Mags leaned over. 'It's OK, Oonagh. These things take a long time to get over.'

'No, God, I'm fine, it's just that...' She trailed off, deciding against telling her GP that she was crying because she didn't have any pals, envied the life she imagined Mags to have and was even fantasising about chumming up with her for girlie nights in the West End.

'Are you trying for another baby? There's no reason why you—'

'I wasn't trying for that one.'

'Sorry.' The colour rose slightly in her GP's face and Oonagh suddenly felt like a shit.

'No, please, it's OK. It wasn't the right time. I don't have anyone special in my life and...' She let it trail off.

'None the less, a miscarriage is never easy.'

How had it come to this? Hitting forty and no pals. She didn't think she should count Tom. And Alec? Well, he had his own life. She longed for some proper female friends. The kind she could lose a Saturday afternoon with over a bottle of wine. The kind she used to have. But times moved on and people moved on. Slowly they changed, or Oonagh changed. Some moved away, most got married, had children, settled down. A couple of them had died. Tragic short lives cut down. It didn't take long to lose touch with people. The new friends Oonagh had made when she'd started working in television had been mainly media types. Itinerant types, desperately moving from promotion to promotion. Oonagh had been lucky, or so she'd thought, staying in her native Glasgow. And the life that she'd craved of late-night parties, adrenalin-filled deadlines and the single-girl freedom of staying in bed until three on a Sunday now just felt hollow and empty.

Mags didn't seem to feel the need to fill the silence. Oonagh let it linger for a few more moments before blurting out, 'Can I get more pills?'

Mags took off her specs and laid them on the table. 'Oonagh, I'm not sure that's necessarily the answer.'

'Just a slight increase in the dosage.' She tried to keep the desperation from her voice. 'I don't feel these are—'

'Have you thought about counselling?'

Shit, not that. 'I've been through most of the good ones within a ten-mile radius. I'm onto the crap ones now.' She let out a laugh as she blew her nose. Mags allowed a faint smile, and her eyes showed she was on Oonagh's side.

'You've had a rough time of it.'

The sympathy was more than Oonagh could bear; her eyes welled up at this display of camaraderie. She felt her heart beat just a little faster. Dr Mags was going to give in. Write her a new prescription for bigger and better happy pills. Ones that worked. Oonagh nodded her head as the tears spilled onto her cheek and pangs of self-pity tugged at the side of her mouth.

'I want you to try CBT.'

'What?' Oonagh struggled to keep the disappointment from her voice. Her new pal was letting the side down.

'Cognitive behavioural—'

'I know what it is.' Oonagh didn't let her finish.

'There's every reason to believe you're suffering from post-traumatic stress disorder. The miscarriage, the attack...'

'Counselling won't help. I could write a book on the different therapies available. I'm sick to the back teeth of therapists with their soothing voices and Laura Ashley curtains. I want more pills!' The last sentence was more aggressive than she'd intended. 'Please,' she added as an afterthought.

'Oonagh, I'm afraid you're already on the highest dose.'

Mags clearly didn't understand. With her perfect life and her perfect husband and her perfect children.

'How much alcohol do you consume each week?'

'For f... goodness' sake. Why does everyone assume I'm an alcoholic all of a sudden?'

'You know alcohol is a depressant, on top of which it really doesn't agree with the anti-depressants that you're on, so if you—'

A slight wave of panic fluttered in her chest. 'Yip, you're right.' She needed out of there. It was happening more and more, with alarming frequency. Butterflies with iron wings reached up and gripped her throat. 'I'll knock the booze on the head.'

Mags' soft smile, which had seemed so caring just moments before, suddenly now seemed smug and victorious.

'And please give the CBT one more go.' She scribbled something down on a Post-it note. 'We can refer you, but there's a waiting list.' She passed the note to Oonagh. 'To be honest, the Priory is probably the best in the country.' Oonagh scanned the piece of paper; it was the name of a therapist.

'I can thoroughly recommend him. He's not cheap,' Mags said, 'but I don't think that'll be an issue?'

Oonagh gave an unenthusiastic nod. 'Thanks.' She felt utterly betrayed, but then Mags had probably never had a day's sadness or uncertainty in her life. She got up to leave.

'Just try him, Oonagh.' Mags dipped her head towards the Post-it note; her voice dropped to no more than a whisper. 'He helped me enormously after my husband was killed.'

Oonagh's mouth moved. 'I'm, I'm so...' Through her shame she mumbled an impotent apology. Mags smiled again as she ushered Oonagh towards the door.

'Come back and see me in a month. And try to stay off the booze, Oonagh.'

11

Glasgow 1975

Andrew Malloy held his hand over the mouthpiece as he spoke. There was no one else around, but just in case. He'd arranged to meet her in a place neither of them would be recognised. She knew as well as he did how vital it was that they kept their arrangement private, but he told her again just in case. She was young and sounded very nervous; understandably really. They'd never met outside work before, well, just that once at the Christmas party, but there had been dozens of others there too so that didn't count.

Dorothy Malloy glanced at the clock, then back at her watch; both settled on 5.50. She caught a taxi from the railway station. It threatened rain and the black clouds meant it was already dark for the time of year. Robbie was tucked up in bed. She'd told the neighbour her aunt had taken ill and she had to visit her in hospital. Her neighbour had no reason not to believe her. He was a good boy, Robbie – more than likely he'd still be sleeping by the time she got back.

The café wasn't somewhere she would normally go, but she took a seat by the window. From here she could see the pub across the road. Had a good view of the front door. No one gave her a second look as she nursed her second cup of coffee. It had already gone cold, but she stirred the top of the froth as she looked out of the window, picking the skin around her thumb until it bled.

Ten past six.

She recognised Andrew immediately. Even with his back to her she'd be able to pick him out in a crowd. The man she slept soundly beside every night. The man who had fathered her only child. The man she'd promised to love, honour and obey. He walked inside, she lost sight of him, but there was only one exit so he couldn't leave without her seeing him. She sat for a further few minutes then saw her across the street. She'd never seen her before, yet recognised her immediately. She didn't belong in this neighbourhood. Her blonde hair hung softly to her shoulders. She seemed barely out of her teens. Her clothes looked expensive, her raincoat a classic design, the plain grey skirt underneath cut on the bias. Dorothy liked that detail. It sat well on her. She walked inside and within minutes was back outside with Dorothy Malloy's husband by her side. He held a protective hand under her left elbow as he ushered her across the road. Dorothy felt the emptiness in the pit of her stomach and realised that she'd already lost him. The girl by his side was almost perfect. Just one tiny flaw. A small ladder on the left heel of her pale-tan stockings. Dorothy guessed she hadn't even noticed it was there.

12

Glasgow 2002

The city had changed so much in the past three decades. Alec Davies had been only a teenager when the first murder had been carried out, but it had dominated news headlines and he remembered it as though it were yesterday. They retraced the steps of the first victim, or what they assumed were her steps. CCTV in the 70s wasn't what it is today. 'D'you think this'll do any good Boss? I mean what're we looking for here?' Davies ignored his partner and kept on walking.

Janet Channing had been a nineteen-year-old medical secretary who'd lived at home with her parents and younger brother. Had had a few close friends and a boyfriend she'd seen twice a week. Then one evening her life had been plucked from the ordinary when a stranger had slit her throat and left her to bleed to death in a back lane just a few minutes from her house. After that Janet Channing had become a household name. The press had made a big deal of the fact that she was pretty and came from a decent family. As though that mattered. In the six months following her death, two more women with the same height and build and hair colour had been killed in the same way. All with the same biblical quote tucked inside their coats. Suddenly Glasgow had had a serial killer on its hands.

A twenty-seven -year-old cold case was a fucking hellish thing to be landed with, but Davies had no choice; he so desperately wanted to do right by Threadgold.

He needed to get a feel for it. Give the killing a sense of place, a sense of time, and that wasn't something he could put into words. He spoke to McVeigh without looking at him. 'Why don't you go back to the office? I'm best here on my own.' By this time, he was crouching near the spot where the body had been found. There had been no reports of a disturbance, no witnesses and no blood or skin under her fingernails. Her carotid artery had been sliced in a clean single cut. McVeigh took a step closer and Davies instinctively pushed him back in case he contaminated the evidence – even though that was an impossibility.

'Fuck's sake, can you just get out of my face here?' He glanced at McVeigh then softened. 'Long day, y'know?' That was the nearest he could bring himself to apologise to his partner.

'Shall I head back and go through the witness statements again?'

Davies nodded. 'Aye, good idea.' Despite McVeigh's tendency to annoy him, he had a good instinct, and often spotted minor details that proved significant. 'Oh, can you make sure someone gets up-to-date contact details for the witnesses?' He took a breath. 'The ones that are still alive.'

*

Oonagh keyed in 'Tainted Blood Scandal' into the search engine; it threw up hundreds of results. Her initial glimmer of excitement dropped like a stone when she saw they were mainly from crackpots and conspiracy theorists, each claim more elaborate than the last. There were a few newspaper articles, the ones which had been archived; it hacked her off that there wasn't more online. There was nothing there that Maura Rowinson hadn't told her already. Her mind and fingers instead wandered to Dr Google. It wasn't that she didn't believe Dr Mags when she said she was already on the highest dose of tranquillisers, but she wanted to double-check. Within moments ads started popping up for online happy pills. Safe, effective and stronger than anything a UK doctor would prescribe. She had no intention of buying them, just wanted to learn more.

Testimonials flooded the page. Happy customers made even happier with each and every dose. Surely there was no way they could sell this stuff if it wasn't safe.

Her finger lingered on the order button. Her basket flashed, urging her to complete the order. She could buy them, didn't actually have to use them. Stuff it, they were only tranquillisers.

13

Glasgow 1975

Her blonde hair hung to her shoulders. There was a shine to it and it probably smelled of apples, but there was no way of knowing that, unless she was closer. Her summer raincoat was pulled tight at the waist with a belt.

Overhead the sky darkened and threatened rain; she walked quickly, obviously used to walking in heels. There was a tiny ladder in her nylons. Just at the left ankle. She probably hadn't even noticed it was there. She looked like the type to throw them away rather than mend them.

Rain would be good. It masked the sounds. The light began to fade and she switched her bag from one shoulder to the other as she looked up at the sky and turned into a narrow side street, then through a lane that was lined with the redbrick walls of the tenement back courts.

She wasn't more than a few yards away now. 'Excuse me…' She turned around. 'Can you tell me…?' Her green eyes flashed for just an instant, then glanced down at her throat; they both saw the street light glint off the long blade. There was no sound as she clutched her hands to her neck, her bag falling from her shoulder onto the ground at her feet. The blood seeped through her fingers as her legs buckled and she fell first onto her knees, then sideways, slumped against the wall. Her nylons were ruined. The blade was easy enough to remove. The rain started as the blood streaked from her wound into her hair and gathered in a little pool.

She looked nice. There was no wedding ring, but perhaps she had a boyfriend. She was bound to have some family and that was a shame.

14

Glasgow 2002

'I appreciate the details may be a bit hazy after all this time.' Davies reached up to take the steaming mug of coffee when the woman faltered.

'Are you kidding? I wish I could forget.' She passed him the mug, careful to twist it so he could take the handle, then sat down on the sofa opposite. 'We were more like sisters than best friends, you know?'

Davies nodded, although he didn't really know. He'd never got on with his own brother, and his cousins were scattered around the country to make anything other than yearly visits out of the question.

Framed pictures were dotted around the room; a black and white photo-booth image of two teenage girls, made fuzzy by the enlargement, was in a silver frame on the console table. She picked it up. 'This is my favourite.' She held it out for Davies to take a closer look. 'Taken at the booth in Central station. We were always goofing about.' She sat back down and waited for Davies to speak.

McVeigh had done a good job tracking down Eileen McLean. She'd moved several times since Janet Channing's murder before finally settling in Edinburgh. She'd also been married twice, changing her name each time.

Davies was trying to find a link between each girl who'd been murdered – other than the fact they all had shoulder-length blonde hair. They must have missed something in the initial investigation. Then the killing spree had stopped almost as suddenly as it had begun. That usually meant one of several things: the killer had died, the killer was in prison for some other crime, or the deaths had never been linked and it was all just a coincidence. But Davies didn't believe in coincidences.

He didn't expect to learn anything from this visit, but he felt he had to start somewhere. Sadly, Eileen McLean was still grieving for her best friend. She was right, her memory was crystal clear, but she just didn't have any information that could lead him to the killer.

'Was there anything different about Janet in the run-up to her death?' Eileen shook her head. 'And the boyfriend, did he seem—?'

Eileen cut him off. 'Alistair was just an ordinary kid. He wouldn't hurt a fly.'

Davies looked down at his feet. He had no idea where he was going with this. Janet Channing's boyfriend at the time of her death was long since dead. He'd been a prime suspect in the early stages of the investigation. The boyfriends or partners usually were, but he'd been out of the country when the other killings took place, which pretty much crossed him off the list. Anyway, the killing was too clean-cut. Too neat for it to be the boyfriend. Partners tended to leave their victims in a mess.

'Was she perhaps seeing someone else? Did she ever mention any other boys?'

Eileen shook her head. A dead end. 'Not that she was short of admirers. You've seen her picture. Stunning, wasn't she?' Davies agreed. 'But she didn't know it. She was quite shy really, was always the quiet one. Her sister was the—'

'Her sister?'

Eileen Mclean topped up Davies's tea. 'Oh, I'm not saying Marjory wasn't nice either...' her face flushed red, as though she'd been caught gossiping '... but she was always much more outgoing than Janet.'

Davies scanned the details he had of Janet Channing. There was no mention of a sister, just her parents and a younger brother. He hated being on the back foot. 'Did she live at home as well?' He tried to sound casual, didn't want to let on he knew nothing about the sister.

'No!' Eileen tutted as though this were the most stupid thing anyone had ever uttered. 'Marjory was in America.' She paused for a few moments. 'I think it was the States – it might have been Canada. Anyway, she was seven years older than Janet and had worked all over the place.'

'Where is she now?' There was nothing in the case notes about a sister, clearly she'd never been interviewed, but had she been abroad at the time of Janet's murder that was hardly surprising.

Eileen McLean settled back into her chair. 'She passed away too from what I gather. She'd come home for the funeral but only stayed until the next day then was off again. Marjory was a bit more, how can I put it...?'

Davies knew he shouldn't prompt her, so let the question breathe for a few moments.

'She just had her own life. Liked to do things her way. Not really a home bird at all.'

'When did she die?'

'Oh, I'm not sure really. I'd heard a few years back that she'd passed away. D'you know I can't even remember who told me that. But aye, only the brother left. It's a sin.'

Davies had left McVeigh trying to track down the brother. They couldn't find any trace of him, like most of the family and friends of the three murdered girls. After all this time they only had a handful of people still alive connected to the case. Even that would prove little use. There were no actual witnesses to the killings themselves. It was hard work. Just old-fashioned plod work, but Davies felt they must have missed something in the original investigation.

'I take it you've lost touch with the family?'

Eileen gave an apologetic smile. 'Although Janet and I were best pals, I never really fitted in. They were a lot posher than us. They lived in the Mearns and we were on the scheme.'

Sprawling estates with council-owned properties were called schemes, the privately-owned ones were always estates. Davies could never work out what the difference was.

'Oh, don't get me wrong, they were always really nice to me, but you know.'

Davies knew only too well.

'We exchanged Christmas cards for a few years, then I got married, moved away and sort of…'

'It happens. Easy to lose touch.' He eased himself out of the chair; last night's five-a-side had taken its toll and his knee creaked like a dodgy dial-up Internet connection. He caught Eileen glance down and once more give him that apologetic smile.

'Thanks for the tea. You've been most helpful—' they both knew he was lying '—and if you can think of anything else, anything at all, no matter how trivial…' He handed her his card. She slipped it into the mirror frame on the mantelpiece and promised to get in touch should that elusive, vital clue suddenly come to mind that would tie up this entire case.

She walked him to the door. 'When you talk to Mike tell him I'm asking for him.'

'Mike?'

'Aye, Michael—' just a nod '—Janet's brother.'

'Will do, and thanks again.' Davies didn't have the heart to tell her they didn't have a clue where he was either.

'Although I'm not sure he'll even remember me. He's done well for himself though.'

Davies paused on the front step. 'I thought you said you'd lost touch with the—'

'Yeah, but let's face it, it's easy to keep track of Mike's progress.'

Davies was lost. Didn't have a clue what she was talking about. His poker face must have let him down.

'Mike Morrison? The painter?' She pointed to a print on the wall. 'That's as close as I'll get to an original, I'm afraid. His work goes for silly money now.'

'I'm not much of an art connoisseur.' Davies wasn't kidding, when it came to art he was clueless, but even he had heard of Mike Morrison. Glasgow boy turned good. His works hung on the walls of the rich and famous across the world. But as usual with these things it was Posh-Glasgow boy turned good. Mike Morrison had been an art-school graduate, but played on his Glaswegian upbringing, playing the working-class-hero card.

Davies was biting his tongue so hard he was sure he'd be drawing blood some time soon. He didn't want to come across as a prick in front of Eileen McLean and let on he didn't have a clue that one of Scotland's most famous artists was the brother of Janet Channing.

The noise won't go away. I've begged them to stop. It's raining. She'll be getting wet. Her clothes will be all muddy and dirty. That's not nice. She didn't suffer. I'm sure of that. I'm praying for her. Praying for her soul. I need to stop this. I need it to stop. There can't be any more. Robbie's safe. I'll make sure he's safe. I must have done something wrong. I don't know what, but it must be a bad thing. I fear Raphael has deserted me. It's been so long since he's spoken to me. I can make this stop. I need to make this stop. Andrew will be home soon. In him we have redemption through his blood.

15

Glasgow 1975

Dorothy wiped her hands on a tea towel and wandered through to the living room. The skin around her once perfect nails was bitten red and raw. The anxiety that had settled in her chest caused the acid to burn the back of her throat.

Her graduation picture was one of a group of family portraits on the piano. She missed teaching. Perhaps when Robbie started school she could think about going back. The shrill ring of the phone made her jump. Her hands trembled as she lifted the receiver. She couldn't bear to hear the words she knew were coming.

'There's been another one.' She didn't answer. The tears stung hot in her eyes, and her breath grew shorter. *'They're just innocent girls.'*

'This has got nothing to do with me,' she screamed. 'Leave me alone.'

She tried to piece together the events of the last few months. But things were hazy. Tried to remember but couldn't. She pulled open drawers to find her diary. She needed to see if there was evidence of a pattern. The radio blared in the background and seemed to grow louder and louder. Panic overwhelmed her chest, which grew tight and squeezed the breath from her.

Drawers were pulled from cabinets, contents scattered around the floor. She didn't even know what she was looking for.

By the time she was finished she was exhausted and sat panting on the floor among the mess. Her shoulder bag hung from a chair. She fumbled inside until she found the small brown bottle, then stuffed two pills into her mouth, hungry for the relief they offered. The dryness coated her mouth and they stuck in her throat. She struggled for breath and scrambled over to the sink on all fours. Pulling herself up, she managed to turn on the cold tap and cupped the water into her mouth. The small tablets, so benign, eventually slipped down.

She wiped the tears from her cheek; the hand of the clock moved so slowly. The ticking counted the seconds, which would eventually turn into minutes, which would allow the pills to give her some relief. Her back was against the sink. The mayhem in her kitchen lay scattered around her feet. The phone rang once more. Loud and shrill, it seemed to echo through the entire house.

'Leave me alone!' Dorothy's scream burned the back of her throat and she placed both hands over her ears, but it did nothing to drown out the sounds. She picked up a plate and threw it in the direction of the phone. It smashed against the wall, the sharp shards spiking the carpet as Dorothy slid down the kitchen unit and sobbed on the floor.

16

Glasgow 1975

The hair was slightly darker, more honey than ash, but still blonde. It was strange how we all woke up each morning, never really knowing for certain if this would be our last day on earth. How many would do things differently if we knew. How many dreams left unfulfilled, how many love letters unwritten. It did no good to be sentimental.

Dusk was descending on the city and the heel of her boots caused a very slight echo as she walked. This was the first day without rain in almost two months; the weather man had said so on the television just a few hours ago. Closer up, evidence of a natural brunette created a slight dark line across her scalp. A single silver bracelet hung loose on her wrist, settling on her hand. She had a confident stride and walked quickly.

Dumbarton Road stretched into the distance, flanked by tenements on either side. A row of shops in the distance. A small clearing of grass just before them. This was a busy road and a bus route. Not the best place for this. She turned left into a side street. Perfect.

'Excuse me, miss.' She spun round and glanced at the one-pound note offered in her direction. 'Did you drop this?'

She patted her pockets. 'No, I eh, no, I don't think so.' She checked the catch on her bag, which was securely fastened. 'Not mine.' She smiled and her teeth appeared to be perfect. Tiny laughter lines creased around her eyes. She looked as though she smiled a lot. Just one flaw. Her nails were bitten down. Made her look vulgar.

'Oh, well, my lucky night, eh?' The pound note was placed back into the pocket from where it came. They were side by side now and fell into step with each other.

'Thank God the rain's off, eh?' She nodded and smiled again. She was probably taught to be nice to others. Always smile. Perhaps she believed girls who smiled politely were more popular.

'Right, I'd best crack on.' A slight look of relief passed her eyes. She seemed glad not to have to continue with the small talk, but she gave a polite smile and a slight nod. 'Oh, just one thing...'

'Yes?' Her eyes once more had that happy-to-help look.

'This.' The blade was across her throat with surgical precision. She fell to the ground before her eyes had a chance to close.

17

Glasgow 2002

Tom was sitting in a booth near the bar nursing a drink. For a moment Oonagh almost didn't recognise him. His hair was cut in a close crop and had slightly greyed at the temples. His clothes were casual but looked expensive and he had a relaxed way that he'd never had before. He waved over and stood up when he saw her approach.

'Father.' Oonagh bowed her head slightly.

'My child.' Tom laid his hand on her head before reaching his arms out to hug her.

'Oh, how the hell are you, Tom?' Oonagh squeezed him tight and couldn't help but notice his aftershave smelt expensive. She eased herself into the booth and sat opposite him. 'You look great,' and she meant it. She tapped her throat with her index finger. 'Not missing the old dog collar, then?'

'Oonagh, I actually liked being a priest...' he looked into his glass '... sometimes.'

She reached across and patted his hand. 'I'm just teasing.' She saw the waiter busy at another table and wriggled out of the booth. 'Same again?' Tom nodded. 'And that would be...?'

'Oh, gin & tonic.'

'Slimline?' He nodded again.

Oonagh stood at the bar and could see Tom behind her in the mirror. She was glad he was looking so well. Initially she'd felt a bit guilty about his fall from grace – after all, she'd been pretty instrumental in the whole decision.

But looking at him now she knew he'd made the right choice. After he'd left the priesthood he'd gone into pastoral care. Oonagh wasn't quite sure what that was but, by all accounts, he was administering good works to a community in Lanark. He caught her looking and gave her a smile, then they were both distracted and cast an eye over a tall chap in a mohair suit who passed the table.

She returned to her seat and placed the drinks on the table. 'So how long are you in Glasgow for?'

'Not long, a couple of days.'

Oonagh was genuinely disappointed. She missed Tom. 'Stay a wee while longer.'

He just shrugged his shoulders and changed the subject. 'So, what're you up to?'

Oonagh let out a slight sigh that made her sound like a horse. 'Don't ask. I've backed myself into a corner with a series on women who kill.'

Tom knitted his brows together. 'Thought that'd be right up your street.'

She stirred her drink with the straw then took a sip. 'Usually, but I don't know, Tom. It just feels...' She struggled for the words; Tom helped her out.

'Salacious?'

She nodded. 'I'm peddling people's misery.' She waited for him to reassure her and tell her what a great journalist she was, but the sod just raised his eyebrows. He let her carry on and she talked for ten minutes to dig herself out of the hole she'd created.

'There's someone who you may be able to help.'

Oonagh held up her hand. 'The last person I tried to help nearly got me killed, remember?' She placed her right hand on her throat and smoothed the cashmere polo up over her neck.

Tom placed his glass on the table between them. 'Hear me out.' Oonagh settled back and waited to be unimpressed.

'I've been dealing with a woman who was incarcerated in Cartland for over a quarter of a century.' Tom was very good. He knew how to press Oonagh's buttons. She hadn't realised it before. Cartland was the state hospital for the criminally insane. The psychopaths who were too dangerous for prison. Oonagh traced her finger around the rim of her glass.

'Carry on.'

'She's now trying to integrate back into society.'

'What did she do?'

Tom took a handkerchief from his pocket and blew his nose. Oonagh shook her glass, allowing the ice to rattle, and said nothing. She knew he was buying time to make his tale more dramatic. Tom raised his glass to his lips. 'Stabbed her husband, cut out his heart—' a beat as he tipped his head back, swallowing the remains of his drink '—then drowned their five-year-old son.' He nodded towards Oonagh's glass. 'Same again?'

It wasn't often Oonagh O'Neil was lost for words. She was only vaguely aware of her mouth gaping open and assumed she must have nodded because he was up at the bar getting the round in. Tom had played a fucking blinder. He must be at it. If that had happened in Glasgow in the last fifty years Oonagh O'Neil would have known about it.

She felt a shift in the balance of power between her and Tom and wasn't sure she was entirely comfortable with this new-found confidence he'd acquired. She rather liked the old Tom. The nervous Tom. The Tom who wore a dog collar and was scared of being a priest. Tom came back and told her the sad story of Dorothy Malloy. 'I don't understand why the press wasn't all over that one.'

Tom raised an eyebrow. 'They look after their own.' Oonagh didn't pick up on the cue. 'The police,' he added. 'They made sure only the scantest of details were released.'

'Fuck's sake! Her husband was a cop?'

Tom thought for a few seconds. 'Not quite – Forensic Pathologist. But he worked mainly for the police and had friends in high places.'

Oonagh took in the enormity of what he'd told her. She made a mental note to ask Alec. He was bound to know the details of this one. Tom gave her the details of Dorothy Malloy's plight. Her entire family had disowned her after the killings.

'Why the hell would she do a thing like that?' She paused for a few seconds, tried to get the image of a wee boy drowning in the bath out of her head. 'I mean, that's pretty fucking brutal.' Oonagh struggled to find sympathy for this woman but could only feel loathing. That aside, she had to admit she'd be perfect for the programme. If she was prepared to speak on camera.

Tom bit the inside of his cheek. Oonagh had seen that look before. 'Tom?'

He drummed his fingers on the table and suddenly the old Tom that she knew and got slightly irritated by had come back. 'It's confidential, Oonagh. I can't really talk about it.'

Oonagh knew that all it took to get Tom to be on her side was a decent red wine or a gallon of gin. She couldn't be arsed going to the bar again and caught the waiter's eye.

'Tom! Behave yourself. You want me to meet this...'

'Dorothy Malloy,' Tom interrupted.

Oonagh nodded. 'Dorothy... so presumably I'll find out anyway.'

'I've had access to her medical notes and she'd been prescribed anti-depressants like they were Smarties.'

Oonagh took in what he'd said. 'Surely that was a mitigating factor?'

But Tom explained things were different in the seventies. Doctors prescribed pills without a second thought and didn't care much for research that suggested that they could cause psychotic behaviour.

'Can I meet her?'

Tom nodded. He was still biting the side of his cheek and Oonagh guessed it would be bleeding by now. Whatever Dorothy Malloy had done, she'd got under Tom's skin.

18

Glasgow 2002

Davies caught the tail end of Oonagh's car driving through the exit gate as he pulled into his parking space in front of the station. Shit. He considered driving after her but decided against it. He had no real excuse to speak to her right now other than he liked talking to her.

McVeigh was waiting for him on the steps, his suit jacket pulled tight with both hands, jumping from foot to foot to keep warm. He opened the door and slid into the passenger seat. 'Jeezus, it's freezing.'

'Did Oonagh say what she wanted?'

'Eh?'

'Oonagh O'Neil, just saw her drive away.'

McVeigh shrugged his shoulders.

'Have you got an address?'

'Yip.' He held a Post-it note above his head, waiting for his boss's approval. He'd have a long bloody wait.

It wasn't a huge surprise that Mike Morrison lived in the West End. A converted church. There was a for-sale sign in the driveway. Davies made a mental note to check the price when he got back to the station.

Huge oil paintings covered the walls; red and green and orange clashed violently with dark purple backgrounds. Naked females with wild eyes and torn distended bellies, malnourished foetuses clawing at their feet, attached by a bloody cord. This was what people paid thousands for. Davies just didn't get it. Morrison must have guessed what he was thinking. 'Not everyone's cup of tea.'

'No, I was just...' Davies struggled to find words, even one word, that wouldn't land him in the shit.

'Passion.' McVeigh's thumb was under his chin as his index finger curved over his top lip. He pointed at an oversized image of a woman tearing open her abdomen to reveal a coquettish girl sucking her middle finger. He turned to Davies and Morrison and tipped his head. 'Aye, there's real passion there.'

Davies wasn't sure if he was taking the piss and currying some favour with the artist, or if he genuinely knew about art. 'I'd say more like pain.' Whatever it was, Morrison wasn't buying it.

'I take it you want to talk about Janet?' He got straight to the point and Davies had no arguments with that.

'We're reinvestigating the case, Mr...'

'Michael, please call me Michael. I use my mother's maiden name. I didn't want to be associated...' He faltered for a few seconds. 'No, that's not quite right. I wanted my art to stand on its own two feet. Didn't want to be that artist whose sister was killed, d'you know what I mean?'

'Aye, I do.' Davies knew only too well. Families of victims of violent crime were forever defined by that very fact.

'So, what is it?' Morrison clearly wanted to get to the point. He was thin but well built. His long hair still had some traces of blond, but was receding slightly and streaked with grey and curled out where it hit his neck. Plain jeans and T-shirt splashed with paint suggested *bohemian* rather than *workie* to the untrained eye.

'We're reopening the case. Well, that's not strictly true, the case was never closed, but we're reinvestigating your sister's death, along with the other two girls who were killed, of course.'

'Oh?' Morrison posed it as a question. Understandable after nearly thirty years.

Davies didn't want to give too much away. Hated giving families false hope. 'We think we may have some DNA evidence that could...' He detected the slightest hint of a twitch in Morrison's jaw line. 'Please don't get your hopes up, but sometimes, in some cases, even after all these years we can manage to match evidence which wasn't available to us at the time.'

Morrison took a deep breath. 'And catch Janet's killer?'

Davies shot McVeigh a look that told him to keep his trap shut. 'Perhaps. But it could be a long shot.'

He pulled at his top lip with his thumb and forefinger. 'I see.'

Davies wasn't sure what to expect, but this was a somewhat more muted reply than usual under such circumstances.

'I'm sorry to bring this all up again, but—'

Morrison cut in before he had a chance to finish. 'What, like you think it ever goes away?'

'Don't suppose it does.' Davies offered the usual platitudes. 'But if there's anything that you think can help us now?'

'Like what?'

'Was Janet pregnant?' McVeigh's voice sliced through the atmosphere like a knife.

'No! What the fuck is that all about? Fuck's sake, you must have the autopsy report.'

'Sorry.' McVeigh took a step back. 'I was thinking out loud. These paintings, they're very...'

'What?'

'Graphic? I just thought perhaps your inspiration was —'

'Fuck off! My art is my business. It's got nothing to do with my sister.' He took a cigarette paper from a tin by his side and formed a thin roll-up. 'Jesus Christ, can you leave her in peace, please? You already fucked up the investigation, so just piss off and leave us to our tortured but at least personal memories.' He flicked his Bic lighter but it failed to ignite.

Davies stretched his arm across. 'Here,' he said, lighting his cigarette. McVeigh remained standing. Seemingly taking in the art.

'DS McVeigh didn't mean anything, he just thought perhaps—'

'It's cool, man.' Morrison ran his fingers through his hair then wiped his nose with the back of his hand. Davies guessed he was trying to act tougher than he was. He knew the type of upbringing he'd had. The type of family he'd come from. They'd never have said 'cool, man', they'd never be the type to smoke, let alone roll-ups. Mike Morrison was desperate to conform into the bad-boy wild child that every artist claimed to be.

'You had another sister?'

Mike nodded, let out a sarcastic laugh. Davies gave him breathing space. 'Not exactly a great help to my poor parents after Janet's... Fucked off back to the States the day after the funeral.'

'Where is she now?'

He shrugged his shoulders. 'Dead, I think. I got word a few years back she'd had a stroke. Don't really care, to be honest.'

'Look, mate, I hate to ask you these questions again but...' Davies went on to ask all the same questions he'd asked Eileen McLean. Was there anything unusual about Janet's behaviour in the weeks before her death? Davies tried not to use the word 'murder'. Did she seem preoccupied? Was there anything that could hint as to why she was killed? He realised that it was a fruitless quest, but one he pursued none the less.

Mike Morrison shook his head and settled with his elbows on his knees. 'She was just a kid.'

There's a pain deep inside that won't go away. There's something there. Something clawing. It lives in my blood. I can let it out little by little. It's the only thing that stops the pain. I lit candles today. As many as I could find. I can still smell them. Raphael says do that which is good and no evil shall touch me. I don't want another one to die. Not tonight. I wish it were my blood that flowed out. I wish my blood poured red and clean like theirs. But mine is black and rotten.

19

Glasgow 1975

'I've done it. I've killed him.'

The handset felt very heavy. She dropped it and could hear the tinny voice on the other end telling her to stay calm as it rocked back and forth before coming to rest on the table. They'd be here in no time. Soon. That was what they said. They'd be here soon. She didn't have much time left.

It took both hands to keep the glass steady and she downed the whisky in one. She poured another, and gagged as she tried to swallow. It did nothing to calm her nerves. And did nothing to take away the terrible taste lingering in her mouth. She didn't know it then, but that taste would be there for good.

The voice behind her was sleepy. He tugged at her skirt, and raised his arms to be lifted. Her brave little man. She grabbed him harder than she meant to and squeezed him tight. Pressing him close against her body. Buried her face into the soft folds on the back of his neck. His little legs dangled by her thighs. The blood on her hands left giant black prints on his pyjamas as she carried him upstairs. Leaving the mutilated body of his father staring at the television in the front room.

The bathroom was on the first landing. She'd drawn the bath earlier in the evening. Before all this. The image of the water lapping against the sides brought an aching lump to her throat and she yearned for normality. Downstairs the television blared; Saturday night game-show giving the lucky contestants the chance of a lifetime. The audience laughed and screamed, yelling conflicting advice to the contestants, oblivious to the carnage in Dorothy Malloy's front room. Her footsteps fell into line with the rhythm. The contestant was just about to make his choice when the deafening thud from downstairs told her they were here. They'd arrived. There wasn't much time left with Robbie.

Later, years later, when she thought about those next few moments, she could never get the order right. Never remember the sequence of what happened next. They tried to restrain her, that she knew for sure. A hand first. Round her throat, dragging her back. Holding her down. It took months for the purple bruise to fade. And even today she could still hear Robbie's screams. And other noises. There were always other noises in her head. The water, the splashing. Robbie's arms stiffening as he reached out. His hands grasping, his little legs thrashing in spasm, his heels banging against the bottom of the bath as he fought for breath, inhaling only a lungful of water. That last fatal breath before he fell silent. Her brave little man.

It wasn't long before the house was full. Full of men. And light. Flashbulbs exploded into her face and her own screams were drowned in the sea of voices.

They dragged her away from Robbie. His arms and legs were limp now. She clawed and kicked and scratched but there were just too many of them and the sudden sharp pain in her arm was quickly followed by a drifting sensation. Her eyes were open as they strapped her down, but her limbs were heavy and impotent. She saw her Robbie one last time. His flaccid body draped in the arms of a policeman, who unashamedly sobbed as he laid him onto a stretcher. Outside the cold scratched her face and they carried her into the van. A young policeman was bent double, retching onto the pavement.

'Aw fuck, sarg, she's killed them both. Her man and the wean.'

It was the last thing Dorothy Malloy remembered of the free world before she passed out into oblivion.

20

Ayrshire 2002

Oonagh struggled to get her head round this. The biggest scandal in the history of the NHS and no one seemed to give a fuck. 'So why now?'

Maura sat opposite her and nursed her coffee. She'd suggested the Ayrshire Pub for their meeting. It was quiet and traditional. A log fire blazed in the background.

'You've been sitting on this for almost thirty years. Why now, and why're you telling me?'

Maura raised one eyebrow. 'I'm not telling you anything that's not already in the public domain.'

'That's not strictly true, Maura, the disk, that had—'

'You could have found that, had you known where to look...' she paused for a moment '... and known what you were looking for.'

Oonagh wasn't buying it, and couldn't help but feel she was being dragged into something dirty. Very dirty. 'OK, so why tell me at all, then?'

'The government has promised an inquiry *if* it can be proven that the victims were given infected blood from US prisons.'

Oonagh knew her way around the legal system well enough to know that in cases like this proving wilful negligence was vital. It wasn't enough that it happened, what was needed was proof that it could have been avoided. One of the key arguments against the compensation claims was that without the blood products the patients might well have died. They were given the plasma in their best interests, and before the risks of HIV were fully known. Therefore there was no real negligence, it was just a case of tough luck. Oonagh felt like a real crumb for all the times she'd thought that very same thing. That the victims had just had a bad roll of the dice. Sometimes that was just what life threw at you. How wrong she'd been on that count.

'So can it be proven?'

'I believe so. I'm a key witness here. I saw it with my own eyes.'

Maura went on to tell her about what she'd witnessed in the Arkansas Department of Correction. It ran the plasma programme until 1994.

'Bloody hell.'

'No pun intended?'

'Sorry! But...'

''S OK.'

'Maura...' Oonagh paused; she had to pick her words carefully. Didn't want to point the finger of blame. 'If you knew the risks were there, then...'

Maura cut in. 'Why didn't I do something about it sooner?'

Oonagh nodded. It seemed obvious enough.

'D'you know what happens to whistle-blowers in the pharmaceutical industry?'

She continued before Oonagh could reply. 'You need to understand what it was like back then. Arkansas was the last state to cease selling plasma from prisoners. There were very powerful people making millions from this. I can't prove it at this stage, but I believe that senior figures in the state prison system were doctoring medical records to claim that the prisoners didn't carry either HIV or hep C.'

'Surely the buck had to stop somewhere?'

Maura nodded. 'The Governor of Arkansas. It happened on his watch. So I suppose...'

Oonagh knew what was coming before Maura opened her mouth. 'You're not telling me...?'

Yip. Big Bad Bill, or President Clinton as he went on to become. By the time he took office in seventy-eight the programme was already a licence to print money. They weren't going to give that up without a fight.

Oonagh could see why Maura had been up against it with this one. 'Jeez, makes shagging Monica Lewinsky seem a rather innocent pass-time in comparison.', The horror unfolded in front of Oonagh like a bad dream. She knew how these things worked. Haemophilia wasn't a 'sexy' illness. No one really cared. In the way that breast cancer got more public sympathy than bowel cancer. Some diseases just didn't make for good column inches.

'Tell me about the Russian involvement. Did the pharmaceutical companies know the blood came from corpses?'

'Absolutely. They drained blood from people who'd died in old folk's homes, state prisons, you name it. There were never any checks on what they died from, or if there were any communicable diseases present. And many of the donors died of Alzheimer's. There's no telling what risks that carries.'

'How did they find out?'

'It's there in black and white. The blood was labelled as a "waste product" and they used it as an excuse to embalm all the bodies. The waste products were sold on. You've no idea what was going on. Harvesting organ donations too. Horrific.'

Oonagh felt ashamed at her lack of knowledge. It was as though Maura knew what she was thinking.

'Don't feel bad at not having a handle on this before. Those responsible designed it that way. It was big business.'

Oonagh raised an eyebrow.

'Have you any idea of the profit margin in a pint of blood?'

Oonagh had no idea at all. Maura didn't wait for her response before telling her that a pint of blood that prisoners were paid seven dollars for was worth over three thousand dollars to the drugs companies. Haemophiliacs had a blood-clotting deficiency either factor VIII or factor IX. This could be manufactured by extracting it from donated blood. Only a tiny bit was needed for each treatment, hence thousands could be used from the same donation. But to extract this essential element the blood was pooled together using blood from up to twenty thousand donors, which increased the risks to haemophiliacs considerably more than the risk factors from ordinary blood donations.

'The Scottish Prison Service was just as bad. They used donors for the best part of fifteen years. And d'you know how they identified the drug users?'

'They asked them?'

'Not that far off the mark. They got them to roll their sleeves up to see if they had needle marks!'

Surely even the Scottish Office couldn't have been that stupid, but sadly Oonagh knew that they were.

'That's scandalous!'

'Concentrating on the American donations meant it took the heat off the NHS, who claimed they weren't responsible. But they were. The whole thing just stinks.'

This was just getting worse.

'Maura, what exactly can I do about this? I mean, what is it you want from me?'

'Even with an inquiry it could take years for the full facts to be made public.' She didn't give Oonagh a chance to answer. 'Yes, I know it's already in the public domain, but d'you know how complicated all this information is? And people need to know where to look for the information. And there's more.'

Oonagh grew nervous. She was really struggling to understand some of the information and knew that to get a programme commissioned on this she'd need credible witnesses. Professionals willing to speak on camera, but most of all victims. Getting people with HIV and AIDS to go public was a hard thing.

'D'you think any of them would be willing to speak on camera?'

'You kidding? I have some who would bite your hand off for the chance to tell their story.'

'You mentioned others – who were they?'

'A friend of mine. He was a forensic pathologist.'

'What was his part in all this?'

Maura's eyes misted over slightly. 'He saw a pattern developing in autopsies from haemophiliacs, which showed that they had signs of severe liver damage. A clear pointer that they may have had hep C. They had to be getting it from somewhere, and the obvious link was the blood products.'

'Did he tell anyone of his findings?'

'He was shot down in flames. After that he believed there was a cover-up so he started doing his own research and saw that a clear pattern was emerging. He stepped on a lot of toes and people didn't like it.'

'D'you have any of his research notes?'

'Very little. I have no idea what happened to them, but that's no great surprise.'

'Oh?'

'The amount of records which have gone missing throughout the years is staggering. Every haematology lab in the country had a hepatitis record book. Every single lab destroyed the record books so it's no great surprise that his notes can't be found.'

'Are you claiming there was a conspiracy?'

'Does that lump me in with the rest of the nutters?'

'No, I'm just saying...'

Maura looked at her watch. They'd been in the pub for less than an hour but she was growing increasingly nervous.

'Can you give me his name, Maura?' Oonagh needed to see if her story stood up.

'Listen, I need to go.'

'I've only just scratched the surface here, Maura.'

She nodded. 'I know, we'll meet again, but I really need to make a move.'

Oonagh realised she needed to toughen up. 'If you want to meet me again I need names, I need some credible witnesses and concrete evidence. I'm not going at this half-cocked. I'd get laughed off the set if I go to my editor with a few half-baked conspiracy theories.' She felt a bit shitty, but she had to play hard ball here. 'I've wasted enough time, Maura. I can't afford to waste any more.'

'I've given you enough information to make a start, surely?'

She had, but Oonagh needed more. 'I'll put a programme outline together, and if you come up with the goods then we'll talk further. But I'm not doing anything without this guy's name.'

Maura bit her top lip. 'Andrew, Andrew Malloy.'

Oonagh slumped back into her seat. 'Fuck me!'

'What? You've heard of him?'

'You tell me what the fuck's going on right now.'

But Maura was already standing, her tweed jacket tucked under one arm. She glanced at her watch but Oonagh guessed the face was too small for her to tell what time it was.

Oonagh stood up. 'Maura, you can't drop a bombshell like that then scurry away.'

'We'll meet again soon, I promise. But for now, d'you mind if we don't leave together?'

'We've been sitting together for the best part of an hour. I think it's a bit late for the cloak and dagger stuff.'

'OK, humour me, then. Give me five minutes, eh?'

Maura Rowinson was halfway out of the door before Oonagh had a chance to agree. She ordered another coffee and tried to make a call to kill time. But there was no signal so instead she watched the flames of the log fire until it was time to leave.

21

Glasgow 2002

There was no real reason for the nerves that had settled in Oonagh's stomach, but they pushed up through her gut and caused tiny ripples of excitement in her chest. The meeting had been scheduled for midday. Apparently, Dorothy Malloy struggled with mornings.

From the outside it looked like any other of the impressive blond sandstone villas in Pollokshields. Oonagh pushed the intercom at the gates and announced her arrival. She had to admit to being impressed. When Tom had told her to meet him at the counselling centre she'd expected it to be a bit drab, municipal and functional but this bore the hallmark of luxury. She was greeted at the door by a smiley-faced woman and led through to a waiting area. Again inside there was nothing to suggest anything other than five-star luxury. Oonagh was looking at the paintings on the wall when Tom walked in looking more serious than their last meeting. A bulging buff-coloured paper file was tucked under his left arm.

'Thanks for coming, Oon.'

Oonagh nodded to the papers. 'They her case files?'

'Yeah, some of the records are pretty scant, to be honest.'

Oonagh wasn't surprised. Mental health patients were often at the bottom of the pile when it came to decent care in the health system – what it must have been like for mental health patients in a state hospital was anyone's guess.

They walked up the stairs and Tom led Oonagh through to a room at the bottom of the first floor. Inside the bay window looked onto Maxwell Park and the sun streamed through, dancing on the green tiles on the fireplace opposite. A plump leather couch dominated the room and several easy chairs were pushed snug against the walls.

Dorothy Malloy was curled up on a wing-back chair by the window. Oonagh drew a slight breath when she saw how tiny and frail she looked. Her legs were tucked up underneath her and she kept her head down, making no attempt to acknowledge their presence. Tom walked slowly towards her, his footsteps barely making a sound on the soft carpet. He crouched by the chair, making sure he was in her sight-line, and laid his hand gently on her arm.

'Dorothy.' His voice was little more than a whisper. She turned her head slightly but still refused to meet his eyes. 'This is Oonagh. Oonagh O'Neil.' A slight pause to allow Dorothy to take in the information. 'Remember I told you she wanted to meet you?'

Dorothy tipped her head a fraction of an inch. Indicating she did remember. 'You still OK to chat?' Another tiny nod and Tom invited Oonagh to sit in the chair opposite.

'Hello, Dorothy.' Oonagh tried to keep her voice as soft and as calm as Tom's. She held out her hand but Tom gave her a sharp look and she quickly pulled it back. 'Thank you for agreeing to meet me today.' She could hear Dorothy's breath growing quicker as she rubbed her palms together. Dorothy's hair was streaked with grey and hung limp to her collar. She wore a simple black sweater and cream jeans, which were miles too big and emphasised how thin she was. Her bare feet were tucked into sheepskin slippers. She glanced up briefly and Oonagh could see the void in her eyes.

'Oonagh just wants to get to know you better.' Tom broke the silence. Oonagh gave a little nod and hoped her smile didn't look too fake. Her heart broke for this poor woman with the dead eyes, but she also knew that there was no way she would be able to feature in a documentary. It would be cruel and unfair to expect her to speak in front of the camera. Tom seemed to read her thoughts. 'Just try and help, Oonagh.'

What the hell Tom expected her to do was anyone's guess and she shot him a look that said, *Later.*

Oonagh tried to associate this tiny, frail, middle-aged woman with the horrendous crime she was guilty of. She tried to cast her mind back, tried to get inside that moment when Dorothy Malloy decided that the world would be a better place without her husband and son. Did she plan it out beforehand? Did she choose the murder weapon carefully, picking a knife that she was confident would inflict the most damage, and as quickly as possible? The sequence of the deaths suggested there was a degree of planning. Had she attacked her son first, no doubt her husband would have intervened. There would have been a struggle. But there was no struggle. No defence wounds on the body of Andrew Malloy. He hadn't even raised his hands to protect himself. He hadn't lashed out, fought back or even tried to grab the knife. From the case notes Oonagh had managed to get from Jim McVeigh's office, everything about Andrew Malloy's death pointed to him being incapacitated by the initial blow.

'Are you originally from Glasgow, Dorothy?' Oonagh tried to make small talk and Tom filled in the gaps as Dorothy stared out of the window. It turned out she wasn't originally from Glasgow, but from Dunblane. Obviously from money, then. She'd come to Glasgow as a student; went to Jordanhill to do teacher training. It had been her dream to be a teacher. Loved children by all accounts. Perhaps just not her own, Oonagh concluded.

Dorothy pulled a tissue from her pocket and as she wiped her nose Oonagh was surprised to see her nails were perfectly manicured. Like tiny little pink shells.

'Oh, your nails are beautiful, Dorothy.'

'Good grooming starts with the nails.' The voice seemed to come from nowhere; its confidence pierced through the silence. Dorothy Malloy rolled a covered elastic band from her wrist and, running her fingers through her hair, tied it back in a ponytail then sat up straight. Crossing her legs at the ankles. Suddenly her clothes seemed to fill out and her mouth eased into a confident smile. The physical transformation in Dorothy Malloy caused a line of fear to crawl down Oonagh's spine. This new woman stood up and reached her hand towards Oonagh. 'I'm so delighted to meet you. Has Tom offered you some tea?'

Oonagh could only shake her head and mumbled something to the effect that she was fine. This personality shift scared the shit out of her and tea was the last thing on her mind. Tom appeared unfazed by this and stood by, hands in his pockets, nodding his head in acceptance.

Dorothy folded her arms across her chest, walked closer to the window and smiled out at the sunshine. 'When I was a child I used to dream of living in a house like this.' She turned her upper body and caught

Oonagh's eye. 'Where d'you live, Oonagh? Are you local?'

Oonagh didn't like this one little bit. The old wound on her throat pulsed as her adrenalin kicked in. She pointed vaguely out of the window. 'A few miles down...' Oonagh decided it would be best not to share too much personal information with Dorothy Malloy and she wagged her finger in some random direction. She stood up, fearing this could all end rather badly.

There was a soft rap on the door and a smiley-faced lady entered with a tray laden with tea and biscuits. 'I'll just leave these here.' She placed the tray on the coffee table and left. Both Tom and Oonagh nodded their thanks and by the time Oonagh turned back the old Dorothy Malloy was back on the easy chair, head down, rocking back and forth, scratching an imaginary stain from her sweater.

Outside Oonagh slapped Tom across the top of the arm. 'What the fuck was all that about?' She pointed her thumb back towards the house. 'She's bloody bonkers!'

Tom looked genuinely confused as he rubbed the top of his arm. 'Well, yeah, she's just out of Cartland.'

Oonagh let out an exasperated sigh as she walked quickly to her car. Tom struggled to keep up. 'Hey, I told you she was still in treatment.'

Oonagh didn't want to admit that she'd been petrified in there. 'There's no way we can use her for...' She rethought her words. 'Dorothy Malloy is not a suitable subject for my documentary, Tom, and fine you know it.'

Tom had climbed into the passenger seat uninvited. 'I know, Oonagh, but she needs help.'

'Too right she needs help.' Oonagh started the engine and eased the car out into the street. 'But if I can remind you, it was her who was supposed to help me with the programme. Not the other way around.' She was shocked to find her right leg trembling and she braced herself to hold it steady. Whatever help Dorothy Malloy needed, she wasn't about to get involved.

'Tom, she butchered her family and she's clearly schizophrenic.'

Tom slapped his hand on the dashboard hard enough for Oonagh to think she needed to make an emergency stop. 'She's not schizophrenic!' He dropped his voice slightly. 'Dorothy Malloy has multiple-personality disorder. There's a huge difference.'

'Not from where I'm standing.' Oonagh pulled up outside Maxwell Park and switched off the engine. In the distance toddlers played by the swings as grown-ups chatted nearby. That very same scene was probably being played out in parks across the planet and Oonagh longed for such normality. The soft touch of Tom's hand on her arm sent a slight shock through her skin.

'You OK?'

Oonagh swallowed hard and was surprised to feel the tears sting the backs of her eyes. '*Wee Thing* would have been about that age by now…' she didn't take her eyes off the kids '… if she'd ever been born.'

'She?'

Oonagh let out a shrill laugh. 'I know it's daft.' Oonagh had always thought of Wee Thing as a girl. Her girl. But she'd lost her when she was little more than a mass of tissue. There was nothing left to grieve for. No trace of the unborn child that should have been hers. Oonagh O'Neil had lost her baby on the very day she'd cancelled her termination.

Tom rubbed her hand. 'It's not daft at all.'

Oonagh started the engine. 'C'mon, let's go for a coffee.' She guessed Tom would take this as a sign that she was compliant. 'You can tell me how I can help Dorothy Malloy and I'll tell you why I won't even think about it.'

22

Glasgow 2002

'I'm not sure what you expect me to do.'

The café had changed hands since Oonagh had last been in and was now sporting some sort of nautical theme, which she didn't much care for. There was a handful of customers and each booth had an imitation porthole backlit with a blue bulb.

'Just hear me out—' Tom pushed the case file across the table closer to Oonagh '—and have a look. If you still don't want to get involved after that, then no harm done.'

'She's not a suitable subject for the programme, Tom.' Oonagh didn't want to admit she was terrified of Dorothy Malloy; she flicked the outer edge of the buff folder open and let her eyes rest on the first page. 'What's post-partum psychosis?'

'Exactly what it says on the tin.' Tom was interrupted by the waitress standing by their table, one eyebrow raised, notepad in hand. They ordered quickly.

'I'll have whatever he's having.' Oonagh pointed to Tom, who ordered a white coffee. 'But make mine black,' said Oonagh. The waitress was about to leave. 'And can you make it tea, not coffee?'

The waitress smiled and nodded.

'Oh, and make it...'

The waitress stopped, still with her back to them. 'What've you got that's not tea?' said Oonagh. 'I'm a bit tea-ed out.'

'We've got wine.' The waitress turned back towards them, placed one hand on her hip and raised her eyebrow. 'That's not tea.'

Oonagh scanned the wine list on the back of the menu and glanced up at Tom, who gave in gracefully. 'I'll have my coffee plus whatever she's having.' Oonagh ordered for them both and the waitress winked at Tom and sashayed away, smiling.

'Can we get back to...?' Tom pointed to the folder.

'Sorry, carry on.'

'It's a rare condition after childbirth where women can experience psychotic episodes.' He paused to look at Oonagh, trying to gauge her reaction, but she wasn't ready to give anything away at this stage. Mainly because her head was pounding and she didn't know what to think. 'It can cause delusions, hallucinations, paranoia... in some cases it can lead to suicide or even attempts to kill their baby.'

The waitress placed their order on the table and started to pour the wine. 'I'll get that.' Oonagh took the bottle from her and smiled. She wanted rid of her as quickly as possible. Once she was out of earshot Oonagh pushed her glass to one side and opened the case file properly. 'Hold on a second. Are you saying Dorothy Malloy suffered from...' she scanned back at Tom's handwriting on the first page '... post-partum psychosis?'

Tom nodded, clearly excited by the fact Oonagh was now taking an interest.

'What does post-partum mean?'

Tom held his hands out in disbelief. 'Are you kidding?'

Oonagh felt a bit pissed off with Tom's superior attitude. 'No, or I would have started that sentence with *have you heard the one about...*'

Tom ignored the jibe. 'It means after giving birth... I thought you'd have known that, being a woman.'

'Yeah, because you're right on it with all things masculine!' Oonagh sat back. 'When it comes to bodily functions I work on a strictly need-to-know basis.' She tried to get her head round this. This wasn't quite adding up. 'I thought her son was five. That's hardly post—'

'Partum.' Tom cut in a bit too quickly for Oonagh's liking.

'I know the word, Tom, but the timeline doesn't quite fit.'

Tom reached across and laid his hands on the file. 'She'd just lost a baby. Stillbirth. She'd been eight months pregnant. The symptoms can present themselves any time from around thirty-two weeks.'

'Bloody hell. Surely that must have been taken into account in the court. That had to be a mitigating factor?' Oonagh had struggled to find a reason why Dorothy Malloy would kill her husband and son. Now she seemed to have one.

Tom nodded and sipped on his coffee. It left a cream moustache on his top lip. 'It's hard enough *now* to get a diagnosis. The world was a different place in 1975.'

Oonagh's mind was racing. She flicked through the notes, trying to make sense of it. 'I take it there are no trial notes in here?'

Tom explained there was no trial. Dorothy Malloy was deemed unfit to plead and subsequently was detained at the state mental hospital, without, it would seem, limit of time.

'What kind of treatment did she get, Tom? Was she given any help, therapy?'

Tom bit the inside of his cheek. There was a pause before he answered. 'Deep-sleep therapy.'

'Don't tell me—' Oonagh wasn't sure if she really wanted to hear this '—that's also exactly what it says on the tin.'

Tom reached into his briefcase and pulled out a pile of papers, which he told Oonagh he'd downloaded from the Internet. 'There's not a whole lot of information online at the moment. But I've managed to get some research papers from colleagues of mine.'

Oonagh cast her eye over the A4 sheets.

Evidence of patients being kept in a medically induced comatose state for weeks or months on end... Lying naked on beds in communal rooms... fed through tubes... convulsive electric-shock treatment administered against their will.

A wave of exhaustion swamped Oonagh. 'This happened here?'

Tom nodded.

'In this country?'

Tom nodded again.

'Scotland?'

'It was first used in the 1930s down south. I think it was Devon, of all places. They found that a narcotic-induced coma for a few hours could help some patients calm down.'

'This isn't a few hours, Tom...' Oonagh pointed to the notes.

'The regulation for psychiatric treatment was, and still is, shite, Oonagh.' Tom explained that some psychiatrists tried to make a name for themselves with this revolutionary new treatment. They used patients as guinea pigs; research indicated that they were often kept like this for weeks on end. Wakened for just a day at a time then put back into a coma.'

Oonagh eased back into her chair and took a deep breath. 'Jesus Christ!'

'There's footage, Oon – these women were like zombies.'

Oonagh struggled to take in what Tom was saying. Footage suggested that the procedure was not carried out in secret, and there was also the suggestion that it was mainly women who underwent this treatment.

'There were psychiatrists across the world desperate to make a name for themselves with this. It was used to treat depression, hysteria, anorexia... PMT... you name it.'

Oonagh felt her eyes sting with tears.

'You OK?'

She shook her head. 'Honestly, Tom? No. Not really.' She looked around for the right words. 'I don't know if I can take much more misery and heartache and...' she caught her breath before she cried '... any more fucking injustice.' Her voice came out slightly louder than intended and a couple at the next table turned to look.

'So, will you help or not?'

'No. I don't know. Maybe.' She held up her hands, aware she was getting carried away. 'OK, hang on. Fine, there's a story here, but it's not one that I can tell, Tom.'

He reached across and touched her forearm.

'Oonagh, I'm going away.'

'Where?'

'Down south. London.'

'Oh, behave yourself.'

'No, seriously. I'm going shortly. Only for six weeks, but it means Dorothy's care will be handed over to someone else.'

'Can't you postpone your trip?'

He shook his head. 'I'm working within the LGBT community, that's the Lesbian, Gay, Bi and—'

'I know what it is, Tom. You don't need to spell it out.'

'I'm setting up a counselling and support centre in Larkhall. I'm going down for training. I'm committed, I'm afraid. You need to get on board now.'

Tom dangled the carrot. But Dorothy Malloy was fragile and volatile and promised Oonagh more trouble than she needed in her life right now. She would be an unstable subject for a documentary and getting a reliable story out of her at this stage would be nigh on impossible. It had disaster written all over it.

'Tell me more.'

23

Cartland 1979

Her arms wouldn't work so she couldn't reach down to feel if the sensation of wetness between her legs was real or in her head. But something felt sticky. Her legs too were useless lumps; incapable of even the slightest movement. A different life played out in her head. One where she had a husband, a son, people who loved her. It seemed so real she could taste it. Twisting her head was all she could do, and the noise; never quite sure if the noise was real or in her head. A boy's screams and his heels banging against a bath. Why didn't someone stop it? Why didn't someone help him, make it stop, save him? But they left him to suffer the way she was suffering and her every waking moment was filled with that poor wee boy's screams.

She'd had a wee boy once. Of that she was almost sure. Or maybe that too had been a dream.

Footsteps broke through the noise and her spine stiffened as they stopped by her bed.

'What the fuck am I meant to do with her?'

'You've got ten minutes, I told you, then get the fuck out of here.'

'She's got a fucking tube sticking out of her hole.'

'It's a catheter, ya twat. She cannae move, so she needs to pee into a bag.'

'I'me not paying you a tenner for some bitch with a tube sticking out of her hole.'

'Shut it. Here, give us a hand rolling her over. Take her up the arse instead.'

Dorothy's body heaved as she was pushed onto her stomach. Her face buried in the stale pillow, making it hard for her to breathe. The weight was on top of her now, pressing down on her lungs. She thought she was going to pass out, and still that poor little boy's screams pierced her brain. It was a different pain than before. Normally it felt hot and sore inside. But this time she felt as though her insides were on fire, as though she was being ripped apart from the inside. Something grunted and heaved itself on top of her. Her hip bones dug into the rough mattress.

Then another scream. This one sounded different. Deeper, more like a growl. It took Dorothy a few seconds to realise the sound was coming from her own mouth, from deep inside her chest, muffled by the sound of the pillow. The beast on top of her pulled at her hair; she knew this was her punishment for not helping that poor wee boy. The one who screamed each day and night. The one who sounded like Robbie.

Raphael had deserted her. He'd promised to help, but instead he'd sent a demon to take his place.

Then the heaving stopped, she was rolled onto her back once more.

'I don't want her again. She fucking stinks.'

'They all stink in here, ya twat. They've been lying in their scratchers for years. Fucking ga-ga, the lot of them.'

'Aye well, she's weird.'

The footsteps walked away from her. She thought she heard them laugh, but couldn't be sure. It'd been so long since she'd heard anyone laugh. She closed her eyes and wondered when Robbie and Andrew would visit. Perhaps they could help that little boy. The one whose screams never stopped.

24

Glasgow 2002

'I can only stay ten minutes.' Alec eyed the drink
Oonagh had ready for him on the table. 'Fifteen at the
most.'

'Don't worry, I've got a meeting in twenty minutes
anyway,' she lied. Oonagh was good at lulling people
into a false sense of security.

Alec leaned over the table and kissed her cheek before
sitting down. 'What's the big mystery, then?'

Oonagh had thought it best if she arranged to meet
Davies in a public place. She was sailing close to the
wind with this and wanted to make sure he wouldn't go
off on one.

'No mystery.' She was desperate to ask him about
Dorothy Malloy but couldn't do it over the phone. She
needed to gauge his reaction. 'Just want to pick your
brains.'

Alec picked up his pint and took a long slow sip.
Oonagh noticed the lines around his eyes were more

pronounced than usual, and he'd lost a bit of weight from his face. He looked drawn. 'I'm all ears.'

'Dorothy Malloy.'

Alec was leaning to place his drink back on the table and stopped midway. Oonagh caught a look in his eye she'd never seen before. 'I take it you've heard of her, then?'

'Why're you asking?'

'Someone mentioned her name when I was researching material for the new programme—' Oonagh poured the rest of her tonic into her gin and avoided Alec's eye '— but I can't really find anything about her. Did she...?' She was hoping Alec would finish off her sentence and spill the beans but his mouth formed into a tight line. 'Did she kill her husband? Is that right?' Oonagh's face flushed scarlet. She was making an arse of this and one look from Alec said that he could see right through her.

'Give me a break, Alec. Someone gave me her case files and...'

A hollow smile tugged at his lips but didn't quite reach his eyes. He let out a laugh. 'Bloody hell, Oonagh, I wish all my suspects were as easy to interrogate as you.' He leaned back and softened slightly. 'What d'you know? Or what d'you think you know?'

'I want to know why I can't find a trace of her in any of the archives. Jesus Christ, a woman butchers her husband and son and it doesn't even make page five in her home town!'

'Come on, I need some fresh air.' Alec stood up and walked towards the door as Oonagh scrambled her stuff together and hurried after him. Outside the traffic was nose to tail and the clouds overhead threatened rain. 'Fancy a walk through the park? I've been cooped up in the office all morning.'

Oonagh nodded and tried to fall into step beside him but struggled to keep up. The mention of Dorothy Malloy had spooked him and she had no idea why. The park gates were only a few hundred yards away but Oonagh was already slightly out of breath and tugged at his arm. 'Can we slow down a bit?' He seemed miles away but slowed down to allow her to match his pace. He didn't say a word until they were sitting on a bench.

'D'you want a look around the orchid house?'

'No, I don't want a bloody look around the orchid house. I want to ask you about—'

This time he cut in before she could say the name. 'It was a long time ago, Oonagh, but it's still fresh for some of the guys who were there.'

This tiny scrap of information took Oonagh by surprise. 'You know some of them? Are they still here? I mean alive? Are they…?'

Alec put his hand up. Stopped her. 'Oonagh, the death of a colleague is never easy. The murder of a kid is heartbreaking. The two together is a nightmare the guys can't shake off.'

This put her on the back foot. Slightly. She hadn't realised quite how close to home this case was for Alec. He might have been a hardened cop, but he lived, breathed and slept the force. It was his life. She softened. Chose her words with care.

'I don't get how such a...' she struggled a bit '... an extreme murder, two murders, could be swept under the carpet... and why? That doesn't make sense.'

'Just because the press didn't get a hold of it doesn't mean it was swept under the carpet.'

Oonagh wasn't grasping this at all. It made no sense. Alec seemed to read her thoughts. 'We put a blanket ban...' He corrected himself. 'When I say we, I mean...' Oonagh nodded for him to continue. 'Andrew Malloy's death rocked the force. He was an absolute gem. His parents never got over it.'

'But why all the secrecy?' None of this added up. 'I mean, he was the victim here.'

'We promised his family they'd be able to grieve in peace. It was the least we could do.'

'Oh, c'mon, Alec, that's bullshit.'

'Really? Have you any idea the effect press intrusion has on a family? D'you think any of them wanted to be related to the woman who slaughtered her husband and son?'

'Yeah, but—'

'This was a very high-profile case slap bang in the middle of the Raphael killings and—'

Oonagh grabbed the top of his arm. 'What's that got to do with this case?'

'Andrew Malloy was the forensic pathologist.'

'And?'

'Well, he was doing the post-mortem examinations on the murder victims.'

Oonagh stood up. 'Whoa. Hold on a second.'

Alec leaned forward and rested his elbows on his knees. He looked exhausted. 'Please, Oonagh, no more conspiracy theories.'

Oonagh's mind was working overtime. Would that seriously be enough reason to put a blanket ban on the press? 'How did you pull that one off?'

'We have our ways, Oonagh. The force was a bit more... forceful then.'

Oonagh didn't like to think of what they could be like. She thought they were pretty forceful now. She badgered him some more but he wasn't budging and insisted that the cops were protecting Malloy's family.

'That bitch really went to town on him.'

'Oi! Alec, don't use that word in front of me. It's offensive.'

Alec stood up, his eyes widened. 'You've got to be kidding me. A poor guy gets butchered in his own home...' he pointed to somewhere in the distance '... his son drowned in the bath. And you're offended at the word bitch?'

The dig stung her, but she stood her ground.

'I didn't mean to offend you, Oonagh, but she really was a crazy mother-fucker.' Oonagh reckoned McVeigh's chat was rubbing off on Davies. Everything around them seemed so normal. People strolled by eating lunchtime sandwiches. On the grass a teenage boy tried to impress a group of girls with his footballing skills. A mother with a pushchair walked past with a mobile phone tucked into her shoulder as she unwrapped some chocolate to appease her toddler's cries. Life went on around them as Oonagh and Alec talked about the crazy lady who slaughtered her family.

It didn't matter how much Oonagh tried to plead Dorothy Malloy's case, Alec refused to believe there could be any reason – insanity or otherwise – for her actions.

'Some people are just born bad, Oonagh, accept it.' Part of her thought he might be right.

'You'd never think she was capable. She's tiny, Alec.'

'Tiny? What d'you mean?'

Oonagh wasn't quite grasping this line of questioning. 'I mean she's small.'

'She's still alive?'

Oonagh looked around. She suddenly felt guilty. She nodded slightly. Alec spoke very slowly. 'Have you seen her?' Again, Oonagh nodded. Slowly.

'She's in a bad way, Alec.'

Alec took a deep breath. 'Promise you won't go back to Cartland, Oonagh.' He held her by the shoulders.

149

'Don't get involved with Dorothy Malloy.'

Oonagh was almost scared to be the bearer of this particular bit of news. 'She's not in Cartland, Alec.'

'Where's she been moved to?'

Oonagh was stunned at Alec's apparent ignorance. 'Don't you know?'

The shrill ring of Alec's phone made her jump. He pressed his thumb on the answer button. 'What?' He listened for a few seconds. 'Too fucking late,' he yelled. 'I've just been enlightened to this fact. By a fucking civilian!'

25

Glasgow 2002

'I didn't like the men.' Dorothy worried a smooth white pebble between her fingers. 'They hurt me. It was sore.'

Oonagh sat opposite. The room was calm and quiet with soft lighting; outside the rain beat gently on the window. She was desperate to ask what men, how had they hurt her, what had they done?

'You're safe here now, Dorothy.' Tom laid a protective hand on the arm of her chair.

Today was a good day for Dorothy. Today Dorothy knew her name and where she was. Today Dorothy could remember some of her time at Cartland.

'They thought I was asleep, but I wasn't.' Dorothy threaded a strand of hair behind her ear then clutched the neck of her cardigan, tugging it closed across her throat.

Oonagh's initial sadness gave way to anger, which settled in the pit of her stomach; she noticed her hands had clenched into fists. Whatever emotion was coursing through Tom's veins, he kept to himself. Instead he reassured Dorothy that she was safe and allowed her story to unfold.

Dorothy Malloy's case notes made for grim bedtime reading; hearing her first-hand account was the stuff of nightmares. 'In the end they left me alone. They didn't like the noisy ones.'

*

Outside Oonagh breathed in the cool air and let the rain fall on her face. The whole sorry episode had left her emotionally exhausted. Tom followed her out to the car. 'You all right?'

She nodded. 'I'm not the one who needs sympathy.' She looked up to the window. 'And neither does Dorothy Malloy. What she needs is justice.' Shit, that was the last thing she'd be likely to get.

Tom folded his arms, clearly pissed off. 'You know how bloody difficult it is to get a rape charge as far as the courts at the best of times?' He paused slightly. 'Add to that a victim who was heavily sedated, has mental health issues *and* poor cognitive functioning,' he said, counting each point out on his fingers.

'You forget to mention the fact she's a ruthless killer.' Oonagh felt shitty about even saying it out loud, but they both knew there wasn't a hope in hell's chance of any of this even making it onto a charge sheet. Even if she was prepared to speak to the police, they'd make mincemeat out of Dorothy.

Tom pinched the bridge of his nose between his thumb and forefinger. Oonagh had had enough. 'I need to go.' She reached over and gave him a hug, then climbed back into the car. She watched him in the rear-view mirror as she pulled out of the drive. He looked broken.

She couldn't face going home. Not yet, not while the sadness and despair of what she'd just heard lingered in her chest.

Both she and Tom had agreed that sticking a camera under Dorothy's nose would be cruel and exploitative, but without her there was no story to tell. She could picture Alan's face if she pitched the story to him without a victim or a key witness. He'd tell her to bugger off.

Without Dorothy, it would be just another general exposé on abuse and the programme idea could sit on the slush pile for months, years even, and might never get made.

A telltale wave of sadness gripped her throat. She drove until she found a secluded spot, pulled over and cried for all the horror and pain suffered by Dorothy Malloy and the hundreds of people like her, banged up in soulless institutions, without a single person to fight their corner. Outside a middle-aged man walked towards her eating chips from a bag. As he passed the car he screwed up the newspaper and threw it on the pavement. The sadness that had moments before engulfed Oonagh gave way to a blind rage. 'You fucking inconsiderate bastard.' She opened the door and jumped out. 'Pick that up, you disgusting piece of shit.' By this time, he was almost half a block away but she was screaming loud enough for him to hear. He turned round. Oonagh stood with one hand on her hip, the other pinching the greasy chip paper at arm's length between her thumb & forefinger.

'You talking to me?' His clothes were casual, but expensive.

'Yes, I am talking to you. And you can drop the Robert De Niro routine. D'you want to stick this in the bin?'

The street was otherwise deserted, and he was closer than she thought. Suddenly he broke into a run.

'Fuck.' For a big guy with a fondness for chips he was surprisingly fast on his feet. She threw the chip paper at him and scrambled back into her car. Her heart was racing as she punched her fist on the central locking just as he slammed his hands on her bonnet.

'Out the fucking motor.' Judging by the vein bulging on his temple, he was a bit pissed off.

Oonagh wisely declined his invitation and, head down, twisted the key in the ignition. For one brief but horrible moment she thought it wasn't going to start. 'Come on, come on.' Her foot pumped the accelerator and suddenly it choked into life. She revved the engine hard as he battered his fist off her side window and, crunching the gear stick into reverse, drove backwards down the one-way street praying it would stay deserted long enough for her to get a bit of distance between her and The Angry Chip Man. She made a quick turn at the corner and winced as the gear stick squealed in protest at her brutal change into first. She sped off, back towards the West End and home, making a mental note not to piss off men eating chips again.

Gradually normal life resumed. As she passed the Botanic Gardens civilisation slowly came into view as apparently law-abiding citizens thronged Byres Road carrying various bags that looked no more dangerous than a week's shopping.

She pulled over outside the record store, which still did a roaring trade in vinyl, and wiped the greasy newsprint off her hands with a tissue as she got her breath back.

Her nerves were in tatters but she felt slightly giddy, intoxicated even at her lucky escape. She swallowed hard; her heart was still beating a tattoo in her chest as she opened her phone. The number was on speed dial, and even for her she knew this was flirting with danger. It rang three times before he answered.

'I've got a story for you.'

26

Glasgow 2002

Oonagh glanced at the clock and did her best to look bored but a wee flutter of excitement played in her tummy; she knew what was coming. The morning meeting was populated with the usual suspects, half a dozen or so fellow journalists with Alan at the helm. He read out the prospects of the day, each member there encouraged to pitch in with a story or an idea. There were very few real news stories; most were the product of carefully worded press releases, doled out by the junior PAs of spin doctors. A trawl through the papers could produce some decent ideas to work on too. It was commonplace for radio and television studios to lift stories from newspapers, put their own spin on it and pass it off as their own. Alan picked up a copy of the *News of the World* from the previous day.

'I take it you've all seen this?' He placed it on the table in front of them, opened at the double-page spread.

Systematic Sex Abuse of Scotland's Most
Vulnerable Inmates

Beneath the salacious headline was the picture of a woman in silhouette sitting alone on a park bench. Throughout the article, several bolded-out quotes read like a horror story.

Screws sold me to their pals for the price of a pint.

Drugged and helpless, I was abused as staff looked on.

'Worth chasing?' He posed it as a question, but what he meant was, *Who's up for it?*

Mutterings from the rank and file suggested historical abuse stories such as this were a nightmare to cover, but irresistible for journalists. They all threw their hats in the ring, but Sandy decided he'd double up as Home Affairs Correspondent for the day and picked up the baton. 'It's a prison story, so I'm happy to chase the Scottish Prison Service for a response.'

Alan nodded. 'Get that kid on work experience to do a bit of phone bashing for you. We need to get former inmates, ex-wardens, cleaners, anyone.' He flicked the top of his pen. 'Try to get victims. Aye, we need victims.'

Sandy was already on his feet, desperate to get onto something new. Oonagh only felt a slight pang of guilt knowing that he'd never find the woman in the picture, but that made no odds. Sandy was an experienced journalist. He could throw everything he had at this story. Had enough contacts in the SPS to get some off-the-record quotes to give this the padding he needed for a decent programme. And he knew that, with a bit of exposure, other victims would be coming out of the woodwork telling similar horror stories. Everything else he'd attribute to 'allegations of', 'reports of', 'claims of', then he could just regurgitate all the information in the article without breaching any laws.

Oonagh was always fascinated by the fact that newspapers had different ethical codes of practice from television; different editorial guidelines. She let her eyes drift over the article. A sickening catalogue of abuse going back years. One woman's tragic story told from the heart. No names were mentioned, and scant details of exactly when or where the abuse took place. None of it could ever be proven. But Oonagh knew it would be enough to prompt a raft of journalists across the country desperate to report on the allegations.

The Home Office would have no choice but to issue a statement saying the claims were being investigated. Heck, there might even be an official inquiry. Their press office would never have the balls to say that there wasn't one claim in that article that could be substantiated or would stand up in court. The public outcry would deafen them. She wasn't much for praying, but perhaps some other poor soul would come forward. A poor soul who was in a position to speak out. A poor soul who deserved the justice that Dorothy Malloy was denied.

Oonagh folded over the paper and slid it back towards Alan. She didn't bother to finish the article – no need, she already knew it word for word. After all, she'd written it.

27

Glasgow 2002

Exhumations were a rare occurrence in Scotland. In this case there was no family objection, but still the paperwork took weeks to complete. The customary white tent surrounded the grave and the digger moved in. Alec Davies stood in the background. As was the legal requirement there were two doctors, two uniformed officers, a state undertaker complete with private ambulance with blacked-out windows and an Environmental Health Officer to ensure the correct grave was opened and that due respect was shown to the deceased. He'd left McVeigh at home. There was no point in dragging him out of bed at this ungodly hour for nothing, and he reckoned he'd need him sharp as a tack later in the day.

The evidence against this suspect was sketchy to say the least. Davies didn't hold out much hope but it was all they had, and it was more than his life was worth to tell Threadgold as much. Willie Mack had been a small-time criminal. Shoplifting mostly, housebreaking and fencing stolen goods. He'd been questioned around the time of the killings as he'd been seen in the area of at least one of the murders. Had claimed it was a case of mistaken identity and had a cast-iron alibi: his wife, who'd vouched that he was at home the entire night of all three killings, and Davies guessed she'd have said he was at home for any future crimes committed too.

Mack had fitted the description of a prowler seen in the area. Sneaking about back gardens. A peeping Tom terrorising women by staring in their bedroom windows as they'd got ready for bed. But the most likely scenario was he'd been trying windows to break in later when all the occupants had been asleep. Davies knew it was very unlikely that a petty thief, a housebreaker, would suddenly turn into a ruthless serial killer. It just didn't fit the MO. But it was all they had – that and DNA from one of the victims. Threadgold was pretty insistent that they close the case. Rumours were rife that he was tipped to be on the Queen's Birthday Honours list, and nailing one of Glasgow's most notorious murderers days before his retirement would be a great piece of PR. Davies feared that no matter what the results were, he'd be encouraged to say the case was now closed. Not actually saying that Willie Mack was the killer, but the suggestion would be there and the press could do the rest.

Davies had known Willie Mack. Had had his run-ins with him. Hands like bananas, a neck as thick as his waist, 'the man they couldn't hang', he'd joked. There was no way Willie Mack had carried out the Raphael killings with such surgical precision. And anyway, he'd had no motive. Davies stamped his feet on the ground and blew into his hands, almost wishing McVeigh would show up with a flask of tea.

Dawn was still an hour away and the bitter cold suited the setting. The Southern Necropolis was slap bang in the middle of the Gorbals, the headstones mirrored the high-rise flats that towered in the distance. It was a fairly small graveyard, as graveyards went, with relatively low walls. Davies could sense the press at the other side of the wall and imagined he could hear the gathering of the locals; but he could be wrong.

They worked by floodlight and Davies said a silent prayer that the coffin would be intact. He'd been to very few exhumations in his career, but at his first the coffin had already been in a state of deterioration and moving the remains to a new casket had been a messy and time-consuming business. And the smell. It had never left him. Thank God he didn't have to actually touch anything. Each person there wore full regulation safety suits, goggles, face masks and a supply of disinfectant was on hand. He rocked back and forth on his heels, wanted the whole thing over and done with quickly.

The guy operating the digger was impressively precise. The hole looked as though it had been cut by hand, neat edges and geometrically squared corners. As soon as the top of the coffin was visible the digger stopped. Not one other piece of earth was disturbed. The driver stepped down from the cabin and Davies was shocked to see it was a middle-aged woman. 'Rest'll be done by hand now.' She nodded to her two colleagues and the three of them got to work to retrieve the coffin from the ground.

No real bad smell. Good sign, indicated it was still relatively intact. It didn't matter too much about the state of the body – all they needed were DNA samples.

Davies waited in his car until he saw the private ambulance ready to leave. He followed it along Caledonia Road taking a right towards Saltmarket and the City Mortuary. It was an old red-bricked building. Hardly fit for purpose, opposite the Merchant City Gates of Glasgow Green.

He knew the forensic pathologist would already be scrubbed up, ready to start as soon as they arrived. As he approached he could see a flicker of light by the front entrance. A security guard sat watching an old black and white portable with the sound turned down. Davies sounded the buzzer; the coffin would have been brought in by the back entrance. Regulation stated it would also be transferred to another bigger casket. He held up his ID to the security camera and waited for the familiar click of the door to open. He flashed his warrant card at the security guy on the way in and nodded a greeting. The guy didn't get up, kept his head down. Davies could only see his face in the mirror and recognised him as an ex-cop from the division. Thrown out for taking backhanders. Davies went along with the game and pretended not to know him.

The mortuary attendant came walking down the corridor to meet him, hand outstretched, white coat flapping behind him. His gut hung over his trousers, which were slightly too long. His shoes could have done with a polish too. He introduced himself as Michael something as he tugged his brown jumper down. Davies didn't catch his second name. He led him through to the waiting room.

'You scrubbing up to go in?'

'No, you're OK.' Davies had no intention of seeing any more than he absolutely had to. He had enough battle scars to give him nightmares for the rest of his life; he didn't need to make any new memories, thank you very much.

He stayed in the corridor and picked up a newspaper, but his bum hadn't even touched the seat when the pathologist came out from the theatre.

'Christ, that was quick.'

'I've not started yet. You need to come in.'

Davies's heart sank. What the fuck did they need him for? It was only the live criminals he was interested in. Someone else could take care of the dead ones.

'What kind of...?' He wanted to know what he'd be seeing in there.

'Skeletal remains. The death certificate shows the deceased had died from pancreatic cancer. There wouldn't have been much left of him in the end.'

Davies followed him through and braced himself. The room was a stainless-steel tomb. The stench of death hung heavy in the air. An industrial-sized extractor fan in each corner of the room could only mask so much. The decomposed body of the suspect lay on the steel slab. Small tufts of hair clung to the skull and the almost perfect teeth jutted from the jaw bone. The remnants of cloth that would have been his burial suit were by his side.

'Here.' The pathologist pointed and Davies gave a very quick glance.

'What?'

'There!' He forced Davies to take a closer look.

'Fuck me.'

'I'll take some more photographs, of course, but I wanted you to see before it's removed.'

On the slab lay the skeleton of their only suspect in twenty seven years. The only organ left intact was his heart, which was wrapped in pages from the bible and preserved in a clear plastic bag.

28

Glasgow 2002

'None of this leaves this room. Understand?' For the first time Davies had a link between the Raphael killings and Andrew Malloy. He'd need to tread carefully here.

'Toria, get onto the undertakers for Mack's funeral. I need the names of every member of staff there, including admin, delivery drivers, cleaners, and check if they took on casuals or freelancers.'

'I don't think they're called freelancers in the undertaking business. I think—'

'So, what, you're an expert now on…?'

'I wish. That's the business to get into, eh?'

'Sorry?' Davies was convinced this girl was a bit on the nutty side.

'Funeral director. I'd love to do that.'

'What? Deal with dead bodies?'

'Doesn't bother me at all.' Toria actually looked as though she was enjoying this conversation. Davies wasn't absolutely sure but thought she might have licked her lips slightly.

'In fact, when I retire from here that's what I intend to do.' Davies and McVeigh both shot each other a look, but she didn't seem put off at all. 'I could do bespoke funerals. I've been pricing motorbike hearses with sidecars, all sorts of stuff.' Davies couldn't tell if she was taking the piss or not.

'Would you do those biodegradable wicker coffin type things?' McVeigh clearly couldn't resist getting in on the act.

'Oh, God, yes, they would all be bespoke... and then I'd—'

McVeigh moved his hand across an imaginary sign in front of her eyes. '*We put the fun into funerals.*'

'That is a fantastic slogan.' She was deadpan.

'Toria, love?' Davies cut in before she had the chance to tell them about the two-for-one deals on stiffs, or the fun-time karaoke wakes. 'How old are you?'

'I'm twenty-three e, sir.'

'OK, love, you've a few years yet before we need to worry about all this, so in the meantime...'

'Just get my arse in gear?'

'Oh, you're one step ahead of me.' He held the door open for her and tried not to lose his patience. She nodded, but didn't seem to realise she was getting on his tits.

McVeigh waited until she was out of the room before he spoke. 'Did the DNA match?'

Davies shook his head. 'No big surprise there. But that doesn't mean he wasn't up to his fat neck in something.'

'Obviously Mack was a lot more clever than we gave him credit for.'

'Not we, me. You're off the hook with this one, McVeigh. You were still at school when Mack died; I've clearly taken my eye off the ball somewhere along the line.'

*

The funeral parlour was in Finnieston, not far from where Davies was born. The area was once a thriving hub of working-class life. Where every man had a job, wore a collar and tie on a Sunday and belted their weans if they stepped out of line. But the decline of the shipyards allowed a river of poverty and neglect to slowly percolate its way through the local community.

There was a large plastic flower arrangement in the window, with a sombre-looking cream curtain. The door pinged a very light bell when he opened it. McVeigh was one step behind. 'You must be Detective Inspector Davies.' The young woman held out her hand and offered a warm smile. Davies was slightly taken aback by how attractive she was, but held back from asking:

What's a nice girl like you doing in a place like this? He nodded and introduced McVeigh as he shook her hand.

'I'm Alison Duncan. Your colleague called to say you were on your way. Please, come through, we can talk in private,' and she led them through to a small room at the back of the main reception area, where Davies guessed Alison Duncan had used her soothing tone and attractive smile to comfort many of the recently bereaved.

'Your colleague only gave me the briefest details, but I'll try to help you as much as I can.' She already had a file on her desk, which she told Davies was the documentation for the funeral of William Casey Mack.

'I don't need to tell you this has to be in complete confidence.' Davies knew as soon as he said it how ridiculous it sounded.

'Rest assured, DI Davies, I have no desire for our long-standing reputation for excellence to be sullied any more than it already has been.'

Wishart Frasers had been in Finnieston for as long as Davies could remember. The sign above their door said 'Established in 1952'. It was a family-run firm and from what the lovely Alison told Davies they handled every part of the process in-house, from collecting the deceased to embalming to dressing the body and they even had their own resident hairdresser and barber. This kind of publicity could close them down for good.

Davies went over the details of what they had found when they'd opened Willie Mack's coffin. Alison Duncan's jaw tightened and Davies detected a tiny pulse throb in her neck.

'Can you tell me if it was an open casket? Was the body on view for family?'

Alison looked as though she was struggling to keep her hand steady as she flicked through the documents on her desk. 'It was a very long time ago and—'

'We really appreciate you taking the time to help.' McVeigh butted in without being invited. 'We understand this is as much a shock for you as anyone.' Alison nodded; a faint tint of red dotted the end of her nose and she swallowed hard as she blinked against the tears that threatened in her eyes.

'This is a family firm. We take a huge pride in the service we offer the local community. It's not easy, you know. Especially now. This place has turned into bedsit land. No one seems to care any more about personal service. And let's face it, you can get buried by the Co-op nowadays and pay it up on tick. Independents like us just don't stand a chance.' The tears she struggled to keep back spilled out over her cheeks, splashing onto the desk. She moved the documents out of the way as she dabbed her eyes with a tissue. 'I'm sorry, it's terribly unprofessional of me to cry but...'

Davies leaned forward, stretching his hand towards hers but stopping short of actually making contact.

'Don't be silly. It's actually refreshing to see someone so committed to their work.' He knew they were in danger of getting off-piste with this and needed to get back on track to find out who the hell would butcher Willie Mack after he'd died.

Alison quickly recomposed herself, dabbing the underside of her nose with a tissue, and wiped an imaginary speck of dust from the desk. She straightened the notes in front her like a newsreader and placed them back on the desk before turning over the first page. 'Every stage of the deceased's journey with us is documented and signed off by a member of staff. I can't possibly believe that such a thing happened here.' She ran her finger down the A4 sheet and Davies detected that tightness in her jaw once again.

'I need a full list of everyone who came in contact with the body at any stage of the...' he couldn't bear to call it a journey, 'process.'

Alison nodded. 'It's all here in black and white.'

'Who's the last person to handle the body?'

Usually our mortuary technicians. It very much depends on whether there's a viewing or if the body has been embalmed or not. But once everything is final then our mortuary technicians will ensure the coffin is fully secured and...'

Davies was about to take the sheet of paper from her hand when she drew it back towards her. Her eyes widened slightly. Davies thought she muttered the word

Christ under her breath but couldn't be sure. He leaned across and pulled the paper towards him.

'The technician in this instance?'

'George McClemand.'

She wasn't giving out any more information than that.

'Is he still here?'

She shook her head. 'No, I'm afraid we had to... we had to let him go.'

As lovely as she was, she was dragging this out and was beginning to get on Davies's tits. He raised his eyebrow, letting her know that he expected her to be a bit more forthcoming.

She played with the silver chain around her neck, rubbing the small pendant with her thumb. 'He just didn't quite fit in to what we expect from a—'

Davies held up his hand. 'Can you cut to the chase here?'

'There was no proof, and we never actually saw him do anything as such, but, well, he was just a bit odd.'

'Odd? Jesus Christ, can you sack people for being a bit *odd*?' He glanced over at McVeigh with his white top lip. He was saying nothing.

'He was found once crying over a recently deceased.'

'Did he know the deceased?'

'No, I mean he was hunched over the body sobbing and crying. Then another time we found he'd taken a lock of hair from someone in our care.'

Davies guessed this was another term Alison liked to use instead of dead body.

'He just seemed unnaturally attached, shall we say, to those loved ones placed in our care.'

'Did he ever mutilate or do anything more severe to any of the other bodies?'

Alison shook her head.

'Not that you know of, anyway,' McVeigh added.

'What?'

'Let's face it, he could have been up to all sorts of crazy shit and you'd never have known about it.'

Crazy shit? Where the hell did McVeigh get these phrases from? But Davies nodded and admitted he could well be right.

Alison Duncan immediately went on the defensive. 'Let me assure you, if there was something going on of a more sinister nature I would have known about it.'

'Presumably you took your eye off the ball with Willie Mack, then?'

'I beg your pardon?'

Davies decided to let McVeigh run with this one. 'Willie Mack. You know. The same William Casey Mack who was entrusted into your care. You know, the same William Casey Mack who, when on his final journey, had his chest ripped open, his heart torn out and wrapped in a poly bag and pages from the bible. You know, that Willie Mack!'

Alison Duncan held her hand over her mouth as she took an intake of breath which caused a tiny gulp in her throat. 'There was nothing to suggest he was doing such, such... extreme things with the bodies.' She'd given up on finding comforting euphemisms for the deceased.

Davies took over. 'D'you have contact details for this George...?'

'McClemand.' She shook her head. 'He left us almost nine years ago. We don't really keep tabs on our ex-employees.'

Davies was hardly surprised but at least they had a name. 'Just give us what you have.'

'I'm sorry I can't be more helpful.' She sorted through some more files on her desk and pulled out a few sheets of paper. 'I mean, he came here with excellent references. There was absolutely nothing to suggest he was, well, odd in any way.'

Davies reckoned anyone who wanted to work in an undertakers was already earmarked as odd, but said nothing. 'D'you have his references there?' Davies didn't need the information to track him down, his National Insurance number would throw up as much information as they needed, but it could save valuable time.

Alison shot him a look. 'Why on earth would we keep information like that?'

'Well, how the hell do you remember that his references were excellent?' This was wearing him down.

Alison Duncan was either incredibly clever or being deliberately difficult.

'Because, Detective Inspector, I only allow those with excellent references to become part of our team of care-givers.'

'Well, just shows, anyone can make a mistake, eh?' He stood up to leave, shaking her hand across the desk. McVeigh offered her a slight nod as he held the door open for Davies. 'If you do remember anything else "odd" about this George McClemand you'll let us know, eh?'

Her arms were folded tight across her chest; she sniffed and nodded at the same time. The colour had drained from her cheeks and she chewed on her bottom lip as she faked a smile.

29

Cartland1985

The stench was so familiar now. The smell of unwashed bodies, people dying from the inside out. The smell of the putrid blood. Grey mattresses lined the floor. The small windowless room was lit only from the lamp at the nurses' station. Dorothy Malloy could no longer count the time she'd been here by the passing of days and nights. So much of her time had been in darkness. Much of it sleeping. She no longer recognised her own hands. The strands of hair that hung loose around her face were no longer chestnut. It was long enough that she could hold it out in front of her eyes and when there was enough light she saw it was coarse and streaked with grey and belonged to a woman much older.

She shuffled along, her feet too heavy to lift, a hand guiding the small of her back. 'C'mon, dear, there we go.' The voice was soft and kind, not like the others. He helped Dorothy down onto the bed. Her limbs were stiff. Her legs felt skinny and fragile, as if they might break from too much pressure. Deep breathing and low moans from the others filled any void in the room. Dorothy lay back and prayed that sleep would come soon. But it didn't. The sleep that had engulfed her was now becoming less and less. Instead her body was paralysed. Her limbs refused to move and the only sensation was in her head. A waking nightmare. Occasionally someone would pass her bed.

She was promised the treatment would make her forget. It didn't.

30

Glasgow 2002

Oonagh spread the sea of papers in front of her. Dorothy Malloy's case notes covered the entire island unit in her kitchen. She didn't have a clue what she was looking for but thought this would be a handy place to start.

Tom had warned her that some of the pictures were horrific. Oonagh had thought it was only in cheesy crime fiction that people cut out their victim's heart and wrapped it in the pages of a bible. She'd deliberately asked Tom to leave those pictures out for now. She had enough trouble sleeping and didn't think that would help any. There were witness statements from Dorothy's GP and the scene of crime officers. Interestingly enough there were none from the neighbours; no one had been asked if they'd heard or seen anything suspicious that night, or indeed in the weeks leading up to the murders. And nothing from Dorothy herself. Oonagh made a mental note to badger Alec for the full police account.

She'd leave it for a few days though. He was still smarting at the news Dorothy Malloy was free and at large in the local community.

Dorothy and her husband had lived in a large sandstone villa on the outskirts of Glasgow with their five-year-old son, Robbie. On paper it would appear they had an idyllic life. Clearly not.

There were some brief details of Dorothy's medical history. She'd been prescribed mild tranquillisers when Robbie was a baby. To help her sleep, apparently. Five years later and she was getting them on repeat prescription. But there was nothing to suggest here that she was capable of this shocking crime.

Photographs were among the papers. Wedding photographs of the happy couple. Oonagh was surprised at how beautiful Dorothy had been. The last picture taken of Dorothy was on the day of the killings. It was a standard police issue photograph. Two sets. One of Dorothy in the clothes she'd worn when she'd been arrested. The other wearing standard-issue hospital white robes. Her eyes looked dead and she stood staring blankly ahead. There were no defence marks on her arms. Clearly she'd incapacitated her husband with the first wound. In the blink of an eye Dorothy Malloy had been transformed from a devoted wife, a loving mum to a ruthless killer.

Oonagh stood up and eased the crick from her back. She was tired, trying to make sense of all this. She stuck the kettle on. Coffee would help. Wine would help more but she was meeting her mum shortly and she couldn't be arsed with the hassle she'd get. And although she'd discovered that chocolate was far better at disguising the smell of booze than chewing gum, she decided today not to take the risk. Well, maybe just one wouldn't hurt.

Oonagh washed the glass, left the papers scattered on the worktop and made her way out. Her mum had already texted suggesting she'd just meet her at the house, but Oonagh wasn't in the mood for visitors and pretended she was already on her way, suggesting instead they meet in the park.

She decided to walk to Kelvingrove Park. It was a nice day and there were a few people out enjoying the early spring sunshine. Her phone buzzed in her pocket. She guessed her mum had already arrived at the café, which was on the other side of the park gates. Oonagh pulled her collar up around her neck and stuffed her hands down deep into the pockets of her jacket. In the distance she saw Fran get out of the car and for the first time she was struck by the resemblance between them. Her build, her hair, her mannerisms. Even the clothes were similar. For her whole life people had told her how much she looked like her mum, but today was the first time she'd noticed. Before reaching the door, Fran turned and caught sight of Oonagh and walked towards her.

'Fancy having a walk first?'

Oonagh nodded and was glad of the fresh air.

'I'm worried about you, sweetheart.' Her mum didn't believe in making small talk.

'Mum, d'you want to get the pleasantries over with first?'

Fran linked arms with her and smiled. 'I just think you're looking a bit pale and—'

I'm fine!' Oonagh cut in before she had a chance to finish. 'Come on, let's go get some tea – I'm not really in the mood for a walk.' The subtext being I'm *not in the mood for a motherly pep-talk*. Fran just gave her one of her looks and they walked back towards the café.

The tables outside were mainly free, apart from one woman trying to placate a toddler in her arms. The boy couldn't have been more than four but struggled to get free and lashed out with his open hands.

'Little shit!'

'Oonagh, he's only a wee tot.'

'Well, he's going to grow up into a big shit if no one tries to control him.'

'You weren't always an angel, lady, let me tell you.'

'But surely I didn't hit you, Mum?'

Fran laughed. 'OK, you never resorted to violence but you were a stroppy little madam at times.'

'I blame the parents.' Oonagh grinned and the middle-aged woman with the shitty little boy had given up and let him walk. She flopped down onto a seat and let him run around the swings, clearly no longer concerned if he ran off into danger.

'They're a handful at that age, eh?'

The woman smiled at Fran. 'Exhausting!' She stroked her neck, which flashed red with tiny slap marks and bore the brunt of little nails scratching her skin. She glanced down at her hands, which also had the making of small bruises from where The Little Shit had lashed out. 'I should get danger money for him!'

'The joys of being a granny, eh?' Fran beamed, totally unaware that her chance of being Grandmother had been washed down the sluice at Glasgow's Western Infirmary little over two years ago. Oonagh felt herself go pale and licked her lips. She looked at the two women, engrossed in innocent chat about babies, and her stomach gave a little roll. Her palms grew clammy, the telltale tightness clasped her throat. She was aware of her heart beating; the rhythm didn't seem quite right. It was too fast, surely. A pulse throbbed in her neck as a trickle of sweat helped the fear makes its way down her back. She wanted her mum to give her a cuddle. Tell her she wasn't going to die. Then the fear intensified and she had to get away. She struggled to keep her breath even. The pulse had moved into her jaw; it was threatening to give the game away. She needed to leave. Fast.

'Mum, I've just remembered I need to be—'

'Oh, my God! Are you Oonagh O'Neil?' The middle-aged woman cut in and pointed. Oonagh nodded, trying not to pant; Fran beamed with pride.

'Oh, my husband loves you. We always think you're so natural on the telly...' She carried on but Oonagh interrupted.

'I'm really sorry, the studio's just texted,' she lied. 'I'm meant to be doing a promo for...' She let herself trail off and Fran jumped up and gave her a quick kiss goodbye. Fran regarded Oonagh's job as something akin to being second in line for the throne. Nothing should ever interfere with it.

'No worries, I'll catch you later, sweetheart,' then she went back to chat to the granny who should be getting danger money.

Oonagh ran down to Argyle Street and flagged down a taxi. Her breathing started to settle, but she wanted home quick. The attack was easing, but she called Alec from the taxi; this couldn't wait. Her heart was racing slightly, but this time for a different reason. She fished her keys out of her bag as the taxi turned onto Byres Road. The traffic was light so she was home in minutes and raced up the stairs and straight back to the kitchen and the crimes of Dorothy Malloy. She picked up the photograph and jumped when her phone rang.

*

Davies nursed his coffee and looked at the sea of papers.

'Where did you get all this?'

Oonagh leaned back in her chair, tried to remain composed. 'And that's important because?'

'Because I can hardly condone looking over files you may have…' he chose his words carefully '… acquired by unorthodox means.' He clearly thought she'd nicked them.

'Oh, for fuck's sake, Alec, drop the Boys in Blue routine.' He gave her a look, which she chose to ignore. 'I didn't steal them, right?' She slid the picture of Dorothy under his line of vision. 'She stabbed her husband, ripped his heart out, then dragged a five-year-old boy up a flight of stairs, held him in a bath of water until he drowned and she doesn't have a fucking mark on her!' Oonagh had to catch her breath and felt a slight tightening in her chest.

At least Alec had the decency to look slightly embarrassed. 'Oon, I didn't investigate this case. It happened over a quarter of a century ago. I've never even seen the medical notes before.'

'But you can see them now?'

Alec nodded and picked up the photograph. Oonagh saw this as her inroad. 'Alec, it doesn't make sense. Look.' She pointed to Dorothy Malloy as though Alec wouldn't know what to look for, but he held up his hand.

'Oonagh, I'm a detective, you don't need to over-egg the pudding here.' He placed his mug down on the table.

'OK, then play detective. Tell me. Does this look kosher?' She thought back to the granny in the park with the scratch marks on her neck.

'This is strictly off the record.'

Oonagh nodded quickly. Desperate to urge him on.

'If I had to make a guess I'd say she took her husband out quickly. The subsequent wounds to his body would have either been post-mortem or he would have certainly been incapacitated.'

Oonagh had already worked that bit out for herself and grew impatient. 'And then?'

Alec drummed his fingers on the table and seemed reluctant to give her any more. Oonagh knew better than to push him and leaned against the worktop, chewing the side of her thumb. She and Alec went way back, but he was no pushover.

'She confessed, Oonagh.'

'So?' Oonagh knew some confessions weren't worth the paper they were printed on. Especially ones from way back. Police procedures were very different then.

'I want to see the pictures of the boy.'

Alec looked up. 'Pardon?'

'Her son. They must have taken post-mortem pictures.' Oonagh's mind was working overtime.

Alec stood up and scraped his chair along the wooden floor. He pushed his fingers through his hair. 'D'you want to calm down? You're a journalist, not a copper. You've got no right to—'

185

'I don't give a shit, Alec.' Oonagh sifted through the paperwork. 'Look.' She held up a sheet of A4. 'This is a doctor's notes from her examination with Dorothy Malloy when she entered Cartland.' Oonagh scanned the paper. 'She never actually says she killed them.'

'Where are you going with this?'

'I don't know, but there's something not quite right.'

Alec nodded. 'OK, for what it's worth I would expect there to have been some defensive wounds on Dorothy Malloy. Not from her husband but from the boy.'

Oonagh looked Alec in the eye. She waited for what was coming next. Alec said nothing.

'And?'

He shrugged his shoulders. 'Not my case.'

Oonagh's lips tightened as she picked up her phone and punched the numbers into the key pad. 'Press Office, please,' she asked the voice at the other end. Alec knitted his brow into a V. She held her phone out. 'If you want me to go through the official channels, I will.'

She should have known better than to call his bluff. 'OK,' he said, 'I'm done here.' He walked towards the door. She hung up and ran after him.

'Please help me with this one, Alec.' Oonagh O'Neil didn't ask for help lightly and Alec knew that. He allowed her to usher him back into the kitchen. Alec was privy to the original police files. He could easily access the pictures of Robbie Malloy's body. Showing them to Oonagh would be a different matter.

'I don't need to actually see the pictures for myself,' she offered as a compromise. 'If you look and think everything's as it should be, then I'll walk away.' She sensed he was softening. 'That poor wee thing must have put up a struggle, Alec.' She was surprised to find her eyes were filled with tears. Her bottom lip trembled. 'He was pinned down under water.' She sat down, exhausted by the false memory; a slight sob hiccupped from her mouth. 'He'd have put up a helluva fight. Whoever did that must have left a trace.'

'You ask a lot, O'Neil.'

31

Glasgow 2002

Her mouth tasted sour and her head was heavy. She struggled to open her eyes and it took a few seconds to register an unfamiliar weight on her right leg. She wriggled free and twisted her head around and groaned as she dropped her head back onto the pillow. 'Who the hell are you?'

The morning was trying to split through the curtains, spilling some light into the room. She screwed her eyes to focus and thought he looked vaguely familiar but was buggered if she could remember his name.

'Hiya.' He laughed as he leaned to kiss the side of her neck and she elbowed him away as she struggled out of bed.

Oonagh scanned the room and realised she was in her own bedroom, but hadn't yet figured out if that was a good thing or a bad thing as she tried to piece together the events of the previous night.

'Listen, you have to leave.'

'I'm in no rush.'

'No, seriously.' Oonagh O'Neil was used to thinking on her feet. 'My husband'll be home soon and he'll go insane if he catches you here.'

The guy propped himself up on the pillows. 'Your husband?' He folded his arms and smirked. 'Really?'

'Yeah.' She nodded as she pulled her robe tight enough to choke any remaining Catholic-guilt that threatened to well up inside. As a rule she didn't do one-night stands and it scared the shit out of her that she had no recollection of the previous evening.

'You told me last night you were single.'

'I lied, OK!' She grabbed random bits of clothes from the floor, throwing them in the direction of the bed. 'I want you to go. I want you to go now.'

'Lighten up! We had a lot of fun last night.' He picked up her mobile from the side of the bed and clicked the down arrow with his thumb. 'You're very photogenic!'

'Is everyone with a phone David Bailey now?' Oonagh felt sick. 'Give me that.' She leaned over but he held the phone out of reach and made out they were playing a game. 'Come on. Come back to bed.' He patted the duvet with his free hand.

'You'd no right to take those pictures.' Oonagh's legs were trembling, and she struggled to stop her voice cracking. She put her hand over her mouth and ran to the en-suite and emptied what little there was in her stomach.

'Christ, you don't look like that when you're on the telly.'

She kicked the door closed with her foot, then brushed her teeth and tried to tidy herself up before going back into the bedroom.

This was such a mess. 'OK, I'm asking you nicely now. Give me that phone, get dressed, then get out of my fucking house.' She leaned against the dressing table to steady herself – her legs were turning to jelly and threatened to let her down. Her hand rested on the small brass miniature of Rodin's Kiss. She felt the cool smooth curves of the couple's embrace.

He gave a slight snort. 'You were a right laugh last night. What's the big deal?'

'Just give me the phone.' Her voice was slow and deliberate.

He pushed the mobile under the duvet. 'Come and get it.' He laughed.

She walked towards him, hand outstretched, pleading. 'Please.' The pictures were sickening. The tears threatened to spill onto her cheek. 'Please, just give me the phone.'

He looked into her eyes and relented when he saw she was serious. 'OK.' He tipped his head and held the mobile in the palm of his hand. Just as Oonagh reached for it he dropped it onto the bed and pulled open her dressing gown, exposing her naked body.

'You fucker,' she screamed as she raised her fist and punched him full across the face.

He fell back onto the pillow, cupping both hands to his head. He let out a soft low gasp, but she guessed it wasn't without pain as the blood seeped from his temple. Oonagh staggered back and Rodin's entwined lovers fell from her hand and dropped at her feet.

'You're fucking for it now, you bitch.'

32

Glasgow 2002

He was at her door within minutes.

'Run that by me again.' He held her by the shoulders. Not quite shaking her, but she felt the intent under his gaze.

'Oh, fuck, what a mess. What am I going to do?'

'Who is he?'

'I don't know. I think he's a cameraman, or a sound engineer or someone. I've seen his face at work... or somewhere.' Oonagh thought she detected a slight look of disgust on Alec's face. 'Don't judge me on this!'

'Oonagh, you just caved a guy's head in, and you think I'm judging you for having a one-night stand?'

'I don't do one-night stands,' she screamed.

'Well, you fucking do now!' he yelled back and the veins stood out on his neck. Alec sat on the stairs, he dropped his head on one hand, then craned his neck up to where the noise was coming from. Upstairs the guy with the caved-in head was battering the door.

'I panicked. I shut him in with the deadlock.'

Alec said nothing, just rolled his eyes as the mayhem from upstairs continued.

'I thought he was going to kill me. Right.'

'So basically you shagged him, smashed his head in then locked him in your bedroom?'

She wasn't really in a position to argue.

'You don't do anything by halves, O'Neil, do you?'

She made her way to the kitchen, trying to ignore the racket from upstairs. 'Can I get you a drink, wine, whisky or… something?'

'Is this a fucking madhouse? It's barely ten o'clock.'

'Well, excuse me for getting this wrong. I'm not really sure how I should behave in this situation. You see, I've never actually committed GBH before.'

'Cool it!' Alec stood up and towered over her. He held out his hand. 'Key?'

She tipped her head towards the staircase. 'It's in the door.'

'You know I can't make this go away, Oonagh.'

Oonagh held her hand over her nose and mouth and nodded as she gulped back the tears.

'But I'll try to make it…' He paused. 'I can maybe do some damage limitation.' She detected a note of sympathy in his voice and her bottom lip quivered and dissolved into her chin as she watched him take the stairs two at a time. He turned. 'For Christ's sake get yourself some coffee and try to sober up.'

Everything was shiny and new in the kitchen; the guys had pulled out all the stops to get it finished when she'd offered them a five-hundred-quid bonus. She tried to pour herself a drink, but was incapable of even opening the bottle. Her hands shook uncontrollably and her legs turned to jelly beneath her. She steadied herself against the sink and held on tight enough to turn her knuckles white as she wretched into the smooth white porcelain. Her head swam with the enormity of it all, and the banging from upstairs seemed to get louder. Then suddenly it stopped.

Oonagh made her way into the hall and clung to the banister as she hauled herself up the stairs. The silence scared her more than the banging. A stream of catastrophic thoughts flooded through her head: he'd be blind in one eye, irreparable brain damage, scarred for life. No matter how shitty that creep was in her bed, he didn't deserve this. As she reached the top step the chaos resumed.

'Fucking psychotic bitch.'

'You'll live.'

'She's fucking mental.'

'Here, let's see. Don't think you'll need stitches.'

She slumped down on the last stair and caught Alec coming out of the bedroom. 'Romeo's going to live to love another day.'

Relief flooded through her entire body. 'You mean... he's all right? I thought...'

'He's not very happy.' He glanced back towards the bedroom. 'Really pissed off if truth be told.'

Oonagh dissolved in a heap on the top landing and sobbed. 'Thank you thank you thank you.'

'You thanking God that he's in one piece, or me for telling you that you're not in trouble?'

Oonagh ignored the obvious jibe and shook as she peeked round the doorway. The nameless guy with the perfect smile was pacing the floor, a wet flannel against his temple. A bruise was threatening its way towards his eye, blushing across his cheekbone.

'You're fucking finished.' He jabbed his finger towards Oonagh.

Just then Alec came back into the room. 'Right, there's a squad car downstairs. They'll take you to A& E, get you checked over, but I'm sure you're fine.'

'I'm going to fucking sue her.' The mobile was clutched in his hand. 'I'm going to sell these pictures to every media outlet in Scotland. She'll be a fucking laughing stock!'

Alec reached across the bed and grabbed the guy by the forearm. 'OK, Simon, play nice,' he said as he frogmarched him into the en-suite. Oonagh scrambled into the bedroom and saw them both in the mirror through the crack in the door. Alec kept his voice low and steady but she heard every word.

'Listen, Simon, I've got your fingerprints, I've got your DNA and I've got a shitload of unsolved cases, some of

195

them quite serious.'

'You can't do that! This is… this is… fucking police brutality.'

'I know. Life's shite sometimes.'

'Prick.'

'Do we have a deal?'

'Wanker.'

'Simon…?'

'Cock sucker.'

'Excellent. I'm glad you've seen sense. Now give me the phone.' The door opened and Simon staggered out of the en-suite, buttoning his shirt from the bottom up. He was breathing hard through his nostrils. 'You're fucking hopeless in bed and farted the whole night, ya manky bitch.' He grabbed what was left of his clothes and stomped out of the room.

'I'm…' Oonagh wasn't sure what she was about to say but stopped herself anyway and slumped down on the bed. She felt Alec's eyes on her and his hand reach towards her. She moved to touch him but he stopped short and dropped her mobile on the bed.

'Get yourself sorted out, Oonagh.' And with that he was gone.

33

Cartland 1996

She longed for the morning and the relief the daylight would bring. Moving her head from side to side was exhausting; bile, its taste sour, stung the back of her throat, and pooled in her mouth, slowly dribbling from her lips. The footsteps got closer. Her teeth clenched and with every effort she forced her head from side to side, trying to thrash it against the stale pillow. They were louder now, two of them, like before. She tried to spit the bile from her mouth, but could only manage to leak it slowly down her chin. Her tongue lolled out; she kept it there. She tried to shout but could only growl.

They were in the room now, one last effort. Just a few seconds. The growling caused her throat to rasp and burn but she was too terrified to stop.

The footsteps stopped at her bed.

'Fuck's sake, man, what's wrong with her?'

'Och, she's mental, 'mon, there's more over here.'

'Her mouth's all minging and slabbers.'

'Fuck's sake, just leave her, eh?'

'Got any young ones?'

And with that they moved on.

Dorothy Malloy let her head sink back, heavy onto the bed. Exhausted. The muscles at the side of her neck ached with the sheer effort of moving. Her head throbbed, her cheeks were wet with tears. If only the noise would stop, but at least this time it wasn't her.

*

'Dorothy?' His touch was soft as his hand rested gently on her shoulder. 'You OK, Dot?' She liked being called Dot. It sounded a happy name. 'You were miles away, love.' He smiled. 'You've got a visitor, Dot,' and stretched out his arm, encouraging Dorothy to follow.

The greenhouse was warm and Dorothy didn't feel much like leaving. She liked it here. They sometimes let her into the garden too when it was dry enough. The soil was soft between her fingers and she could see the sky. Outside the noise of a train thundered in the distance. The train to Glasgow, someone had told her. There had been a time when she would have torn at the walls to get out and onto that train. To get away, but that had been a long time ago and now she had nowhere to go.

The nurse smiled as he led the way, opening the heavy metal door with a key that hung from a metal loop on his belt. He was nice. He'd told her his name. Several times. But she could never remember. His uniform, a tunic and trousers, was black, with thick black shoes that reached up to his ankle. A far cry from the nurses she'd remembered as a child, who were always women, and wore crisp starched aprons with snow-white caps on their heads.

His arm bore a tattoo of a fox with a red rose underneath. Dorothy could see it through the thick brown curly hairs; the fox seemed to be smiling. Above his left wrist the names *Louise* and *Mike* picked out in elaborate writing. 'My wife and my boy', he'd once told her, tapping his finger on the names. Dorothy had had a boy once.

Her legs no longer felt heavy and she didn't seem to sleep as much. She was allowed into the garden too and managed to grow things. They said she was good at that. She never answered them, wasn't sure if she still had a voice. Perhaps they'd taken that away.

'Come on, love.' His voice was kind and soft as he closed the heavy door behind them. 'D'you know what day it is, Dot?'

Even if she could speak she wasn't sure she'd say, in case she got it wrong. It might have been Wednesday, but maybe not.

'It's your birthday, Dot.' He smiled again. He was nice. So few of them were. Another key, another door.

My birthday?

'And you've got a special visitor.'

He gave her shoulder a gentle pat and suddenly the door slammed shut. Dorothy turned to grab his arm. The nurse with the kind voice, but he was gone.

'Hello, Dorothy.'

He sat in the soft chair by the window, legs crossed, the sun behind him so she couldn't see his face. But she knew who he was.

34

Glasgow 2002

She drove north towards Maryhill then turned right into Lochburn Road. The block of art deco flats was on her right, built on the site of the old Magdalene Institution. Oonagh wondered if pain and sadness could linger in the soil and her thoughts drifted back to Irene Connolly. She continued up towards the cemetery and took a sharp turn at the roundabout. The sprawling graveyard suddenly came into view and the Campsie Fells were prevalent in the distance. It was April and they still had a light dusting of snow on their peaks. Oonagh dropped into second gear as she negotiated her car through the wrought-iron gates and drove slowly along the narrow road flanked by gravestones. The older ones were the most impressive. Towering monuments to remember the dead.

She pulled over and switched off her engine. There was barely enough room for another car to pass but she guessed it was quiet enough that that wouldn't be a problem. She walked over to the third grave on the left. Plot number 1906.

'Hi, Dad,' she whispered, and wiped some grass clippings from the top of the small headstone. Her heels sank into the grass, which was soft from the previous evening's rain. She laid a small daisy chain over the top of the gravestone and was almost glad he wasn't here to see the mess she was making of her life.

*

Fran was already waiting in the coffee shop; Oonagh knew she'd be early. She stood up when she saw her daughter and reached her arms out and held her tight. 'Hello, darling angel, how's my girl?'

'I'm great, Mum,' she lied. 'Bloody hell, you look fantastic.' This time she meant what she said. Fran looked ten years younger, and Oonagh told her so.

'I'm ten years happier, darling.'

Oonagh felt a stab of envy. She didn't begrudge her mum happiness but it would be nice to know the secret. 'Here.' She thrust a parcel towards her mum, hurriedly wrapped in tissue.

'Oonagh, you need to stop buying me things.' Fran pulled the tissue away to reveal a soft brown leather handbag, the Prada logo glinting discreetly at the top. 'Oh, no, this is too much.' Fran clasped the bag to her chest, apparently breathless.

'Mum, behave yourself, it's a bloody fake! It was peanuts, honestly.' Her mum hung the bag on the crook of her elbow like a badge of honour then leaned over to kiss her daughter again. Fran O'Neil was probably the only woman on the planet who carried real-deal designer handbags and boasted to all her friends they were fakes.

'Still going well with Owen?' Oonagh changed the subject away from the bag and Fran smiled for the affirmative.

'What about you?' she asked, scanning the menu without looking up. Oonagh shook her head, and tried to catch the waiter's eye, ready to order.

'Have you thought about a dating agency? They do it online now.'

'Sorry?'

'A dating agency.'

'Mum, I heard, I just couldn't believe you suggested it.'

'Moira's doing it.'

Oonagh had no idea who Moira was and couldn't be arsed finding out.

'She's been out for dinner three times this week. Saved herself a fortune. All she's had to buy is a tin of corned-beef.'

'Mum! That's enough. Bloody hell.'

'What about Alec?'

'Alec who?' Then the penny dropped. 'Davies?'

Fran nodded.

'Are you kidding?'

'No, why not?'

'Well, no! I mean, there's nothing wrong with him… he's nice and…'

'You could do worse.'

And I have done, Oonagh thought several times a week. But for now, all she could think about was the look of disgust on his face after her one-night stand with the cameraman she thought she'd killed. 'I'll just order at the counter.' She stretched her legs and wriggled out from the table.

'Don't rule him out just yet…' Fran yelled and Oonagh allowed her mother's voice to be drowned out by the coffee machine. That was one road she'd never go down. She was still mopping up the aftermath from her affair with Jack, if you could even call it an affair.

By the time she'd ordered and come back from the loo the coffee and cakes were on the table. Oonagh could murder a glass of wine, but Fran would go mental if she thought she was drinking during the day.

It was true her mum was looking better than she had done in years. Oonagh felt like a shit for the way she'd carried on when she'd discovered Fran had a boyfriend. But Owen, as it turned out, wasn't after Fran's money, didn't appear to be a serial killer and, judging by his teeth, he seemed to floss twice a day, so what wasn't to like?

'I'm glad you've found someone, Mum,' and she was surprised to find she meant it. 'Tell him I'm asking for him the next time you see him.'

But Fran looked as though she was only half listening; her concentration was on something outside the window. 'Why not tell him yourself?' She scraped her chair back and waved towards the door as the brave man himself walked inside and pulled up a chair beside them.

He dropped a kiss effortlessly onto Fran's cheek. The intimacy of the gesture pinched the back of Oonagh's throat. She eased back into her chair and watched their obvious affection as they chatted together.

'Tell Owen about your new project, Oonagh.' Suddenly Oonagh was six years old again and being made to put on her tap shoes, or her skating dress, or twirl her baton or whatever hobby she was practising at the time. 'Mum!'

'Oonagh's writing a book.' Fran didn't even try to disguise the pride in her voice. 'A novel.' Oonagh slunk further into her chair, sure that the outside world could bore into her very soul and see the scant progress she'd made with her *bestseller*.

Owen raised his eyebrows. 'Very impressive.' There wasn't even a hint of sarcasm in his voice, which made Oonagh feel worse.

'Early stages.' She sipped her coffee and looked at her watch, using it as a prop. 'Listen, I really need to shoot.'

Small talk no longer came easy to her and she feared Owen would ask her more about the book.

She gulped down her coffee and said her goodbyes, leaving Fran to show off her new bag to Owen. 'Honestly, I don't think anyone would ever be able to tell this from an original…'

On the drive home Oonagh's thoughts wandered back to work. Where the hell would she find six female killers who would be willing to talk on camera? She pulled off the main road up the one-way system for home. She reckoned two of the programmes could cover historical crimes, which would negate the need to secure fresh material and she could use archive interviews, library footage and 'experts'. She knew that was cheating slightly, but she needed this series secured pronto. Those episodes could be scheduled towards the end of the series, and with a bit of luck she might be able to find other subjects and not have to use them at all. They couldn't go right at the end. The first and last episode of any series were always the money shots – the pick of the crop.

The rain was light enough not to smear the windscreen and patches of blue sky struggled through the cloud.

For the first time in a long time Oonagh felt the nostalgic feeling of happiness. It took her by surprise. She slowed down to take a corner, the sun was low in the sky and flickered dazzling light as she passed the railings of the high school. The light pierced the side of her eye and a slight wave of nausea stirred in her stomach. Her mouth suddenly felt dry and parched. Then blackness.

35

Glasgow 2002

A dead weight crushed her chest and she thought she could hear a siren in the distance. An overwhelming scent of burnt toast filled her nostrils and the taste of vomit lingered in her mouth. The wetness between her legs was cold and she prayed to God she hadn't peed herself. Her right eye was forced open by someone's hand and a white light shone in her eye. 'Can you hear me? Can you tell me your name?'

Oonagh pushed the hand away and looked down. The airbag had inflated and forced against her chest; the bonnet of her car was pressed neatly into a lamp post. 'Shit.' Her voice sounded strange: thick and muggy. She wiped the saliva away from her chin. The paramedic leaned over and slid her seat back, releasing her from the constraints of the airbag.

'Are you in pain anywhere?' He touched her neck and down her shoulders with his thumb.

Oonagh looked round. 'Did someone rear-end me? What happened?' But there were no other cars nearby. She tried to piece together the events leading up to the obvious crash as she struggled to get out of the car.

'It would be best if you didn't move for now until we've checked there's nothing broken.'

Oonagh tried to smile. 'Believe me, had I broken anything you'd know about it.'

Her legs trembled as the paramedic led her to the back of a waiting ambulance. Her black jeans disguised the damp patch at her crotch. 'Well, you'll need to get checked over just in case.'

'And breathalysed.' The second voice seemed to come from nowhere. The uniformed officer got into the ambulance and sat opposite her. 'It's just routine.' He held the kit to her lips and Oonagh O'Neil vomited all over his standard issue copper's shoes.

*

'Have you ever blacked out before?' There were more lights in her eyes and she was rigged up to a heart monitor in a small single ward.

'Why do hospitals always smell like cabbage?'

The doctor glanced at the screen then back to her. He allowed a brief smile. 'Oonagh, please.'

'No, never.'

'Do you drink?'

She fell back onto the pillows, which felt scratchy on her back through the gap in the hospital gown. 'For God's sake! The breathalyser proved positive...' she thought for a moment '... or negative... What's the good one?'

'Negative.' He looked at her notes and went through a battery of questions. She wasn't really listening so answered no to all of them.

'Any history of epilepsy?'

'No.'

History of strokes, family history?'

'That's it, I'm going.' She swung her legs out of the bed and staggered slightly as she tried to stand.

The doctor guided her back onto the bed and carried on. 'Are you on any medication?'

She faltered slightly. 'The, the em, the contraceptive pill...' innocent enough '... and I'm on...' She made the tranquillisers sound as benign as possible and elected not to tell him about self-medicating with stuff she'd bought on the Internet.

'Often these episodes are a one-off occurrence, but we need to run a full CT scan to find out what's going on.' He smacked his lips and gave her a cheesy grin. 'D'you have someone who can drive you home?'

'I can drive myself home. The breathalyser was negative. Remember?' She stood up, then suddenly realised her car was wrapped around a lamp post somewhere off Byres Road. But sadly that wasn't what the doctor was talking about.

'Oonagh, sit down, please. You won't be able to drive until we find out what's wrong with you.'

'There's nothing wrong with me. I skipped breakfast and fainted at the wheel.' Nerves fluttered in her chest and she began to wish she had been drunk. This was scaring her.

He nodded as though he wasn't really listening. 'Did you have any tingling in your arms or legs? Tightness in the jaw?'

She sat back down on the bed; her head spun as she pieced together the moments before the crash. 'No, I don't think so. In fact...' she recalled the sun streaming through the car window and feeling good '... in fact the opposite. I felt really... good. Happy.'

He nodded again, but this time seemed to take in what she was saying. 'Any feelings of butterflies in your tummy, unfamiliar smells, tastes?'

She wanted her mum. 'I thought I could smell... toast?'

'It could be temporal lobe epilepsy. Patients often describe a feeling of euphoria prior to a seizure. Often accompanied by hallucinations, strange smells, vivid memories. Common in children.' He was prattling on about Dostoevsky suffering from it, he was on a roll and Oonagh reckoned he'd researched this for his final papers. She zoned out until he delivered the killer blow.

'Your licence will be suspended until it's determined you're fit to drive—'

'Whoa. Wait a wee minute here,' but the doctor was in full flow.

'You seem to have had a complex partial seizure. Now these episodes can and often are solitary in occurrence and we may never know...' The doctor's voice faded into the background as Oonagh's stomach moved and the blackness enveloped her once more.

36

Glasgow 2002

It wasn't like McVeigh to keep him waiting. Davies looked at his watch again: quarter past. He'd got the voicemail almost an hour ago now, asking to meet him at the office, said it was urgent. He tried calling but no reply. He was losing his cool when his phone rang, number withheld.

'Davies.'

He didn't recognise the voice on the other end: 'Is that DI Alec Davies?'

'I've just said as much, who's this?'

'I'm calling from Workplace Wellness. It's about your colleague DS—'

He didn't give her a chance to finish. 'Shit, what's happened? Is he OK?' Davies was surprised to feel the slight stirring of nerves in his gut.

'Well, it's a bit…'

'D'you want to just tell me what's wrong?'

'We have him here at our chronic illness and stroke rehabilitation unit. He's had a bit of an... well, let's call it an episode whilst trying out one of our machines.'

Fuck. 'Is he OK? What's the score?'

'The emergency services are on their way, but he asked me to call you, said you'd be worried.'

'Right, where is he? I'm on my way.'

'We're right across the car park in the ancillary building. The mobile breast screening is parked right outside, you can't miss us.'

'Tell him not to worry, I'm on my way.'

'Don't worry, he's perfectly calm. We're looking after him...'

Davies let the annoying whiney voice trail off as he ignored the lift and took the stairs two at a time. He ran across the car park, there was no sign of an ambulance yet, but there were enough trained coppers to deal with most CPR emergencies until the big boys arrived. His own heart thumped through his shirt; the cold air caught the back of his neck, turning the sweat on his back icy cold. He clearly wasn't as fit as he should be and made a mental note to shift a few pounds. McVeigh was as thin as a whippet and, as far as he could tell, fit as a butcher's dog. If he could take a stroke, there was little hope for the rest of them.

He pushed the swing doors open and was greeted by a flushed-faced occupational therapist. The badge on her chest said Morag; he couldn't be arsed reading the rest.

214

'Where is he?' His voice caught the back of his throat, he was more breathless than he should be after that short burst, but the adrenalin had kicked in too and gave him some much-needed energy. Morag took his arm and gently guided him through to a small room. There was no sense of urgency in her manner; he feared the worst.

'As I said on the phone, Jim's had a bit of an episode...'

And there he was. The colleague who'd got on his tits every day for more than two years, standing on the state-of-the-art health monitor, dressed only in his T-shirt and boxers, arm encased in the blood-pressure cuff.

'What the fuck?'

'Oh, boss, thank God you came over.'

'The fuck are you doing? I thought you were dead!'

Morag tried to calm troubled waters. 'It seems Jim was a wee bit enthusiastic about using the machine. He seems to have got himself stuck in the blood-pressure sleeve. It's electronic, very tight, you know.' The sleeve, as she called it, was a solid metal tube sticking out from the body of the machine.

'I wasn't enthusiastic, I was just taking my blood pressure.' McVeigh tugged his arm to prove his point, but it wasn't budging.

Davies felt the colour rise in his cheeks. 'Could you not have told me that on the phone, you stupid fucking cow?'

215

Morag stepped back, clearly horrified by his outburst. 'You put the phone down on me before I had the chance to explain.' She held her hand across her chest, waiting for an apology. Morag clearly didn't know Alec Davies, otherwise she'd have known she'd have a long wait.

By now McVeigh's head was in his free hand, the other arm swallowed by the machine up to his bicep, which was turning slightly blue as the electronic cuff inside grew increasingly tight. The three-day-old ginger stubble trying its best to cover the white tan line under his nose.

'Is there anyone in charge in this fucking nut-house?' Davies looked at McVeigh. 'What happened?'

'It wasn't me! I was just checking my blood pressure and stuff when the thing stuck and jammed my arm inside.'

'Where's all your gear?'

McVeigh tipped his head towards the chair where his clothes sat folded in a neat pile.

'You're best to get weighed without clothes. It says so.'

'Jesus, Mary and Joseph, I've seen it all now.'

Morag was patting McVeigh's free hand, telling him he'd be fine as someone from maintenance was on their way. She drew Davies daggers for his outburst. 'I'll be taking this further,' she said to him under her breath. Morag didn't look like the type of woman to be messed with. McVeigh just looked mortified as Davies walked to the other side of the machine and cut the power from the supply at the wall. The machine bleeped twice, before the sleeve deflated inside the cuff, freeing McVeigh.

Davies picked up McVeigh's clothes and handed them to him. 'D'you want to get back to work, Houdini? And, Morag?' She looked at him. 'Why don't we both just keep schtoom about this one, eh? And I suggest you get that machine away to fuck out of here.' This time she drew McVeigh a stinker, and stormed out of the room.

Back at the ranch the office looked like a carefully crafted bomb site; cardboard boxes covered every available floor space. The desk was piled high with paperwork, but each bundle neatly ordered. McVeigh was rubbing his arm, left swollen from his close encounter with the mad-machine. Davies did his best not to laugh, but found despite the situation he was starting to warm to his colleague.

'Right, what've you got?'

McVeigh continued rubbing one arm, trying to get the circulation back as he took the notes from the desk. 'Raphael's calling card.' The original evidence was stored at Forensics, but the photocopied prayer card read the now familiar line: *Do that which is good and no evil shall touch you.*

'Yeah?'

'I've went through this with a fine-toothed comb. Got Toria to double check it. This wasn't mentioned in the

217

original police report into Janet Channing's murder.'

'She was Catholic, McVeigh – they're always carrying wee trinkets and pictures of saints and stuff. The cops originally thought it was hers.' And that was true. The prayer card had been tucked into the pocket of Janet Channing's raincoat, and everyone had assumed at the time it'd belonged to her. It had only been when the second girl had been found and the same prayer card left on the body that the significance had taken hold.

'So why wasn't it listed among her belongings?' McVeigh held up the file that presumably listed the murder victim's belongings.

'Oh, gawd, this is a total mess. This case was mishandled from the start.' Davies waved his hand over the boxes lying across the floor. 'It's a fucking disaster zone.'

'We've checked, sir, and double-checked. There's no sign of it anywhere in the original report, yet it's down on the forensic list. It'd been bagged and tagged along with everything else.'

'Go on.'

'I think it was planted afterwards.'

'Be careful what you're saying here, McVeigh.'

'I'm not saying deliberately, sir, but...' he took a deep breath '... well, yes, I am saying deliberately. Had this been found on Janet Channing's body and thought significant enough to store as evidence then it would have been listed in the original report.'

Davies was slipping up. How the hell could he have missed that? 'Get the original from Forensics. I want a look at it.'

'It's already on its way.'

*

Evidence from a cold case was a copper's worst nightmare. Toria came in and laid each of the polythene bags on the desk. She looked more nervous than before and glanced at McVeigh who gave her a little smile. 'It was Toria who noticed it first Boss.' Davies nodded his thanks and she appeared to relax.

Each prayer card had been carefully documented, dated and with its own reference number.

'Well?' Davies could see at a glance it wasn't right.

'Couldn't even be arsed using the same pen.' McVeigh waved his hand loosely across the table. Each item belonging to Janet Channing had been logged in the same handwriting and signed off by the same forensic officer. Except the prayer card. That was clearly written by someone else.

37

Glasgow 2002

She asked the taxi to drop her off at the south side of the park, a good twenty minutes' walk away from the hospital but she could do with the fresh air. A breath of warmth eased its way through the thin cloud, bringing a promise of a good day ahead. Oonagh didn't feel like sunshine today. She wanted mist and damp and cold and rain. She needed the bitter chill of a cold November day. A *Big Issue* seller stood on the corner, tilting his head up towards the threatening sunshine, daring it to match his grin. She stuffed a tenner into his hand, trying to appease the guilty queue-jumping pleasure that her private health care offered her.

The hill leading to the centre of Queen's Park gave a panoramic view of the city. Oonagh stopped for a few moments taking it in. Her breath caught slightly in her chest and she wondered if her heart was beating faster than it should do. Ever since her blackouts she viewed each breath, each heartbeat with deep suspicion;

accusing her body of letting her down. Wondering which organ had betrayed her. The heart, the brain, the lungs? Or maybe it was the central nervous system or the respiratory system that had decided it didn't want to play ball any more. Had bailed out, refusing to be part of the team. The sense of treachery overwhelmed her. The anger all consuming. Was this how transplant patients felt? Let down? And how would they ever trust another kidney, heart, lung again if their own let them down so badly? How could they trust the organ of a stranger if their own could just pack up and decide to leave without a care for the consequences?

She'd ditched the Internet-sensation tablets after the blackouts; further research down Dr Google's wormhole had brought similar tales of unsuspecting people blacking out, memory loss and one poor bugger said he'd had a fit. The sudden withdrawal had left her feeling sick, miserable and even more anxious. She couldn't tell anyone, least of all her doctor. She prayed that the medication was indeed at the root of her fainting fits but the sickening fear that there was something seriously wrong with her had already gripped her abdomen.

The tears that had been welling up for days gathered in a pool and threatened to spill out onto her cheeks. She blinked hard and pressed the tissue into the corners of her eyes as she crossed the road. The Victoria Infirmary loomed in the background; thick black smoke belched from a tall chimney. Oonagh wondered what useless organ or limb was being incinerated today. What other poor sod was being told that their body had decided to pull the rug out from under them and bail out or had sneakily let cancer in the back door?

Her phone buzzed in her pocket, her mum texting her to say she was on her way. Initially she'd thought against telling Fran; she knew it would freak her out, but she needed some support. Needed her mum's arms around her. She made her way up to the main entrance. This place should have closed down years ago. It reeked of decay and neglect that no amount of cash could ever put right. A culture of despair seeped from every pore.

Fran was already waiting by the front door. Eyes wide, chewing on the inside of her cheek. She stopped when she caught Oonagh wave to her and faked a smile, which almost convinced Oonagh there was nothing to worry about.

The waiting room had seen better days. An elderly man sat propped up in a wheel-chair, a white, waffle hospital blanket over his knee. He glanced at Oonagh, gave her a wee smile then stared back at the floor. She guessed he hadn't been fast tracked through the system for treatment like she had, and wondered how long he'd been on the particular list. Oonagh's consultant had assured her it was commonplace to send private patients to NHS hospitals for certain tests, but she couldn't help feeling shitty about it and wondered if it was worth the grief. She drained the last of the weak coffee her mum had bought from the W.I. shop downstairs, while Fran picked away at the edge of the polystyrene cup with her nail until the entire rim was in tatters.

'Mum!' Oonagh grabbed at Fran's wrist and already felt a pang of guilt but couldn't stop herself. 'Can you not do that, please?'

'Sorry, sweetheart, I didn't...'

'It's making me feel sick.'

Fran just nodded and reached to stroke Oonagh's arm.

Oonagh's stomach heaved and an involuntary spasm tightened her throat. She didn't hear her named being called; it was only when Fran raised her hand to indicate where she was sitting that Oonagh realised the nurse was looking for her. He looked friendly enough, young but efficient. She couldn't deal with any platitudes right now and she hoped he wouldn't try out his bedside manner on her. Live in hope, die in despair they say. The young nurse, Gary was his name, wittered on endlessly in the seemingly never-ending corridor. He ushered her to a changing room where a standard issue hospital gown, paper knickers and foam slippers awaited. Oonagh was sure that the kit was the design of months-long consultation by senior surgeons desperate to find the best method of keeping patients in line. What better way than the antiquated hospital gown, buttoned up the back? It was very difficult for patients to become unruly, rebellious and complaining if their arse was hanging out for the entire world to see.

Once in the system she became a name and serial number. Led from room to room, a plastic bracelet giving her name, date of birth and hospital ID number.

She filled out another form asking if she had any piercings – ears, nipples or otherwise – whether she wore dentures or indeed had a wig on. That bucked her up slightly. The fact she had her own teeth and showed no signs of male-pattern baldness slipped her into the super-league bracket of patients.

Oonagh hardly noticed when the girl touched her arm. 'Oonagh? I'm Kelly. I'm your radiologist.'

She led Oonagh into the room for her MRI scan. 'There's nothing to worry about. It will be noisy at times, but here—' she handed Oonagh a set of headphones '—you can listen to music and that helps.'

Oonagh's quick wit and sarcasm went on a tea break as soon as she saw the massive piece of kit, which in her eyes looked like an iron lung. 'Has the procedure been explained to you?' Oonagh nodded. 'You may feel slightly claustrophobic, but I can stop the test if you feel overwhelmed.' Kelly must have guessed what Oonagh was thinking. 'Here…' she sat her down on the chair '… take a few moments, you'll be fine. D'you want your mum to come in?'

Oonagh shook her head. 'No, thanks, I'm OK, honestly. As long as you don't play Kylie when I'm trapped in there I'll survive.' Kelly smiled as Oonagh lay down and allowed herself to be swallowed by the machine.

38

Glasgow 2002

Oonagh could see Jim McVeigh's outline against the frosted glass and rapped on the door. She knew Davies wouldn't be there – she'd already spoken to him on the phone. The office was dingy with polystyrene ceiling tiles, and the sunlight streaming through the window only served to highlight the gloom as dust settled on every available surface. McVeigh was perched on the edge of the desk but stood up as soon as she entered.

'The boss isn't here.' He looked a bit flustered and was surrounded by countless box files, tattered paper wallets and a seemingly endless sea of paper.

'Crikey, is that the files for…?'

McVeigh nodded. 'Aye, I need to sift through it and go through the witness statements again.'

Oonagh stood slightly on tiptoe and peered over the desk. 'Don't suppose there'd be any chance of…?'

'No!' McVeigh gently ushered her back from the desk with his arm. 'You kidding? He'd have my head on a plate for that.'

She wasn't surprised but, still, a slight pang of disappointment pricked her chest.

'I see you shaved your top lip.'

McVeigh just tutted.

'Don't let him bully you, Jim.'

He looked a bit uncomfortable so she steered the topic back to the investigations.

'Making any headway?'

Oonagh had already gained copies of as much of the press coverage of the crimes as possible, radio archives, television news bulletins and newspapers. Almost every article focussed on the fact that all the girls had been *pretty blonds*. As though in some way that had made a difference. Killing beautiful women was less palatable to polite society and there was a greater need for their killers to be caught. Beautiful women had earned their right to survive. She wondered how often the media would include a male victim's looks when reporting a murder. *The handsome, blue-eyed father of three...* just didn't have the same ring to it, and it made her feel slightly sick. Even those useless vox-pops so prevalent now after an atrocity carried the same message. 'She was such a pretty girl... she was so nice... always had a smile on her face.' Beautiful people didn't deserve to die that way.

'Fancy a cup of tea?' McVeigh held his cup aloft and Oonagh looked at her watch.

'It's taken you almost three minutes to ask!'

McVeigh grinned. 'What kind?' He was legendary for his tea and could talk for hours on the subtlety of each flavour.

'Oh, go on, surprise me.'

He gave her a look that she couldn't read. 'Oh, I may do just that.' This time it was his turn to look at his watch. 'I'll be gone for about—' he pursed his lips '—four minutes?' He turned the statement into a question.

'I hadn't realised tea making was so precise.'

He looked at his watch again, then glanced at the sea of paperwork. 'Four minutes.'

With that he was gone and it took Oonagh a few seconds for the penny to drop. *Shite!* She lunged at the desk and pulled random pieces of paper from files, trying to take in what was the most important. It was impossible to decipher what was the most vital and she knew her golden opportunity had a very small window so she took pot luck. Nothing else for it. She jotted down numbers, names, anything that she thought would be of use.

Jim's notebook lay open on the desk. Beside it was an A4 sheet of Glasgow University headed paper. It was DNA results. Impossible for Oonagh to read. She tried to scribble down the details as she ran her eyes over the results but couldn't really take it in. Her eyes scanned the room, then out through the slight crack in the door, and spied the photocopier. The clock was ticking. Four minutes suddenly didn't seem like a very long time. On-air a four-minute silence was a lifetime, at the dentist with a drill rattling against your teeth four minutes seemed an eternity, but this seemed like the race of her life.

The main office outside was empty. She made a dash for it, slammed the statement into the machine, pressed 'copy' and waited. There was a faint electronic click then the lights on the machine flashed red: error, error, error. She could see McVeigh's telltale red hair at the end of the long corridor; he was walking towards her. 'Oh, fuck!' She looked around for inspiration then kicked the photocopier hard enough to hurt her foot. Suddenly it whirred into life. Perhaps it was used to police brutality. 'Oh, thank you!' she uttered, and wondered if there was a patron saint of photocopiers.

McVeigh was now visible through the set of double swing doors and held a mug in each hand. Oonagh could see the slight edge of crisp white paper feeding out of the other side of the photocopier. Her right foot tapped on the ground as she willed it to move faster. She held it between her thumb and forefinger, pulling with just enough force to ease it closer to her. McVeigh backed against the doors and kicked them open with his heel, three quarters of the document was now visible, he then spun round with expert precision to avoid the doors swinging into his back as Oonagh tore the paper from the photocopier and stuffed it into her bag.

Her face flushed red and she swallowed hard to stop the rising panic in her chest. 'Jim—' she made a big play of looking at her watch '—I'm not going to be able to stay for tea after all...'

'No worries, Oonagh.' She leaned up and kissed him on the cheek, aware that she was slightly out of breath. 'If ever you don't want another cup of tea feel free to pop by.'

39

Glasgow 2002

No matter how long he'd been in the job, no matter how embittered he'd become, or used to the sight of death, the murder of a child still chilled him; affected him like no other. The case was over a quarter of a century old, and, as far as the legal definition was concerned, solved and therefore case closed.

He looked first at the scene of crime pictures of Andrew Malloy to give him an appetite for death before moving on to the boy. The 1970s didn't seem that far away. It was living memory, yet, in the background of the pictures, several sets of bloodied footprints from the scene of crime officers were dotted around the corpse and a policeman's hat sat on the sideboard. Contaminating vital evidence.

Andrew Malloy's body was on a leather armchair. His head tilted back and to the left, his throat open from a single wound, which started from his Adam's apple and ended just under his right ear. The wound, which had proved fatal, had been inflicted from behind. Poor bugger wouldn't have known what hit him. It was a clean cut, sliced through the carotid artery. That would have put Malloy out of the game. No chance to retaliate, hence the lack of defensive wounds to his arms. His eyes remained open. His mouth, too, gaped as his chin dissolved into what was left of this throat. His arms hung limp across each side of the chair. One leg stretched out in front of him. Davies wondered if Malloy's last sight had been of his devoted wife slicing through his chest into his heart.

The blood from the initial wound had sprayed in an arc, hitting the wall behind and reaching the edge of the fitted carpet. By all accounts she'd let him bleed out before hacking open his chest. Rumours that she'd taken out his heart and wrapped it in pages of the bible weren't quite true. Malloy's breastbone was still intact. It would take more than a kitchen knife and a pissed-off wife to break that. Instead Dorothy Malloy had stuffed pages of the bible into her dead husband's chest cavity, ensuring they covered as much of his heart as she could. Davies wondered if there had still been a faint heartbeat as she'd performed this final ritual. Coppers had a macabre joke that the quickest way to a man's heart wasn't through his stomach, but straight through the chest with a kitchen knife.

The charge sheets for Dorothy Malloy were in a different envelope. He glanced through them. The police statement was there, no witness statement and of course no statement from the accused; she hadn't been in a fit state. The Malloys had lived in a suburb in the south side of the city, where things like this didn't happen. Davies looked again at the paperwork. Something jarred. Dorothy Malloy was taken from her home and straight to Cartland in Lanark, over thirty miles away. It was the only state mental hospital with a segregated female ward. He slipped the paperwork back into the envelope, put it in his drawer and locked it.

He then braced himself before looking at the pictures of the boy. Of Robert Malloy. Their son Robbie. Just five years old. He'd have been thirty-two now, had his mother not killed him. A grown man, with all the happiness and sadness and mundane shit that all the other grown-ups had to deal with every day. Davies could never shift that utter sense of devastation, the absolute loss with the death of a kid. A life yet to be lived. Dreams unfulfilled. Was there a woman or a man out there somewhere missing a soulmate because of the premature death of Robbie Malloy? Was there an undiscovered cure for cancer that died with him? Or a work of art never to be realised or a great statesman who would never be? Davies chose not to consider the fact a murdered child might just as easily have grown up to be a rapist, a serial killer or just another fucking waster who didn't give a shit.

He looked at the post-mortem examination results first. There was only one single page. He sifted through the rest of the papers to retrieve more but found none. It was little more than a death certificate. There had been no toxicology report, no detailed examination of the boy's organs; not even a fingernail scraping. His height, weight and cause of death, *drowning*, were all that was recorded. He couldn't read the signature of the pathologist who signed it off, but it would be in the records.

Davies slid the photographs from the A4 envelope, laid them side by side and immediately felt a chill from the back of his throat slide down towards his chest. He dropped his head into his hands. 'Fuck's sake.' He stood up as the adrenalin caused a slight shift in his abdomen then surged through his body; he punched the door of his office hard enough to cause a searing pain through his right knuckles. He rubbed his wound as he rocked back and forth on his heels wondering what the fuck to do next. He caught sight of McVeigh's ginger hair through the glass and snapped his fingers, even though he was too far away to hear, gesturing for him to come quick without catching his eye. McVeigh was used to being on high alert and opened the door.

'You want me, boss?'

'Get your arse in here quick and shut the fucking door.' He drummed his fingers against his thigh, his left foot dancing on the ground as he pointed to the pictures, denying McVeigh the luxury of reading the post-mortem report first. Davies leaned back on the window sill and held his right hand over his mouth, hiding the tiny beads of sweat that had formed on his top lip. His eyes shifted from the photographs to McVeigh, who remained perfectly still but was betrayed by the tightening of his jaw and the single vein pulsing on his temple.

'Who is it?'

'Doesn't matter.' Davies hadn't kept McVeigh in the loop about this one. McVeigh shot him a look, and he suddenly felt a bit shitty for exposing him to pictures of a child's corpse without prior warning. 'Of course it matters.' He softened slightly. 'I mean, for now, please just tell me what you see.'

Robbie Malloy's bloated body was grey. There were no scene of crime pictures. Instead he lay on a metal slab. The blue tinge around his lips still evident. His eyes, thank God, were closed and his hair smoothed down at the sides.

McVeigh folded his arms in front of his chest. He hesitated slightly.

Davies was growing impatient. 'It's not a trick question, McVeigh, just tell me.'

He cleared his throat. 'Child, aged...' he paused '... six or seven?' he said; an obvious question waiting for his boss's approval before continuing. Davies nodded.

'Five.' Robbie Malloy was tall for his age. 'Carry on.'

McVeigh picked up one of the pictures for closer examination. 'Clearly—' he took a deep breath '—the child was murdered, killed.' He began to relax into the job in hand. 'Finger marks, bruises, to the upper arms, neck area suggest he was grabbed from behind. Can I ask?' Davies tipped his head, gestured for him to continue. 'Did he drown?' Davies nodded. McVeigh was shaping up to be a good cop. He was thorough and could slot vital pieces of evidence together like a jigsaw. 'Bruising around the ankles, too, shows that a degree of force was used.' He was getting into his stride. But paused again, momentarily. 'Boss?' Davies let him continue. 'Do we know *where* he drowned?'

'Bath. At home.' Davies knew McVeigh was already forming the scenario in his head. Had the child been thrown into a body of water and left to die the bruising would have been caused by the initial restraints. In the bath suggested he was held down.

'A significant degree of force was used,' he repeated.

'Can you tell me anything about the killer?'

'Oh, no.' He held up his hands. 'I'm not going there. You need forensics for that.'

Davies knew he wasn't playing fair, but who said life was fair? McVeigh had joined him as part of the graduate training scheme for coppers and had a special interest in forensics. 'Just humour me, eh?'

McVeigh looked nervous as he picked up the set of photographs. Taken from every angle on the pathologist's slab. Bruises on the heels indicated he'd kicked against the bottom of the bath for as long as he'd had life in his body. Bruising on the ankles but lack of bruising on the ankle bone itself suggested he'd been restrained from lashing out sideways with his legs. Apart from purple bruising on his buttocks, presumably from bucking his body against the attack, his torso was clean. Not one handprint or finger mark was present on Robbie Malloy's body.

'So?' Davies stared at his colleague.

'I'd need to see more, boss, I mean—'

Davies cut in. 'Fuck's sake, the case is closed. I know who the fucking killer is – it happened twenty-seven years ago. Just go out on a limb here.'

Despite Davies's outburst McVeigh seemed relieved to be off the hook with the realisation that the case did not rest on his opinion. 'OK,' he ventured, 'the pattern of the bruising suggests his legs, arms, throat were restrained or grabbed simultaneously.' He leaned over the desk, resting his weight on one hip; the pictures he rearranged from top to bottom, his eyes darting between each one. 'This kid was attacked, possibly by a male, judging by his hand-span.' He read the notes, which stated Robbie Malloy was three feet ten inches. McVeigh held his arms wide, judging the distance, then leaned over, simulating the scene; holding his arms in front of him reduced his arm span considerably. 'Mmm… six foot plus, or…' He hesitated.

'Or what?' Davies cut in.

'Or two people held him in the bath?' Again it was a question. McVeigh turned slowly. 'But...'

'What?'

'You wouldn't hold a kid down in a bath, would you?'

Davies said nothing, let his colleague continue.

'Would it not be easier just to force his head under the water?'

Davies hadn't known of many deliberate drownings; of those he did know about, none of the victims were killed face up. McVeigh was right. Face down. Hand on the back of the head.

'I'd say the kid put up a bit of a fight.' He paused. Davies knew what was coming but wasn't sure if he wanted to hear this. 'And more than one person was involved, given the fact there seem to be several sets of finger-mark bruising.'

Davies looked at his colleague, who offered him a weak smile, apparently hoping he'd passed the test. At that precise moment he had no way of knowing the huge, big can of fucking worms he had just opened.

<u>40</u>

Glasgow 2002

Davies's bed offered little in the way of sleep, so he thought it the lesser of two evils to go into the office before the day shift arrived. He pulled on a pair of jeans and a shirt, badly in need of an iron, then jumped in the car whilst it was still dark. It was only when he arrived at work he realised quite how early it was: 3.30 a.m.

The duty desk sergeant was the only other soul around. He didn't look overly surprised to see him. 'Another sleepless night, Alec?'

He just nodded and rubbed his hand across the stubble on his chin. He'd known Bill a long time. They'd worked in the same division for almost thirty years. Bill had been happy to stay in uniform, and worked his way into a desk job, always said he couldn't be arsed chasing criminals. And it was more than just rumour that he spent most of his shift in his slippers, with his Docs tucked out of sight in his locker; hardly worn.

'Cuppa?' Again Davies nodded. 'D'you want a wee dram in that?' Bill glanced at the clock. 'You're all right, Alec, it's still night-time.'

A whisky would take the edge off things. 'Go on, then, since it's you.' He pushed through the double doors and turned. 'Thanks, Bill.'

He kept a few things at the station, meaning that he could usually shave and shower when the long shifts extended into even longer shifts and bled into each other, until some days he only knew what day it was by the newspaper in front of him.

He chewed on the end of his pen as he drummed his fingers on the desk, fidgeting with his mobile with the other hand. It had been a few days since he'd last heard from Oonagh. There was no real reason for her to call – aye, they were friends, but their friendship still had its boundaries. He missed her. Hated admitting that, but he did. Despite her problems she brought an element of fun into his otherwise dull personal life. A tiny knot of something, not exactly jealousy, made a wormhole in his chest when he thought of her and that prick in bed together. He switched on the radio, Classic FM, and let Vivaldi fill his head instead. The music washed over him like a comfort blanket as he put his feet up on the desk, closed his eyes for just a moment and settled back in his chair.

'Comfy?' The voice sliced through his slumber.

He blinked the sleep from his eyes and sat bolt upright. 'Shit!'

Threadgold was sitting opposite. 'Long night?'

'Sorry, sir, I was just...' He glanced at the clock: 8.30 a.m.

'Resting your eyes. I know.'

Fuck, this was all he needed. Threadgold catching him asleep at his desk. He was supposed to be using up his holiday leave before hanging up his truncheon. The fact he was prowling around the station at this hour wasn't a good sign.

'Relax, Alec. Bill told me you've been in since the wee small hours.'

He smeared a handkerchief across his mouth, aware of the stale smell of whisky and the line of drool that had escaped down his chin. 'I thought if I came in early I'd...'

Threadgold held up his hand, telling him to calm down. 'You know, Alec, I've been in the force for almost forty years. It doesn't do to be married to the job. It's tough enough.'

Davies nodded, not quite sure where this was going.

'Don't be afraid to let your hair down now and again. Lighten up a bit.'

Jesus Christ, he must be a right uptight pain in the arse if the Chief Constable was telling him to lighten up.

'So. How's it going?'

'The case?' Davies felt that telltale burning in his gut. 'It's ehm...' He hadn't quite got round to telling Threadgold of the latest developments. That Willie Mack wasn't so much resting in peace as resting in pieces, and that it was growing increasingly likely that someone was tampering with the evidence. 'There's been a bit of a development.' Threadgold raised his eyebrow and Davies let the scenario unfold. He gave his own edited version, deliberately leaving out the part about the evidence tampering. 'I was going to call you today. To let you know.'

'I'm on *garden leave*, Alec, you don't need to tell me everything.'

Davies knew he was talking shite. Threadgold had ordered this cold case be re-opened. His balls were very much on the line here.

'So, what d'you make of it?'

He didn't seem altogether surprised that Willie Mack's heart had been wrapped in polythene with pages from the bible stuffed inside, but then Threadgold had seen a lot in his years as a cop. He let Davies witter on about his chat with the undertaker. 'I've got a lead on where the mortuary attendant may be now, so I'll go talk to him today.'

'And the DNA?'

Davies had almost forgotten about that. 'Mmm, inconclusive.'

'Sorry?' Obviously Threadgold had heard but was looking for a different answer.

'Sir, the evidence is too contaminated...'

Threadgold stood up and leaned his hands on the desk. 'Well, get more evidence, then.'

'And Mack had a cast-iron alibi for at least two of the killings.'

'Listen, Alec, I want this case closed by the end of the week.'

'Are you fu... are you serious? The end of the week? That's impossible.'

'You've got bags full of evidence, some of it must fit. D'you hear what I'm saying? That fat bastard did it, case closed. Organise a press release for next week. Do it after budget day – folk'll be too busy moaning about the price of beer and fags to bother about much else.'

Davies ran his hands through his hair, surprised that he had any left at this rate. 'But you could drive a coach and horse through the case against Mack.'

'Get down off your high horse, Alec. There's not going to be a court case. Mack has one living relative left: a daughter that says he's the killer. At least this way the families of those poor girls get closure. It's win win all round.'

'This is far from closed.' His voice came out louder than intended and he fought to keep it in check. 'What about Willie Mack's body? What the hell's that all about? Hacking him to bits in his coffin?'

'If you find who did it, charge them with desecration of a corpse and move on.'

Davies rubbed his hand across the pulse on his neck. He couldn't shift the nagging doubt that Threadgold knew exactly what was behind the mutilation.

'There are bigger things happening in the city now, Alec, than finding out who had a grudge against Willie Mack.' Threadgold made towards the door. 'Go home, get some rest, son, you're heading for burnout.'

Davies watched him walk down the corridor, head and shoulders above the rest of the foot soldiers who had finally turned up as the office sprang to life. McVeigh entered stage left. 'Bit early for a social call from the Chief. Everything OK, boss?'

'Does everything look OK?' Davies had given up keeping a check on his anger. 'But in case you really are as stupid as you look, no, everything is not OK.' He didn't know where to start. 'I'm going for a shit and a shave – any chance of a decent cup of coffee when I get back?'

McVeigh turned and Davies thought he heard him tut slightly as he walked out of the door. 'And, McVeigh, I hope you had a good night's kip. We've got a long fucking day ahead of us.'

41

Glasgow 2002

Oonagh stood on the doorstep and pulled her collar tight against the biting wind. The sky was crisp and blue but the sun provided little warmth in the cold east-coast wind. Typical of Edinburgh, it was always bloody freezing.

It was an expensive neighbourhood; she had no idea why that surprised her. She stamped her feet and was about to chap the letterbox once more when she heard shuffling footsteps from behind the door and the telltale clink of keys being turned in the lock. The heat was the first thing to hit her as the door opened just a few inches.

'Graham?' She dropped her head to the side, bringing her eyes in line with his. It was difficult to guess his age. His face was thin, his skin and hair almost the same grey pallor. He nodded and afforded her a smile as he opened the door just wide enough for her to squeeze past. It was only as he locked the door behind her that she realised she hadn't actually told anyone where she was going, or who she was meeting. Oonagh palmed the car keys in her pocket and wedged the sharp end between her index and middle finger in case she needed a makeshift weapon, but, looking at Graham, she reckoned a bad cold would floor him.

'Thanks for agreeing to see me.' She gave him a little smile but tried not to look happy. He ushered her through to the living room, where the source of the intense heat in the form of a wood-burning stove was.

'Sit down, Oonagh.' His familiarity took her by surprise; even though she'd set the tone by calling him by his first name. 'Tea?'

She weighed up her options and decided to buy some time. 'Go on, then.'

He left the room and it gave Oonagh the chance to take in her surroundings. The room was immaculate and, although sparsely furnished, every piece was expensive and well crafted. There were few pictures; nothing that suggested a back-story. Within minutes Graham came back with a tea tray; he'd clearly had it ready prepared for her arrival.

'So how did you find me, then?' He handed her a china mug and let her help herself to milk and sugar.

'I have my methods.' She slipped her coat off her shoulders; her host made no attempt to take it from her.

'Can't have been easy for you these past twenty-five years.'

'Twenty-seven,' he corrected without looking at her.

Oonagh worried she was coming across as patronising. But she felt a genuine ache for Graham Semionoff, a man whose life was robbed through no fault of his own.

'It's not exactly been a bed of roses, no.' He shrugged his shoulders; gave her a *who cares?* look.

'Are there no support networks, people you can speak to? People in the same boat as yourself?'

He laughed at this last comment. 'And what boat is that, then, Oonagh O'Neil? The Good Ship up the Creek Without a Fucking Paddle?'

She blew on her tea and put it on the coffee table without drinking it. 'Sorry,' she said, and meant it.

'No, I'm sorry.' He didn't sound as though the word fuck came easy to him; he braced himself slightly and gave Oonagh a weak smile. 'So what d'you want to talk to me about?'

Oonagh took the mini-recorder from her bag and placed it on the table. 'May I?' She flicked the on switch with her thumb.

'No, you may not.' He shook his head and she realised she'd overstepped the mark. 'An informal chat, that was all I agreed to.'

Finding Graham Semionoff had not been easy. After his sister had butchered her husband and drowned her son, he, like the rest of the family, had gone into hiding. Guilt by association had robbed Graham of the normality of a family life enjoyed by his peers. As it turned out, his wife had left him, taking their two children with her. No forwarding address. Graham had never tried to find them, he told Oonagh. It was better all round if they could enjoy a new life without the guilt or the stigma of being related to Dorothy Malloy. The mad bitch who killed her husband and son. The apple didn't fall very far from the tree, they said.

'I still miss her.' Graham ran his fingers through his hair, and Oonagh caught a glimpse of the man he once was.

'How long had you been married for?'

He looked up. 'Not my wife. I closed that door a long time ago. My sister.'

Shit. Oonagh saw a resemblance around the eyes. 'But you visited her at Cartland?' It was through the visitor records that Oonagh had traced Dorothy Malloy's brother. He was her only visitor in almost three decades.

'That woman in there—' he pointed to a faraway place '—that wasn't our Dot.' He stood up and took a photograph from the top drawer and handed it to Oonagh. 'She was a great kid.' He held his index finger to his nose and a trace of grief tugged at the corners of his mouth. 'It killed my mum and dad, you know.'

Oonagh knew, for some people, shit like this just never went away. For most it was a front-page headline, a story at the top of the hour. But once the cameras were gone and the fuss died down the pain settled and festered for those left behind.

Graham Semionoff told Oonagh that after the killings he'd changed his name from Anderson. 'Just opened the Yellow Pages and picked the most unusual name I could find.' Apparently he'd thought that would make him harder to trace. 'I do mainly private commissions now.' Oonagh looked puzzled. 'Oh, I'm an architect,' he explained. 'The odd job here and there keeps the wolf from the door.' Judging by the neighbourhood and the handcrafted furniture the wolf wouldn't be visiting Graham Semionoff's door anywhere in the near future.

'Can I talk to you about Dorothy?'

His tongue darted across his lips. He gave her a brief nod.

'Were you...?' She wasn't sure how to word this. 'Did her behaviour...?' Oonagh took a deep breath. 'Was there anything to indicate why she would do such a... such a terrible act?'

Graham sat back in the leather armchair and let out a long sigh.

'There's a suggestion,' Oonagh spoke slowly, 'that she was suffering from post-partum psychosis.'

'I saw my sister's sanity unravel before my very eyes.'

Oonagh said nothing. She allowed the situation to breathe. Graham took a notebook from the drawer to his right. The same drawer that housed the photograph from earlier. 'I kept her diary. I know that seems a bit...'

he thought for a few seconds to select the right word '… sentimental.'

Oonagh smiled, but her heart pounded in her throat.

Graham flicked through the pages. 'She claimed she was receiving messages from a…' he looked at Oonagh, then dropped his gaze to the floor '… from a disciple.'

'Shit.'

'Yip.'

The silence between them forged a bridge. 'My sister was a beautiful, intelligent, creative girl. She adored her family, and I loved the bones of her.' A lifetime of memories washed over Graham Anderson. 'But within the space of a few months she turned into a maniac who killed her family.' His chin trembled and he lost whatever battle he was fighting with the tears that spilled down his cheeks.

Oonagh stepped towards him and crouched by his side. 'Here.' She held a tissue by way of an olive branch in his direction and stroked his arm; a lifetime of loss swam in his eyes. He opened the notebook that served as Dorothy Malloy's diary.

'Her handwriting was immaculate.' Oonagh couldn't disagree. Every page offered perfectly uniform script and she tried to think of the last time she'd held a pen to write something other than her name or a signature on a credit card. Dorothy Malloy's diary was a work of art. 'Take it.' He pushed it towards Oonagh's hand, and for the first time she realised that he was looking for as many answers as she was.

'Graham, d'you want to see your sister?'

By this time, he was clutching both her hands in his. He shook his head. 'Just promise me you'll look after her.'

'You can see her. You can speak to her yourself.'

He freed his hands and stemmed the tears from the corners of his eyes. 'I can't, not just now.'

Oonagh squeezed his hand and stood up, clutching Dorothy Malloy's diary. 'I'm not sure what I can do.'

Graham Anderson slumped back in his chair. 'Look at me.' He tipped his head around the room. 'I don't have much time left.' Oonagh took a sharp intake of breath, ready to tell him he was talking nonsense, when he interrupted. 'Och, stop it! Look at me, I said. I've got months, weeks, shit, maybe even days.'

Oonagh felt a tug at her spine. 'You know more than you're letting on.'

Graham eased himself out of the chair. 'You need to leave.'

'I want an answer.'

'Oonagh, you've got the whole world in your hands.'

'For God's sake, give us a break here. This isn't *The Silence of The Lambs*.'

'Tough titty.' Again the phrase, the words sounded rehearsed. As if he was trying to be tough.

'Please, Graham. If you're dying, just... just say. What d'you know?'

'Somewhere out there I've got a son and a daughter. Maybe even a grandchild or two. You work it out.' Oonagh hadn't noticed that he'd ushered her into the hall. He pressed his hand at her back. 'Take care.' Suddenly she was back in the street, tugging her collar up against the biting wind, with Dorothy Malloy's diary clutched in her hand.

42

Glasgow 2002

It had been surprisingly easy to find George McClemand. His widow was still in black, something you didn't always see nowadays. McVeigh was giving her his best charm offensive, which Davies had to admit was very good.

'Mrs McClemand, we are so sorry for your loss, but we need to ask you a few questions.' He paused for a second. 'But if you'd rather wait until a more convenient time, then we'll come back, or if you want a friend to sit with you then let us know.'

She'd made them tea, and, judging by the curled-up corners of the sandwiches and the tinned ham inside, George McClemand wasn't quite cold yet.

'He was a lovely man, salt of the earth. You know, when our Geraldine got pregnant he wouldn't let another sinner say a word against the girl. Stood up, proud as punch of her, the way he was with all our weans.'

Transpired of the five *weans* Geraldine now had four kids of her own, doing very well by all accounts; of the other four, one was a corporate lawyer, two ran a successful haulage company and the other was a plumber who was about to relocate to Australia.

Mrs McClemand was fierce in her defence of her family; Davies wondered if that loyalty supported her husband too.

'Mrs McClemand—'

'Call me Al.'

Oh, fuck, this was proving to be a long day.

'Al, we just need to ask a few questions about your husband's time at Wishart Frasers.' Davies looked over at McVeigh, who was chowing down on the day-old ham sandwich. He stopped mid-chew when he realised his boss was watching and delicately dabbed the side of his mouth with his middle finger.

'Did he ever mention knowing a Willie Mack?'

George McClemand's widow shook her head, worrying the twisted paper hankie between her hands.

'You see, we have reason to believe he may have witnessed someone...' Davies had to choose his words carefully; so far Al was on their side and he needed to keep it that way '... someone interfere with Willie Mack's body.'

'Sexually?' Mrs McClemand didn't even try to keep the disgust out of her voice.

'Oh, no, nothing like that,' McVeigh interjected, although to be honest no one had a fucking clue as to what he'd been doing with the bodies on their final journey. They'd hardly been in a position to blow the whistle on him. 'Willie Mack's body had been... cut... in a way that was inconsistent with any post-mortem examination, and we're trying to find out why.'

'Well, my George had nothing to do with that. For goodness' sakes, he'd performed enough of them in his time to know what he was doing.'

Davies and McVeigh shot each other a look. Once again Davies took over. 'Your husband performed autopsies? Where? I thought he was a mortician.'

Mrs McClemand got up and poured more tea; it had gone cold but she didn't seem to notice. She nodded. 'When he worked at the forensics department at Glasgow Uni. Most of the technicians did the initial cutting during the post-mortem in preparation for the forensic pathologist.' There was a slight hiccup in her voice as she wiped her nose. From what she told them George had clearly talked about his job often enough. 'He loved that job, he took great pride in the fact...'

'So what happened? Why did he leave the uni?'

'Couldn't stomach it, not after his boss died. Really got to him, you know.'

Davies hardly needed to ask the next question, but the dates tied in. 'Did George work with Dr Andrew Malloy?'

Again the widow nodded her head. 'It really affected him when Andrew died. I'd never seen him like that before.'

'In what way?'

'George dealt with Dr Malloy, you know, on the slab. Never, ever told me any details, but it must have been bad. After that…' She struggled to remain composed, 'well after that he suffered a complete breakdown. Couldn't eat, couldn't sleep. He was a nervous wreck.'

'I'm so sorry Al. Had he been particularly close to Dr Malloy?'

She immediately seemed brighter at the memory. Just for a moment. 'Oh, Dr Malloy was such a gent. A *real* gent, always treated my George with such respect. You know how some doctors can be real snobby bastards? Well, not him.'

'Did your husband ever seek help for his emotional problems?'

Again a slight nod. 'Our GP did the best she could, but other than tranquillisers said there wasn't much she could do. Then he got made redundant from Wishart Frasers and that was him on the scrapheap.' The emotion trapped in her chest escaped in one convulsive sob and the tears spilled down her cheeks. Her hand shook as she fished in her handbag for another tissue.

'Al, I hate to ask,' Davies gave the widow a few moments to compose herself, 'But how did George die?'

'Throat cancer. Only diagnosed ten weeks ago. Horrible way to go.'

Davies felt a wave of relief wash over him. He might not be able to quiz Georgie Boy about his post-mortem pass-times, but at least he wasn't another one to add to his headaches with this case.

McVeigh stood up and placed a comforting hand on Al's shoulder as he crouched beside her. 'Is there anyone we can call? You shouldn't be on your own.'

'It's OK.' Her voice was coming out in little spasms. 'Our Sandra'll be here soon.'

Davies eyed McVeigh and they stood up to leave. He needed to digest this, but it seemed there was little more that George McClemand's widow could give them. 'Thanks for taking the time to speak to us, Al. We know how hard this must be for you.'

'He was a good man, my George.'

They both nodded in agreement and left the widow to grieve in peace, unaware that her George had cut Willie Mack's heart out.

43

Glasgow 2002

The notebook was bound in a William Morris print, the inside pages neatly lined. She tucked it safely into her handbag. Every instinct told her to call Alec Davies. Tell him what she'd discovered. Or what she thought she'd discovered. Oonagh switched on the ignition and pulled her seat belt tight across her chest and clicked it into place before switching off her mobile; something she rarely did. She hadn't made an appointment, and wasn't even sure they'd let her see Dorothy Malloy without Tom being present. She didn't even know if Dorothy Malloy would still be there. Oonagh wasn't very well versed on the rights of ex-inmates of Cartland. Were they permitted to see whoever they liked? Was there a 'handle with care' order on them?

She drove to the south side; the traffic was unusually quiet. Once or twice her left hand drifted onto her handbag and she eased it open slightly and took a peek inside to make sure the notebook was still there. There was nowhere for it to go, but just in case. She'd been up half the night and could feel the tiredness scratch at the corners of her eyes. The sky was grey and a few drops of rain played on the windscreen, but never developed into anything more. Oonagh felt a shiver and put the heating up a few notches, even though the gauge told her it was already twenty-two degrees inside the car. She stopped off at a florists under the railway bridge near Pollokshaws and selected three bunches of tulips, then nipped next door to the deli and bought an enormous family-sized gateau, a box of home-made macaroons and some Orkney fudge wrapped in cellophane. Apparently, Orkney was famous for its fudge; she'd had no idea. Oonagh got them to box it all and wrap it. They didn't have a ribbon, but she guessed she could pick one up easily enough before she made her way to see Dorothy.

She stood at the door armed with her goodies and pressed the bell. She felt a bit crumby, bribing her way in, but she reckoned some nice goodies would make whoever was on the door a bit more sympathetic to her request. Truth be told she'd been too scared to phone ahead in case they'd said no.

The Smiley-Faced Lady opened the door, just as happy as the last time. The goodies seemed to work. 'Oh, hello. You here to see Dorothy?'

Oonagh nodded. 'Is that OK? I was passing and...' She decided to quit while she was ahead, and pushed the

259

obvious bribes towards Mrs Smiley-Faced.

'Dorothy's in the garden.'

Oonagh took this as a good sign. The garden fence was relatively low. If she was really dangerous they wouldn't let her out on her own.

'She's in good form today, in one of her happy places.'

Oonagh wasn't sure exactly how killers found a happy place, but followed Smiley-Face to the back of the house and out into the grounds.

'Tom told me you'd more than likely pop by to see us,' she said as she opened the back door. That explained the willingness to let Oonagh in, no questions asked. It wasn't the warmest of days, but Oonagh guessed Dorothy had had her fill of being cooped up.

The garden was well tended, and bursting with the promise of spring. Snowdrops were already over, dropping their heads, offering their faded blooms to the ground. Daffodil heads bulged, not quite ready with colour yet, and an air of anticipation enveloped every bud. Dorothy knelt on a pad at the far corner; even from this distance she had an air of confidence. Very different from the Dorothy Oonagh had met the last time. She didn't much care for the fact she was holding what looked like razor-sharp secateurs. A set of loppers, capable of taking off a finger or two, lay at her side.

'Would you prefer I spoke to Dorothy indoors?' Without Tom by her side she felt suddenly vulnerable and swung round quickly, making sure Smiley-Face was close by.

'Not at all,' said Smiley-Face and rested her hand on Oonagh's back, ushering her towards her like a reluctant play-date. 'Now can I get you tea, coffee?'

'Whatever's quickest,' she yelled. It came out louder than intended and Dorothy Malloy twisted from the waist, pointing the secateurs in Oonagh's direction.

'Dorothy?' Smiley-Face yelled the length of the garden. 'Tea?'

Dorothy nodded and Smiley-Face trotted back indoors, leaving Oonagh alone with a crazed killer, some lethal garden tools and a packet of *home-made* macaroons. She swallowed hard and walked towards her, trying not to stare at the makeshift weapon. 'Tom told me these were your favourites.' She held the packet towards her. An olive branch.

Dorothy dropped the secateurs, ran towards Oonagh like an excited child and teased open the top of the cellophane. 'Meringues?'

Shit.

'Em, sorry,' Oonagh said, 'they're macaroons.'

Dorothy flashed her eyes – they were vibrant green – and pursed her lips slightly to disguise her smile. 'I'm teasing.' She popped a macaroon into her mouth and dabbed the crumbs from the corner with her ring finger, giving Oonagh a flirtatious sideways glance.

This all-new, all-singing-and-dancing version of Dorothy really threw Oonagh, who felt ill prepared to be outwitted by a killer who was taking the piss. There was something familiar about her actions that unnerved Oonagh. She seemed to walk slightly on tiptoe, and flicked her head to the left, allowing her hair to fall behind her shoulder. She'd had it cut too. And coloured. The grey, lank style was gone and replaced with a precision-cut chestnut bob, which she most certainly didn't get on the NHS. Her clothes too were classic and well cut; Oonagh guessed they might well have been Dorothy's own clothes from more than a quarter of a century ago. All in all, this Dorothy Malloy was a far younger model than the one Oonagh had met previously.

'Looks well, doesn't she?'

Oonagh spun round and was relieved to see Smiley-Face back with the tea tray. Dorothy drifted off to the back of the garden again, brushing her hand along the tips of the shrubs. She walked slowly but confidently with a deliberate sway of her hips. She tilted her head back and gave them both a smile before returning to her flowers.

'She's certainly...' Oonagh thought for a moment '... different.'

'Oh, she's harmless enough. All of her personalities seem to be nice.'

Apart from the one who slaughtered her husband, Oonagh thought, but decided against saying it.

'Good, isn't she?'

'What?' Oonagh wasn't sure what Smiley-Face was referring to.

'She's been watching you a lot on the telly.' Smiley-Face poured the tea. 'Even asked Tom who cut your hair. Milk and sugar's on the tray.'

A mixture of annoyance and fear pricked the back of Oonagh's skull. She tried to sound casual. 'Is she impersonating me?'

'Oh, don't worry, she does it with everyone, but she does seem to have taken a particular shine to you.'

Her ego, or it might have been her vanity, refused to let it go. 'Eh, do I act like that?' she asked as Dorothy Malloy teetered around on tippy-toes, swinging her hips and tossing her hair to one side.

Smiley-Face smiled and sort of hunched her shoulders up at the same time, but Oonagh realised it was the cake she was more interested in as she opened the box to reveal the goodies inside.

Oonagh pushed her fear to one side; she needed to get back in control. 'Would it be OK if I spent some time alone with Dorothy?' She didn't wait for an answer and left Smiley-Face to her tea and cake routine as she approached Dorothy.

'D'you enjoy gardening, Dorothy?'

Dorothy clutched one hand to her chest. 'Oh, it's my absolute passion.'

Somewhere in there was a petrified and abused woman. Oonagh wasn't quite sure how or when she should reveal the notebook to Dorothy. After all, it was her personal diary, albeit twenty-seven years old.

'Fancy a seat?' Oonagh strolled over to the tea and allowed Dorothy to follow. Her heart was beating faster than intended and she was glad she'd taken her inhaler before she'd left the house. She sat down and Dorothy started pouring the tea. She put the milk in first and gave Oonagh three sugars without asking; clearly she'd remembered from their last visit.

'Thanks.' Oonagh smiled and wondered what was going on behind those eyes. 'Dorothy, can we chat?' The other woman nodded as she sipped her tea then picked her way through the cakes in front of her.

It was time to bite the bullet. 'I have something here that belongs to you.' She should have taken a copy of it, she should have told Alec what was in that diary, she should have called Tom. Instead Oonagh reached into her bag and took out the notebook. Dorothy's eyes flashed just for a moment, then her head dipped and her arms folded across her chest as she rocked back and forth on the garden chair. Apart from the hair, the old Dorothy Malloy was back, nervous, physically smaller and scared as hell. Oonagh had never witnessed such a physical transformation of anyone before.

'I've spoken to Graham, Dorothy.' She thought she owed her an explanation as to how she acquired the diary. 'He misses you.'

Dorothy tipped her head very slightly to say she understood. Her right hand reached across her mouth as she chewed on the web of skin at her thumb.

'Has anyone else seen it?' The question displayed a degree of cognitive reasoning that gave Oonagh some reassurance. She assured Dorothy the contents had remained private.

'But I'd like to speak to you about it, Dorothy – would that be OK?'

Again she shrugged her shoulders. Her eyes not leaving the notebook. Then a tiny nod.

Oonagh had bookmarked three pages, all towards the end of the book. She wasn't sure if she should say it or not, but did so regardless. 'Dorothy, can we chat about these three pages in particular?' Oonagh opened a page and began reading.

'He was with me again tonight. He's angry. He wants vengeance. Their innocence shall redeem their souls. Dying can end all pain and all suffering. I'll pray she meets the Holy Father in Heaven once her time in Purgatory is over...'

'Who did you mean, Dorothy? Who were you writing about?'

Dorothy warmed her hands on the teacup but didn't answer. Oonagh leafed through to the next marked page. It held a similar message.

'...for the innocents death holds no fear. The Holy Father shall redeem...'

Still Dorothy Malloy said nothing. Another page.

'...the evil needs to be wiped out. The devil hides in plain sight amongst us all. She didn't suffer and will be lifted up to the Holy Father...'

Each diary entry was dated. Oonagh had read the whole book, thoroughly, and felt she was witnessing the sad demise of the life of Dorothy Malloy as she descended into madness.

'Dorothy?' Oonagh was careful to speak softly and slowly. Dorothy looked up. 'Dorothy, each of these entries was written on the day a young woman was killed in Glasgow.'

Dorothy rubbed her hand over her mouth. Oonagh struggled to hear her. 'I prayed for them. I wanted them to be OK.'

Oonagh considered her next question very carefully. 'Did you know any of the girls?'

The other woman shook her head. 'Read about them. The papers.'

Instinct made Oonagh reach across and take Dorothy's hand. 'But their deaths wouldn't have been reported until the next day. You wrote this the day they died.'

'Did I?' Dorothy seemed genuinely surprised. She put down her cup and seemed to be happy holding Oonagh's hand. 'Can I try on your watch?'

Oonagh moved Dorothy's hand away from her wrist. 'Later, Dorothy, this is important.' She dipped her voice so no one else could hear what she had to say. 'I'm really sorry, Dorothy, but I need to ask you.' She took a deep breath, but the words wouldn't come out.

'Her nylons were ripped.'

'What?' She looked into Dorothy's eyes but couldn't read her expression.

'Just here.' Dorothy pointed her index finger onto her left ankle.

Oonagh didn't have a clue what she was talking about. 'One of the girls who died?'

Dorothy nodded.

'I thought you didn't know the girls.'

'It's not nice to wear laddered stockings. It's... it's vulgar.'

Oonagh had come to visit Dorothy Malloy for this very purpose, only now she was almost too scared to ask the question.

'Dorothy, did you...?' She wasn't sure she wanted to know the answer. 'Dorothy, you know who the killer is,

267

don't you?'

Dorothy looked around, but said nothing.

44

London 2002

The queue for the red-eye snaked its way from the boarding gate. Mainly men in suits. Oonagh had opted for hand luggage only. She'd be back up this evening and if not she could buy a few essentials in London. She was sure they'd have shops there. Tom had said he'd meet her at the airport but she'd insisted on taking the Underground on her own. She feared Tom would be a liability.

It'd been a while since she'd been in London. Two years at least. Odd, the anonymity such a vast city offered. She stupidly got off at the wrong station and grabbed a black cab for the few blocks to King's Cross, where they'd arranged to meet. The traffic was thick and heavy; quicker walking, but she was wearing heels and wasn't quite sure which direction. The fare was less than what the meter displayed.

'I always give the Scotch a good discount.' The driver winked and smiled.

Oonagh grinned back and handed over a tenner. 'And I always give London cabbies a decent tip.' She knew it was probably a ruse to get more cash out of her, but she didn't care.

Tom was exactly where he should be, waving frantically lest she didn't notice him. Ten a.m. and the station bar was already open and densely populated. They made their way inside and tried to catch someone's eye. Normally in Glasgow waiters fell over themselves to serve Oonagh. She was instantly recognisable there, but here, well, here she was just another face in the crowd. A short face at that, struggling to get served.

'It's a shame you're not famous down here.' Tom gave a laugh, eventually attracting enough attention from the barman to be told he'd need to wait.

'Yeah, funny that. Imagine only being famous in Scotland. What a bummer.' Oonagh spied a table. 'Listen, I'll grab that table, you try to woo old blue eyes there and get us a drink.'

'He's got brown eyes actually.'

'Just get the drinks in.'

Oonagh had copies of some of the most important files from the dossier that Maura Rowinson had given her. As well as photocopied extracts from Dorothy's diary. And her own notes, of course. Tom eased his way through the crowd and sat opposite her. 'Good to see you.'

'You too. You're thriving, Tom.' And she meant it.

She took a shot in the dark. 'You know the police have reopened the Raphael case?' Oonagh picked her way through the bowl of olives on the table, tried to look casual. So far she hadn't mentioned her suspicions to Tom. His reaction was right on cue.

'That's a bit convenient.'

'In what way?'

Tom tipped the tonic into both gins and handed Oonagh her drink. 'They reopen the case within weeks of Dorothy being released from Cartland?' Clearly he had more than a hunch that Dorothy was in some way connected. Oonagh drummed her nails on the table; she hadn't even considered the timing before. She was about to say it was just a coincidence but thought against it and instead took the bull by the horns.

'You already knew, didn't you?'

Tom dabbed the plate with his finger, picking up the last drops of olive oil, and popped the last olive into his mouth. 'I had my suspicions. And at the moment that's all they are, suspicions.'

'D'you think she was involved? Did she know the killer?'

Tom shook his head. 'Not quite, but...'

Oonagh thought this might be the perfect opportunity to tell Tom about the diary, but decided to wait and see what his take on it was.

'Are you going to the police with this?' Oonagh felt the nerves swell in her stomach.

Again he shook his head. 'Hardly. They already seem to be ahead of the game with this one.'

'I think Threadgold's trying to cover this up.'

'What would be the point?'

'The cops have covered this up from the beginning. They banged Dorothy away and kept her out of sight for nearly thirty years. No trial, no reporting of the case, nothing.'

Tom put down his drink. Oonagh had decided against telling him of her own troubles. The blackout behind the wheel, the fact she'd thought she'd killed someone. Thought it best if they concentrated on poor Dorothy Malloy.

'I know, despite the fact Andrew Malloy was butchered by her, they didn't want it made public that his wife was a nut-job serial killer.'

'Oonagh, those sorts of descriptions aren't very helpful to people suffering from mental health issues.'

'Really? Neither is festering in your own filth in a secure unit for twenty-seven years, but you're right. Let's not offend anyone with our choice of words.'

Tom clearly wanted to steer the conversation back to the case in point.

'OK, so what've you found?'

'The truth? I don't know. But something's just not right here.'

Tom nodded. Didn't look surprised.

'I just don't know how to make sense of it all, Tom.'

None of it made sense. There were too many loose ends. Too many unanswered questions. She fished her hand into her tote-bag, felt the diary was still there.

'You planning to do *another* exposé on this?'

'You read it, then?' She hadn't told Tom it was her behind the prison abuse scandal that had dominated every tabloid for the past week, but he was no fool. Her heart skipped a slight beat in case he thought she'd sold Dorothy Malloy down the river, but there had been nothing to connect either Oonagh or Dorothy to the story.

'You played a blinder there, Oonagh. Let's hope it's put enough wind up enough people to at least raise awareness.'

Oonagh nodded, but she knew next week the story would be replaced by another scandal and people's outrage would be directed elsewhere.

'There's a bigger story here, Oonagh.'

She let him speak, wanted to know what he knew.

'Dorothy's case,' he said, 'it was a miscarriage of justice.'

'Well, it was a *no-justice*, to be more accurate. No trial, no justice.' She hadn't yet told him about Marjory Channing, or Andrew Malloy's involvement with the tainted blood scandal.

'Exactly! No trial. And have you reached the same conclusion that I have yet?'

273

Oonagh finished off her drink. 'Tom, how the hell do I know? You haven't *told* me anything yet.'

'I think Dorothy found out her husband killed those girls in Glasgow and that's why she killed him.'

Oonagh's heart raced. 'What evidence d'you have?'

'I'm not a policeman, Oonagh. I don't need evidence, but I know how scared she was. I know her sanity was hanging by a thread. She was scared for a reason.'

'Did she tell you that?'

'Not in so many words, but...'

'She's not always 100 per cent lucid, Tom.' Oonagh held back on her own theory for now. 'Her memory of that time is scant.'

'That's all to do with her DID.'

Oonagh raised one eyebrow.

'Her Dissociative Personality Disorder. There are huge gaps in her memory. Something too traumatic to remember, she just blots out.'

Oonagh thought how lovely that would be at times and pulled a large buff envelope from her bag. 'Here.' She pushed the copies of Dorothy's diary towards him. She'd retyped some of the more pertinent pages. The ones that really mattered.

'Tom, the dates tie in. Every psychotic episode Dorothy had coincided with a killing in Glasgow.'

She held back from telling Tom about her own suspicions. Instead tried to gauge his reaction as he read through the diary extracts.

'What're you saying?'

In truth she didn't really know what she was saying. Suddenly her suspicion that Dorothy Malloy killed those girls felt like the ultimate betrayal. 'Tom, I've uncovered a whole can of worms here. A big giant family-sized can of worms.'

Tom sat back. Said nothing. Gave her space to say her piece.

'I can't work out how it all ties in. But it does.'

'Not everything's a conspiracy, Oonagh.'

She chose her words carefully as she told him about her meetings with Marjory Channing. Desperate not to come across as overzealous. Stuck to the facts.

'Bloody hell. I know! Andrew Malloy was about to blow the whistle on the biggest scandal in the history of the NHS but conveniently dies before it could be made public.'

'Well,' He pondered for a few moments, taking it what she was saying, 'I can't see how there could be a connection. Sometimes shit happens.'

'Tom!' She drummed her fingernails on the table. She knew how annoying it was. 'I need you in on this, Tom. You can get more information out of Dorothy than I can.'

Tom pondered for a moment. 'What kind of information?' He was dragging this out. Making her say the actual words.

'I think *she* might have killed those girls.'

'You want me to get Dorothy to confess to killing those girls? That's unthinkable, Oonagh.'

'I'm not looking for you to coerce a confession out of her. As you say, you're not a copper, but you need to get inside her head. Find out what the hell was going on.'

She still wasn't sure what she was looking for. Or indeed why Dorothy would start a random killing spree of young blonde girls in Glasgow. 'We just need to know why.' She let him absorb it for a few moments. Tom's loyalty to Dorothy was obvious. He didn't want to act the snitch. 'Listen, Tom, let's get real here. Even if she does confess she's done her time. We don't need to pass this on. It'll be case closed.'

'Then why pursue it?'

'Because she didn't just do this for the hell of it. Something triggered her off.' Oonagh spread the copied pages from Dorothy's diary in front of them. 'There's an entry from each day of the killings. Each time she talks about Raphael. Receiving a message. Purifying the world from bad blood.'

'Raphael was one of the archangels.'

'I know. I didn't think she was getting messages from one of the fucking Ninja Turtles!' She was growing increasingly frustrated at Tom's insistence on spelling everything out to her.

'And Patron saint of physicians.'

'Now that I didn't know!' She gave him that one.

'OK, I'll talk to her again. But...'

'But what?'

'It's too random. She would have had to be stalking these girls to know their movements. She'd need to have established a link to give her a motive. I don't know.'

Oonagh wasn't giving up on this. 'Tom?' He looked up, waiting for what was coming next.

'I think the messages were real.' He raised his eyebrow, a gesture for her to continue. 'Oh, I don't mean from the Archangel Raphael, but I think Dorothy was getting messages, phone calls, whatever. She was being gaslighted.'

'Gaslighted?'

'You know, from the movie? When Ingrid Bergman's convinced she's going insane but really her husband is manipulating everything, making her believe she's losing the plot.'

'Why would that happen to Dorothy?'

'I don't know yet, but she was being made to believe she was hearing voices from the other side.'

'Who would do that?'

'No idea, but whoever it was wanted Dorothy Malloy out of the picture, for good.'

45

Ayrshire 2002

'How well did you know Andrew Malloy?' The recorder was already on the table and switched on. Oonagh hardly waited until Maura was seated before starting her questions. 'And why were the blood products so damaged? I mean, surely then everyone who's ever had a blood transfusion would be at risk?'

'Can I grab a coffee first?'

Oonagh nodded, embarrassed slightly at her own enthusiasm, and eyed the waitress to come over. It was off season, and everything in the seaside town looked a bit sad. Judging by the décor the café had seen better days. The cream walls were tinged with decades of nicotine. The Formica tables suggested a bygone age full of teenagers tasting first-time coffee, kisses and cigarettes.

Maura slid into the booth and cupped the steaming mug with both hands as soon as it was on the table.

'Were you having an affair with him?' Oonagh cut to the chase. Couldn't be bothered with the bullshit any longer. Not for the first time she guessed Dorothy Malloy had slaughtered her husband because he'd been playing away from home, and those poor girls had got caught in the crossfire.

Maura let out a sigh. The tip of her nose stung red. 'OK, one step at a time. The blood products were so *damaged* because, to extract the plasma, blood from up to twenty thousand donors had to be pooled together, therefore the risk was higher. Just simple arithmetic. Coupled with the fact that the blood came from skid-row donors, it's little wonder that factor VIII was a lethal injection.'

Oonagh was anxious to talk more about Malloy, but allowed Maura to set the pace. For now.

'So, have you any good case studies?'

'I can put you in touch with a mother whose seven-year-old son died after he contracted HIV through contaminated blood.' She sipped on her coffee. 'Is that good enough?'

'Oh no.' This would be manna from heaven to most journalists, and would have been for Oonagh not that long ago. There was a time she would have gorged herself on that information, but she'd lost her appetite for other people's misery and felt sick at the thought. Perhaps she was losing her edge.

'The doctors had suggested that the boy's father had had a homosexual affair. Said the boy probably contracted the disease whilst still in the womb.'

Oonagh pressed her right hand onto her thigh to stop it from shaking. 'Presumably the family took legal action?'

A small laugh escaped from Maura's lips. 'The husband was found dead in his car. The old rubber hose onto the exhaust pipe routine.'

'Oh, my God, so he *was* gay?' Oonagh took stock and quickly corrected herself. 'Not that there's anything wrong with being—'

Maura cut in. 'Of course he wasn't gay.' Oonagh wasn't used to being the slow-witted one. 'The stress of it all drove him to it.' She paused; it looked to Oonagh as though she was holding back the tears. 'Can you imagine what it's like to watch your baby die a little more each day, and have every family member, every friend, every medic and nurse in the hospital point the finger at you?'

Of course Oonagh couldn't imagine it. She found herself saying something for the second time. 'And this happened here?' Maura nodded. 'In the UK?' Again Maura nodded. 'In Scotland?'

The tears that had welled up in Maura's eyes spilled over and fell down her cheeks. Oonagh passed her a tissue. 'Did you know the family?'

'No, thank God. That would have been worse.'

280

Oonagh nodded but didn't really know what Maura meant.

Maura gave Oonagh a pitying look. 'You're not quite grasping this, are you?'

'Well, no, not really!' Oonagh struggled to keep her temper in check. Now was not the time for a bit of petty point scoring. 'Perhaps you could...' She wasn't sure where she was going with this and was glad when Maura cut in.

'We could have stopped it.'

'You and Andrew?'

'There were a few of us, not just him – we started piecing things together. We knew something wasn't right.'

The buzzing of her phone made her jump. It was her mum. Shit; they were supposed to meet for lunch.

'Is it OK if I take this?'

Maura nodded.

'Hi.' Pause. 'Oh, Mum, I'm so sorry, I was just about to call you...' She looked at Maura, offered a weak smile. 'I'm tied up here in the studio and may not get out for a few hours yet...' Maura was staring out of the window, looking at something beyond the rain-smeared glass.

'Thanks, Mum, yeah, honestly, I'm good. I'll give you a buzz tomorrow?' She pressed her thumb on the end-call button before Fran had a chance to answer.

'Who are the others? Where are they now?'

281

'Most of them are dead by now.' Oonagh wasn't sure whether to believe her. 'There was a morgue technician who worked with Andrew – he'd been warned off and soon scarpered. They gave him a hell of a time.'

'Oh? How?'

'Rats in his lunch box, pictures of his kids with a noose around their necks. These evil bastards were ruthless.'

'Maura, assume I'm a bit stupid.' She tried to keep the sarcasm out of her voice. 'Can you just tell me in plain English what the fuck is going on?' She paused, not sure she knew what to ask. 'Who were *they*? And why're you acting like a scared rabbit?'

'I live with this every day. That horrible feeling that I could have done more. But they were bigger than us. And you don't mess with the big boys.'

Oonagh had a million questions and knew she'd have to tread carefully. She stretched her hand across the table. The door opened and an icy blast caught them both by surprise. A young girl, no more than a teenager, came in; a toddler resting on her hip. Maura looked miles away. Oonagh looked down at the recorder. 'Maura?'

The coffee was still hot, she gulped it down, then looked Oonagh in the eye. 'I can trust you, can't I? It's odd but I see another damaged soul in you, Oonagh O'Neil.'

Oonagh felt the colour rise in her cheek. Wanted to tell her to fuck off, she couldn't be arsed with the psychoanalysis crap, but instead she bit her tongue.

'We've all got our tale to tell. So, come on…'

'I killed my sister, Oonagh.'

'Fuck.'

'Oh, I didn't stick the knife in myself, but I might as well have.'

Oonagh let her back rest against the chair and let Maura talk. 'She was helping me pass on the information from the States to my contacts in the UK. Don't forget, as I say, we didn't have mobiles or emails or anything then.' Maura looked tired. Dark circles had formed around her eyes and her mouth was set in a hard line, which didn't suit the softness of her face. 'She was my baby sister and I didn't do enough to protect her.'

'So what happened?'

'They found out she was the go-between for me and the others in the UK and they took her out. Plain and simple.'

The same icy blast caught the back of Oonagh's neck. But this time the door was closed.

'I'm sorry.'

Maura simply shook her head. 'She was a medical secretary and passed on information to Andrew.'

Oonagh stiffened. She took in Maura's heart-shaped face, the oval eyes, the blonde hair scraped back off her face. 'What was your sister's name?'

Maura looked around, thrown off guard by this change of pace.

'And your name? Your real name.'

Maura knitted her brows together. 'What?'

'I ran a search – you've no passport, no national insurance, you're not on any electoral register.'

Maura looked into her coffee, bit her lip, played for time. Oonagh reached across and touched her hand. 'You need to trust me here, Maura.' She paused for a moment. 'Otherwise there's no point in taking this any further.'

Oonagh tipped the last of her coffee into her mouth and made out she was leaving. Her gut instinct told her Maura would play ball, otherwise she wouldn't have gone to so much trouble to set this whole thing up in the first place. She was slipping her jacket over her shoulders when Maura spoke.

'Channing, Marjory Channing.'

'Janet Channing's sister?'

She knew the answer before Maura nodded her head and Oonagh slumped back in her chair. It felt as though she was the last one in on the joke and didn't know where to start. What a complete fool. She guessed it was no coincidence that Marjory Channing had contacted her with this tainted blood story the same week the police had reopened the Raphael case. It was all from the same stinking cesspit.

'My sister was—'

'Give me a minute here,' Oonagh cut in, didn't let her finish. She was too far in to get out. Didn't want out, if truth be told, but she needed to get back in control.

'You could have gone to a hundred journalists with this story. Ninety-nine of them better qualified to grasp the nuances of a medical story. Why did you pick me?'

Her answer came just a little too quickly. 'You were the obvious choice. People respect you, they admire you for being in touch with—'

'I'm flattered. Tell me you can't believe I'm hitting forty and I'll roll over and let you tickle my tummy.'

Maura looked confused.

'Cut the crap, Maura, or Marjory, or whatever it is you like to call yourself. You targeted me for this.'

'I don't know what you're—'

'Cut the fucking crap, sister.' Oonagh reached over, switched off her recorder and slipped it into her bag.

'Please...' Marjory Channing didn't finish her sentence. Oonagh could feel the colour rise in her cheeks. Hoped she looked angry and not embarrassed.

Marjory dipped her head slightly. Couldn't look her in the eye. 'I found out you were going to see Dorothy Malloy.'

'How?' Oonagh didn't try to hide the anger rising from her gut.

'Seriously. That doesn't matter. I have my sources.'

At least she admitted it. Admitted it wasn't just one huge ball of coincidence that rolled it altogether and for now Oonagh would have to be happy with that.

'Oonagh, this is what I meant when I said the shit was about to hit the fan. Dorothy Malloy's out of Cartland and who knows what's going to come out?'

Oonagh grabbed the recorder from her bag and put it back on the Formica table between them. Her mind frantic, trying to connect it all together.

'How well did Andrew Malloy know your sister?'

Marjory Channing shrugged her shoulders, didn't quite grasp the question.

'Was he shagging her? Is this what all this was about?' Oonagh struggled not to raise her voice. 'He was slaughtered, his whole family destroyed, and for what? A quickie?'

The tears that had threatened for so long eventually spilled over onto Marjory's face. 'No, it wasn't like that, I promise.'

Oonagh chewed the inside of her cheek; a faint taste of blood coated her mouth. This was getting grubby. As far as she knew the police had no evidence of any association between Andrew Malloy and Janet Channing, or indeed any of the girls who were killed. She tried to gather her thoughts as her heart ached in sympathy for poor Dorothy Malloy, who killed a poor young girl and slaughtered her own family because her husband wanted his end away, despite Marjory Channing's conspiracy theory.

Oonagh softened, got herself in check. At the end of the day this woman's sister was murdered and that was a sore one. 'Marjory, you know Andrew was killed by his wife. She, admitted it. They put her away' She reached across and took the other woman's hand. 'Janet, it would seem, just sort of got… caught in the crossfire.'

Marjory looked her in the eye, demanding an explanation.

'Andrew's wife, Dorothy, she's in a bad way. Completely unstable.'

'What're you telling me here?'

'Trust is a two-way street, Marjory; you need to give me your word here.'

Marjory nodded. Oonagh wasn't convinced but she felt she'd suffered enough, and guessed she wouldn't be running to the police any time soon. 'Marjory, there was no conspiracy. It's looking more and more likely that your sister was killed by Dorothy Malloy.'

Marjory sat back, almost laughed. 'Where did you get that nonsense from?'

'Hear me out. Dorothy believed Andrew was… having an affair with your sister.'

'That's well out of order.' She raised her voice but there was no one in the café who cared. 'Janet wouldn't have gone near a married man.'

'I'm sorry, Marjory. I'm not saying they *were* having an affair, but Andrew's wife clearly thought so and killed them both.'

'That's fucking ludicrous.'

'What about the others, Marjory?'

Marjory said nothing, instead waited for Oonagh to explain.

'There were three girls killed in total. None of the others had any links to this tainted blood thing. The only thing they had in common was they all looked similar.'

By the looks of Marjory's expression, she wasn't grasping Oonagh's train of thought.

'They were all Andrew's type.'

'Nonsense. The police must have missed something. They don't know what they're supposed to be looking for. Dig a little deeper. You'll find a link.' There was an air of desperation in her voice.

'I'm sorry, Marjory, Andrew might have been a really good friend, even a nice guy on the surface, but his wife thought he was screwing around and went postal.'

Marjory put her hand across her mouth but it did little to stifle her cries. The waitress glanced over but quickly turned away when she caught Oonagh's eye.

'It wasn't your fault, Marjory. Janet's death had nothing to do with you.'

Marjory slammed her hand on the table. 'Are you kidding? This makes it even worse. Jesus Christ, I introduced them.' She pressed the tissue against her eyes, wiped her nose and took a small flask from her bag. Oonagh didn't need to know what was in it, but guessed that Marjory Channing's demons were kept at bay through a mixture of drugs and alcohol.

'Sorry.' Her hand shook as she slipped the flask back into her bag.

'Hey, I'm the one who should apologise. Landing that on you with no warning. But, Marjory...' time to change tactics '... this tainted blood story. We can do things with this.'

Marjory hesitated. God knew what was going on inside her head right now.

'Marjory?'

Marjory nodded. 'Of course, I'll give you as much information as you need, on one condition.'

'Go on?'

'My sister stays out of it. There's nothing that will slur her name.' She suddenly hardened, gave Oonagh a look. 'Do we understand each other?'

'Of course, Marjory.' Oonagh agreed to play ball and ran with it. 'Have the police spoken to you yet?'

'No, they think I'm dead.'

Oonagh raised an eyebrow; she needed to hear this.

Marjory got up to leave. 'I sort of spread the word that I'd taken a stroke. No big deal, just let the rumour mill do its business, and it worked.'

Oonagh gave her a smile. 'Smart move.' Then raised one hand as Marjory glanced towards the door. 'I know, you don't want us to leave together.'

Marjory smiled and Oonagh reached out to shake her hand, but instead she bent down and placed a kiss on Oonagh's cheek. 'Take care of yourself, Oonagh O'Neil.'

Oonagh decided to order another coffee

*

She gave it fifteen minutes before leaving the café and took the A71 east towards the A74. The flat Ayrshire countryside stretched out for miles. There were few other cars on the road and she eased her foot onto the accelerator, taking each curve of the road faster than she should have. Speeding was her only vice. Well, that and smoking, and maybe drinking, and perhaps the odd wee swear word. But on the whole, she was a clean-living gal.

Marjory Channing's story really did beggar belief, but she'd manage to dig around a wee bit herself to know that it wasn't as far-fetched as it sounded. The sun through the windscreen warmed her face and the familiar thrill of exhilaration caressed her chest as she eased her car around a hairpin curve, watching the needle nudge up to sixty. Then slammed the brakes on hard as she saw the roadblock ahead. The screech of the brakes pierced the tranquillity as she stopped just yards from the uniformed copper. Shit.

He gestured for her to take the B road to her right. She put down the window and asked what the problem was. In her head she weighed up the options of waiting it out until the incident was over. The fact there was a plod on duty indicated that this wasn't a long-term closure for roadworks. Rather some short-term problem that could well be over soon; however, if she took the diversion route she knew it would add over an hour onto her journey and she couldn't be arsed.

The plod made his way over. She fished around her bag for her press pass and hoped it would curry some favour in getting information. The press pass could swing both ways: sometimes it did, other times it pissed people off.

'Hi.' She flashed him a smile. 'Is the road likely to be…?'

He was young, looked inexperienced, but tried to look like a proper grown-up. 'Crash, I'm afraid.'

'Has recovery been arranged? Will the road reopen soon?'

He looked around, not sure how to deal with a question. 'Mmm, probably not, could be several hours yet.'

Oonagh's heart sank. That usually meant a fatal. No matter how long she'd been in the job she could never get used to the fact that some people woke up in the morning and had no idea it was their last day on earth.

'OK, thanks.' She started up her engine and took a hard right onto the single-track road. As she steered round the bend the wreckage from the accident came into view. Single vehicle, no other cars in sight. Head first into a tree. No one could have survived that. The winding road took her slightly closer to the scene, which was now to her left-hand side. She recognised the British racing green MG sports car immediately. Only the back had escaped unscathed. The rest was a mangled wreck. Police and ambulance flanked either side. But Oonagh knew by the stance of the paramedics standing idle by the side of the road that Marjory Channing would have been pronounced dead at the scene.

46

Glasgow 2002

Her hand shook as she turned the key in the lock. She didn't remember the drive home. All she could think about was the sight of Marjory Channing's car wrapped around a tree. She clutched Marjory's research notes to her chest, terrified they'd somehow disappear, just like Marjory. Once inside she checked and double-checked every lock on every window, and ensured the alarm was switched on. She rattled the box of dried cat food near the back door to encourage Cat to come in early from his neighbourhood jaunt. But the little shit refused to come in. Suit yourself, she thought, and locked the cat-flap out of spite, then unlocked it just as quickly, knowing she was just being shitty.

She flicked through the various news channels but there was nothing about the crash. Maybe too early to be reported. Or perhaps the city was busy with other crimes tonight and another fatal on the roads just wasn't newsworthy any more. Or would be put 'under the line', used as an 'and finally' if the sports guys were a bit late with their cue. The arbitrary nature of news sickened Oonagh. If there were five minutes to fill, there would be five minutes of news. If the slot only allowed three minutes, then that was how much news the viewers or listeners would be allowed.

She spread Marjory's notes across the island unit in the kitchen and looked out of the window into the darkness. Tried to take in the connections between Dorothy Malloy and the tainted blood scandal. She was sure Marjory had got it wrong. Andrew Malloy couldn't have been killed to shut him up. There was no doubt that Dorothy had dealt the fatal blow. The fate of the other girls was pure conjecture at this point.

She called Alec. He answered after two rings. 'Hey, sorry to bother you… looking for some info on a fatal in North Ayrshire.' She tried to sound light-hearted, matter of fact. Not letting on she was personally involved. And there was no way she could tell Alec at this stage who the victim was.

'Eh…' He paused for a moment. The area was out of his patch, but Oonagh knew Alec Davies could get information on most police matters across the whole of Scotland. 'Can you try Jim? I'm up to my eyes in it here, Oons.' He hung up before she had a chance to say cheerio. She hoped Jim would be a bit more forthcoming. He was.

'Oh, hi, Oonagh, how goes it?'

'Great, Jim. Listen, can you get me some info on a fatal RTA from tonight?'

'Aye, what kind of info?'

Oonagh realised she didn't have a clue what she was looking for. 'Eh, causes, et cetera...?' That was a long shot. Accident investigation work could take days.

'Right, hit me.' Jim McVeigh made Oonagh laugh with the way he spoke. Liked to try to use phrases he'd picked up from old reruns of *Kojak* or *Starsky and Hutch*. She played along.

'Right, here's the low-down.' Again she took great care to ensure she had no connection to the victim. 'A71 eastbound at the junction with the A719, single vehicle RTC. Single occupant, driver *obviously*. Female.'

He let out a laugh. 'Once a traffic reporter, always a traffic reporter, eh? Right, what d'you need to know?'

She thought for a few seconds. 'Not sure really – do we have a name, age for the victim? Was she pronounced dead at the scene? Cause of the crash? You know, the usual?'

'Why?'

'Why what?'

'Why d'you need to know?'

'Oh, I passed this tonight, doing a piece later in the year about carnage on Scotland's roads, thought it would make a good starting point.' Lying was becoming second nature to Oonagh; perhaps when the media chewed her up and spat her out she could flirt with the idea of becoming a politician.

'Roger. Leave it with me.'

It could take hours or even days before Jim got back with anything concrete. She studied Marjory's notes again. Struggled to make sense of them. Something wasn't adding up. She tried to put Andrew Malloy and Janet Channing to the back of her mind. Their deaths were clouding the issue at the moment.

This shouldn't be such a cloak and dagger operation if all the information was already in the public domain. From what she could gather prison services both here and, in the US, had used inmates as a constant supply of blood, which had then been sold on to pharmaceutical companies, who in turn had pooled the supplies and extracted factor VIII and factor IX crucial for the treatment of haemophiliacs. Evidence that the procedure carried risks appeared to have been ignored. With further evidence that the diagnosis of inmates with blood-borne diseases had been played down, or even hidden. Trouble was much of the research and evidence had been destroyed, probably deliberately, but it hampered any investigation into who was responsible. Also the claims that haemophiliacs would have died without the treatment added to the confusion. The authorities claimed they were acting in the patients' best interests and without the intervention of the blood products the patients would have died years before. They'd actually prolonged their lives.

The whole thing was murky and stank of cover-up after cover-up. The one detail that was significant was the fact that Andrew Malloy had reported an increased recurrence of haemophiliacs with liver disease, which had given rise to the diagnosis that they had in fact been suffering from hep C, brought about by contaminated blood products.

This was more than Oonagh could take in. Among the files were old newspaper cuttings. Tabloids. *Every Haemophiliac in Scotland Has Aids* was the headline. Oonagh had a vague recollection of it at the time. Her face burned red with shame that it had been no more than a passing headline. No more than a salacious, attention-grabbing line that tore families apart. Left lives in shreds and kicked people out of work, out of communities for fear of contamination through ignorance.

She needed to contact some of the victims; Marjory had already given her some names. Said they were eager to tell their story – those who publicly campaigned would surely be willing to speak to her for an in-depth interview. Oonagh still had no idea how the programme would be formulated, or what angle she would take, but she wasn't leaving this to gather dust.

The soft banging against the back door made her jump. It was Cat refusing to use the cat-flap. She yelled at him, but he continued to tap the door with his paws. That cat was driving her bloody nuts, and she acknowledged she didn't have too far to travel on that score. She was about to open the door when her phone rang. Jim McVeigh's number.

'Hey, Oonagh, got the low-down for you.'

'Ooof, that was quick.'

'Off the record?'

'Yes, yes.' She wanted him to cut to the chase. Confirm her worst fears: that Marjory Channing's brakes had been tampered with, that Marjory Channing's steering column had been severed, that Marjory Channing had been chased off the road by an unknown assailant. She guessed he wouldn't be telling her any of this. Oonagh reckoned that Marjory's luck had just run out. Hit a bad bend on a road notorious for accidents.

'OK, waiting for official confirmation of name and age.' She could hear the rustle of the fax paper in Jim's hands. 'Local guys still trying to track down relatives so this *has* to be off the record.'

'Of course.'

'And this still has to be rubber-stamped, but the cause from what we can see?' He was dragging this out; it was his style. 'Classic case of drunk driving. She was pissed, Oonagh. Four times over the limit. It's a wonder she even managed to walk to her car, let alone drive it.'

'Fuck off, Jim!'

'Eh?'

'Drunk? I was with her less than fifteen minutes before. She was stone-cold sober. Unless she got in her car and downed a whole bottle of vodka, then she was not drunk.' Fear pricked at her skull. There was something bigger going on here.

'I'll double-check, but it'll take a few days for a full blood count to be signed off and—'

'No worries, Jim, thanks for checking.' She was about to hang up.

'Who was she? Local cops are trying to name her.'

'Sorry, Jim, I didn't catch her name. I'd just got chatting to her in a bar earlier. I'd been down doing research into a story and was looking for some local gossip.'

She had no idea if he believed her or not and didn't really care, to be honest.

'Oonagh, there's an appeal for witnesses, so…'

'No can do, Jim, off the record works both ways.' She hung up and walked to the fridge. Rain tapped against the window and she felt a pang of guilt for leaving Cat out longer than was necessary. But she needed a drink. What the hell was going on? Her hand shook as she poured. Even for her it was a large glass. Shit, shit, shit. The sea of papers on her worktop seemed to grow in volume. Her heart pounded and she tapped her chest lightly with one hand as she tried to steady her breathing. Taking small sips of air through her nose, holding for three, then out for three. It was the only practical advice that helped subdue her panic attacks. The tapping at the door grew louder. She downed a mouthful of wine and opened the back door, ready for Cat to head-butt her shins.

It wasn't clear at first. The blood looked black, not red. It took a few moments for her to focus. Someone had hung a piece of meat in her back porch. It swung back and forth like a pendulum. She swerved to avoid it hitting her. As the light from the kitchen brought it full into view Oonagh saw Cat's mutilated body hanging by its neck, his legs had been hacked off and placed neatly on the step underneath.

47

Glasgow 2002

'Oonagh, open the door. Oonagh. Oonagh.' The door shook from the force of the banging.

She inched her way towards it, wiping her nose with the back of her hand. 'Put your ID through the letter box.'

'What the hell's going on? Open the—'

'I said put your ID through the letter box.' She gripped the poker in her right hand. It felt heavy and gave her a crumb of comfort.

'Oonagh…?'

'Just do as I ask.'

The letter box flickered slightly then a Strathclyde Police warrant card edged its way through; just enough for her to see Alec's picture and half of his name. Her left hand shook as she turned the Yale lock and opened the door just an inch. The safety chain was on, but she knew one good boot from a size twelve would put paid to that. Alec Davies was on the other side. Oonagh released the catch from the chain as he eased his hand against the door, encouraging it open. 'It's OK, Oonagh. It's me.'

She dropped the poker behind the back of the door, hoping he wouldn't notice. As soon as he was inside she lost every ounce of her false bravado and dissolved into a flood of tears. He draped his arm across her shoulder and ushered her through to the kitchen as she pointed her right index finger towards the back door. He said nothing, but she saw the pity in his eyes. He thought she was a nutter. He sat her down and filled the kettle.

'Shit, you're not making me tea, are you?' All she could think about was Cat hanging from the back door just a few feet away.

'Well, now that I know you don't need either CPR or a S.W.A.T. team I thought I'd make myself a coffee – is that OK?'

She nodded and felt a bit shitty for snapping at him. 'There's wine in the fridge.'

'Really?' He made no attempt to keep the sarcasm out of his voice.

She held her right hand on her knee to stop her leg shaking uncontrollably. 'Alec, I really don't need this shit just now.'

'D'you want to tell me what's going on?'

Her earlier resolve vanished as her throat hiccupped. 'Cat's dead.'

He held the fridge door open, his mouth gaping slightly in apparent disbelief. She knew what he was thinking. 'Alec...' she tipped her head towards the fridge '... can you close the door? The motor'll burn out.'

'Sorry, Oon.' He closed the fridge door and sat down across the table. 'Your cat's dead?' He let out a slow exhalation. 'I thought something had happened. I thought—'

'Oh, God, Alec, someone killed him.' She pointed to the back door and covered her eyes with her hands. 'He's in the porch. I can't look.'

Alec stood up and opened the back door slowly, naturally looking down to the mat. It took a split second for him to catch sight of the dead animal swinging on the rope. 'Aagh...' He closed the door again quickly. 'I'm sorry, Oonagh. Look, go upstairs and I'll deal with this.'

'No, we need to bury him.'

'Of course, but I need to get the place dusted for fingerprints. You know, it was probably just kids. I blame these flipping video games, but we'll get it checked just to make sure.'

'It wasn't kids, Alec.' She'd given up on the thought that a coffee might soothe her nerves and was tipping the remaining contents of the wine into her glass. 'That was meant for me.' She told him about Marjory Channing. She struggled to remain calm and blurted it all out in one go. She knew she wasn't making much sense. She picked up the dossier from the table. 'It's here, evidence. It's all here.'

It took her a couple of seconds to read the look on his face.

'Channing? Any relation to...?'

'Sister. But this is bigger than—'

'You better be fucking kidding me on! You've been in contact with Janet Channing's sister and didn't think to let me know?'

'I only found out her real name tonight.'

Alec leaned his hands on the worktop. Dropped his head. Oonagh could see the swell of his shoulders as he took a deep breath. He was clearly pissed off, but giving little away.

'So, you're saying someone had her killed then the cops doctored the results of the breathalyser?'

Oonagh knew this was far-fetched. 'I was talking to her fifteen minutes beforehand. She was stone-cold sober!'

'It doesn't take very long for someone to get drunk, Oonagh. She might have had booze in the car.'

Oonagh elected to keep quiet about the hip flask; there was barely enough booze in that to do any damage. She drank more than that some mornings to sober up. 'We both know that's shite, Alec. She was onto something and someone wanted to shut her up.'

'Maybe it wasn't fifteen minutes, Oonagh. Maybe it was nearer twenty-five minutes or forty-five minutes

304

beforehand. This isn't the Bronx.'

'Yea, but we're not a million miles away from South Yorkshire either.' It was a low blow, but the tarnished reputation of South Yorkshire was legendary. Journalists knew they'd fabricated evidence on the Hillsborough deaths, but could do nothing about it. Rumour that they were actively ignoring paedophile rings in Rotherham went unreported for fear of repercussions and Oonagh vividly remembered pictures of front-line bobbies on the force waving wads of tenners in the faces of striking miners who were so strapped for cash the arse hung out of their trousers. Alec looked down, said nothing. She couldn't tell what he was thinking, but guessed he knew of a few other misdemeanours that had taken place under the watchful eye of that particular force.

The wind picked up outside and once again Cat's body swung in the breeze, banging against the back door. 'Can we just get him down? Please?' Oonagh took a fresh towel from the linen cupboard. 'Here, wrap him in this.' She took a knife from the block on the worktop and Alec grabbed her wrist.

'Hey, what're you doing with that?'

'I'm going to cut the rope?'

He blushed and let go. 'Here, let me.' He took a Swiss Army knife from his pocket and closed the back door behind him, saving Oonagh from any more bloodshed. He came back in carrying a bloody bundle that used to be her cat. Oonagh did her best not to cry.

'Pigs, doing that to an innocent wee thing.'

'Aw, you're not trying to tell me you think the police were involved in this too?'

'Eh?' The penny dropped. 'No! I mean, animals, bastards...' she struggled for another word as Alec laid the bloodied bundle on a black bin liner '... cunts, that's what they are, total fucking cunts. With a K!' She saw him raise an eyebrow at the C word but he said nothing, just wrapped Cat up in the polythene.

'We can have a vet perform a PM, but I doubt it'll tell us anything.'

'D'you think he suffered?' What a stupid bloody question – he was mutilated; his limbs hacked off and hung. But she needed some reassurance.

'I'm sure it was really quick, Oonagh. Whoever did this...' His voice trailed off; there were probably only so many lies he could tell with regards to this. 'I've called it in. We'll have the prints guys out very soon.'

'Poor wee Cat.'

He nodded in agreement, but Oonagh could tell his mind was on other things.

<u>48</u>

Glasgow 2002

Oonagh set her plate down on the table beside him.
'Hiya, anyone sitting here?' He'd just taken a mouthful
of food and she sat down before he had a chance to
answer. They'd worked together on and off for years.
Sandy Murray had somehow elevated himself to Health
Correspondent, and on a quiet day he'd doubled up as
Home Affairs Corr.

'Can I get you a coffee? They've a new machine.' She
nodded over to the stainless-steel monster hissing away
behind the counter. 'Go on,' she said, 'before someone
from Health & Safety comes and takes it away.'

Sandy let out a laugh and eased a bit of bacon back
into his mouth with his pinkie. 'On you go, then. Get me
a slice of caramel shortcake while you're there,' he
shouted, almost an afterthought.

She loitered at the counter, putting the coffee on a
tray, planning the best strategy in her head. She got on

well with Sandy, but he could be a funny bugger if he didn't want to play ball.

'So, what you after?' He sipped the coffee through the foam and broke off a corner of the biscuit.

'Nothing! Can't I buy you a coffee just for the hell of it?' She was clearly losing her touch.

'Last time you bought me a coffee, O'Neil, you were looking for some guy's phone number.'

She could feel her face going red. 'That was a long time ago. Anyway...' she decided to use the direct approach '... the tainted blood scandal.'

Sandy put his cup on the table, raised his eyebrow, giving her the OK to continue.

'I want to interview some of the victims, and thought —'

'That bunch are a nightmare.'

'Sandy! That's a hellish thing to say.' She was genuinely shocked, and surprised that she was hurt by his outburst, but she needed him to fill in some gaps.

She didn't go into detail about the programme at this stage, just told him that she was looking at medical negligence stories in general.

'Well, steer clear of that mob. They're just impossible to deal with.'

'From what I can gather they've been dealt a really horrific blow.'

Sandy wiped the foam from his lips with the back of his hand. He liked to give the impression that he was a laid-back, can't-be-arsed type of journalist, treading water in a cushy number to see him to retirement. But his years of experience alone meant for the most part he knew his stuff.

'Listen, there's no doubt they've suffered. It must be crap for all of them. I'm not denying that. But they're so busy fighting among themselves that they're alienating themselves from anyone who could maybe help.'

'Explain.'

Sandy didn't tell her much more than what she knew already: basically those affected by the infected blood were categorised into different groups. He pushed his plate to one side and pulled the sugar bowl towards him. 'Right, here you have every patient affected.' He glanced up to make sure Oonagh was paying attention. He took out a handful of sugar sachets and placed them in front of the bowl. 'Some of these were infected with hep C in the late seventies and would have died without the factor VIII. Next—' he grabbed another handful, smaller this time '—we have the poor sods who were infected later, once the risks were known.' The last handful of sugar was smaller again. 'Then there are those non-haemophiliacs who were infected during transfusions after operations and the likes.'

'Right, so we've got a table full of sugar, people are dying and the problem is?'

'There's a whole load of stuff as to how the blood became infected. Some of it was never properly heat treated to make it safe, others because it came from suspect sources…'

Oonagh was anxious to get to the heart of it all. 'So what's the bottom line?' She hoped he'd leave the sugar alone. It was getting on her tits and reminded her of how much dumbing down there was in television.

'Well, some are dying, an increasing amount are dead, there's no one single reason or person to blame and no criminal charges.'

'This doesn't really explain it, though, Sandy.'

'The bottom line, Oonagh, is none of the campaign groups can agree on a compensation figure. They've been offered different amounts in line with how much their lives have been affected – but in return they need to drop the negligence claims.'

'That's deplorable.'

Sandy nodded. 'Yeah, but that's life, eh? Some want to take the money as at least it's better than a kick in the chukkies, others are furious and say the compensation doesn't even amount to a year's wages. You know as well as I do how compensation works. Joe Public thinks there's money to burn. But in real life it's not like that. One poor sod crippled from hep C, cannae get up the stairs, can't work. But he's a haemophiliac. His life was already hanging by a thread. It's just a different type of shite that he was dealing with before. He can hardly claim loss of earnings when he had a disease that meant he was unable to leave his front door most days anyway.'

'Yes, but that can't be the same for all of them. There must be some who were—'

Sandy cut in. 'That's my point, Oonagh. There are just too many variants within the victims to get a one-size-fits-all compo arrangement. And if one group turn it down then none of them get the cash.'

Oonagh liked Sandy, she liked him a lot, but this left a bitter taste in her mouth. She couldn't imagine any other scenario where victims were accused of being so complicit in their own downfall. 'So basically you're telling me that because the victims can't agree then they're snookered?'

Sandy nodded and placed the sugar sachets back in the bowl. Carefully ensuring they all faced the same way.

'It's just too complicated, Oonagh, and at the end of the day it's a pain in the tonsils. I could spend three weeks making a single package about this that's on air for less than four minutes. In that time, I could have covered five different stories for the network.'

It broke her heart, but she knew he was right. Very few duty editors would sign off such an assignment. There just weren't the resources. She'd already resigned herself to the fact that most of this programme would be made in her own time. It was a good job she didn't have

311

anyone to go on holiday with as she made a mental note to cancel all leave.

'I still want to interview some of the victims.'

Sandy just shrugged. ''S up to you,' and stood up to leave.

'I've got a contact for Eva Muirhead?' Oonagh posed it as a question.

Sandy slid the sugar bowl towards Oonagh with his index finger. 'There are hundreds of victims who I reckon would speak to you, Oonagh – why d'you want to talk to the one bampot that's too crazy for the sugar bowl?'

*

'It was my fault. They get the gene from the mother, you know.' She smoothed the soft white Babygro on the bed. 'We brought him home in this. It was miles too big. Funny how you have no idea you're defective until it's too late.' The clothes seemed to be laid out in chronological order: baby to toddler, smart infant school uniform and the immaculate wee black brogues, without even a scuff.

'He was so excited the day we bought these. He promised me he'd keep them good.' She held them to her chest. 'I don't want his school shoes to be good. I want them wrecked and scuffed and broken. He was seven.

Seven years old and he never got a chance to wear his school uniform like the rest of the kids.'

Oonagh struggled to keep it together as the wee boy's life was laid out before her. This was so fucking unfair. She reached out and touched Eva Muirhead's shoulder. The mother's loss was palpable. 'It doesn't get any easier. People think after a few years it eases, fades into the background, but it doesn't.' The sob in her throat clawed its way out of her mouth. 'He was my wee boy.' Her cry was visceral and Oonagh broke every rule in her book as she wrapped both arms around Eva Muirhead and held her close.

The sun streamed through the window and the light glinted off the bedside table. Eva's sobs subsided, but Oonagh guessed they were never far from the surface.

'People think we're nutters, you know. Crackpots screaming about compensation. Justice. Perhaps we are, but no one's listening.'

'Eva, what kind of help are you getting?'

She just shrugged. 'None really. Oh, there are support groups for people who've lost children, and others from the tainted blood scandal, but I just feel…'

She didn't say hers was a special case. There was no hierarchy of grief from Eva Muirhead, no special claim to be worse off than any other grieving mother. But Oonagh knew she was.

Eva made her way back into the main living room, away from her dead son's things. She had prepared for

Oonagh's visit; folders apparently containing every scrap of paperwork and information on Mark's medical condition were on the table.

Oonagh feared this was a bigger story than she could handle. She'd need a helluva lot of help and backup. A separate researcher, one she could trust, and a production team that could deliver the goods. This wasn't a programme that she could put together in a few weeks; this would take time. Every new piece of information led her down a wormhole until she felt she was drowning in data.

'Eva, I'm so sorry, I need to ask some really upsetting questions.' Oonagh didn't want to add to her pain.

'There's nothing you can say or do that would make me feel any worse. I've got nothing inside. I don't even have bitterness any more. Just nothing.'

Oonagh thought back to the times she'd read out a news item on the tainted blood scandal. She'd hardly even taken in the words. Another victim dead, another group calling for a public inquiry. But Eva Muirhead's pain would go on long after the studio lights went out.

She told Oonagh that Mark had been diagnosed with haemophilia when he was just six months old. There had been no known family history and prior to that Eva had been oblivious to the fact she carried the defective gene. 'When I think back to the times I'd injected him, and he was trying to be brave. It was sore. I could see it in his face, but he was such a wee soldier. He was being brave for me and I was killing him. Injecting him with that filthy poison.'

'Eva, please; you put your trust in the medical profession. They were the ones that let you and your family down. Don't torture yourself like this.' Oonagh's words felt hollow, but she just didn't know what else to say.

Mark Muirhead was seven years old when he died. He was HIV positive. After his diagnosis the doctors in the children's unit quizzed Eva about a possible heroin habit when she was pregnant. Had she injected?

'I was a thirty-two-year-old chartered accountant when I got pregnant. I could have written a book on being dull, yet they were asking me all this stuff.'

Could it have been Mark's dad? they'd asked. Had he been having unprotected sex with prostitutes? Was he frequenting gay bars, picking up rent boys?

'Brian lost his job as soon as it got out about Mark. He was a catering manager and they said it was too risky. There was a huge article in one of the tabloids with the headline: *'Every Haemophiliac in the UK has AIDS'*. Friends I'd known for years wouldn't let me near them. Pulled their kids to one side as I walked past. Mark loved swimming, but we were banned from the local pool. We were treated like lepers. And all the time I was trying to find out what was wrong with my baby. I used to worry that haemophilia would hamper Mark's life. Maybe stop him having kids of his own one day. He wasn't supposed to die before he'd had a chance to wear his school shoes.'

This time Eva Muirhead didn't cry. She grabbed one of the folders and flicked through the pages. 'Look; it's here in black and white.'

Oonagh scanned the document in which a Canadian pharmaceutical company pleaded guilty to labelling blood as coming from donors in Sweden when in actual fact it came from Russian cadavers. Oonagh read and reread the last line.

'They've actually admitted this?'

Eva nodded. 'The blood was then repackaged and exported to Europe to make factor VIII.'

According to Eva there were never any criminal charges brought about, instead they were being pursued in the civil courts.

'It was as though he was slipping through my fingers. Gradually he was getting sicker. There was nothing I could do. He was so ill. In the end we brought Mark home to die. Wanted him to be surrounded by his favourite toys, in a house where he was loved. He looked like a wee old man. His skin as thin as paper. That night Brian held him. I lay beside them both in the bed, stroking his cheek. I was whispering goodbye and telling him how much I loved him. D'you know what he said?'

Oonagh's chest tightened as Eva tried to suppress her sobs.

'He said, "Mummy, where am I going?" And the only thing I could think to say was to tell him he was going on a big adventure with ET. Up into the sky. Why the hell did I say that?'

By now Eva's cries were convulsing in her throat, and Oonagh did nothing to stop her own tears, which stung her cheeks.

'Our wee boy, he didn't deserve that. D'you know how sick I feel thinking that I might've injected him with blood from a Russian corpse who died of God knows what?'

Eva's cries subsided, and Oonagh reached for her hand. 'If this is known, well documented, what's the…' she struggled to find the right words '… why's there such a problem with getting justice?'

Eva waved her hand over the sea of paperwork. 'I've pored over this for almost two decades. Each year the files get bigger and bigger; more mess come to the surface. I practically know every case by heart, but d'you know what those bastards say in their defence? Said Mark was going to die anyway, and at the time they didn't know the blood was infected. That's why we can't get any justice. There's no bottom line here. No one to take ultimate responsibility. No one to sue.'

'I need to play devil's advocate here, Eva.' Oonagh felt like a shit, but there were some things that needed to be said. 'Could they have been right? Were they at least giving him what they believed was a fighting chance?'

Eva's knuckles whitened slightly as she gripped the arm of the chair. She'd obviously been asked that question before. She tapped her index finger on the table next to the files. 'Every single sufferer in here is different. And for some that may well be the case. I firmly believe Mark's condition was more than manageable. D'you know how many paediatricians are familiar with the disease?' She didn't wait for Oonagh to reply. 'Very few. They maybe see one or two patients throughout their careers. Sometimes none at all. They were as much in the dark as we were. I don't blame them. It was the haematology departments who were playing God. Bastards. I can't prove it, but I know my boy was deliberately infected with HIV. Those bastards needed a guinea pig.'

Oonagh reached out and held Eva's arm. 'Surely not.'

Eva pulled away. 'D'you know how many people look at me as though I'm mental when I say that?'

'I don't think you're mental, Eva, but I genuinely want you to be wrong.' Oonagh meant what she said. Eva's theory was too horrific.

'Oonagh, I'm sorry, but somewhere along the line some bastard signed off a consignment of blood from Soviet mortuaries and state prisons. That I can prove. The bottom line is I injected my only son with blood from corpses, drug addicts and killers and I'm just meant to think that's a bad roll of the dice.'

'What about Brian? Are you two still together?'

Eva dropped her eyes and shook her head. She walked over to the window sill and picked up a framed picture of the three of them. A happy family: Eva with her dark blonde hair slightly over her face, Brian grinning with Mark in his arms. Taken during happier times. Before Mark's illness claimed the best of his childhood. Bastard, thought Oonagh, leaving Eva to deal with this on her own. She kept her trap shut on this one.

'D'you know there are people thought we'd made it up?'

Oonagh must have looked confused.

'Made up the tainted blood scandal. I've had poison-pen letters from people saying Brian had AIDS and gave it to Mark. Or that I'd been sleeping around. They said the most vile things.'

It was dawning on Oonagh that a decent production team was the least of her worries. The studio lawyers would be working overtime for six months to pass any of this to go on-air.

'Were you ever tested for HIV?'

Eva shook her head. 'We both refused. If either of us had contracted it from Mark then, well, I'd rather not know.'

'Eva, what makes you think that Mark was deliberately infected with HIV? That's a pretty serious allegation.' Eva Muirhead shot her a look; Oonagh hurried to explain herself. 'I mean, isn't there the possibility that he contracted the disease through the infected blood? You said so yourself.'

Once again Eva referred to the documents on the table. 'There's a cluster of kids here. They're all fairly similar to Mark in the way that the disease presented itself. They all had what's known as mild haemophilia.' She went on to explain, 'Severe haemophiliacs bleed into their muscles and joints, and bleed spontaneously. It's all to do with the amount of clotting agent missing from the blood. It's a horrible disease.'

Oonagh could see Eva Muirhead was a self-taught expert on the subject.

'Moderate sufferers will have problems after surgery or dental work. They tend not to bleed spontaneously. Mark was at the mild end of the scale. Yes, he'd have had a problem with surgery, or an open-wound injury, but that was it.'

'And you're saying…'

'There's a cluster of half a dozen kids, all similar age to Mark with mild haemophilia, and they all contracted AIDS around the same time.' She caught the question in Oonagh's expression. 'Yes, all dead.'

Not for the first time Oonagh felt out of her depth.

'None of these kids ever really needed Factor VIII. I believe that they were used as lab rats and deliberately infected with this new blood-borne disease.'

This was a bit of a leap. It was becoming difficult to separate what might be a crackpot conspiracy theory from the real deal. But her gut told her to trust Eva Muirhead and her mother's instinct.

'Why would they do that, Eva? Why would any doctor be so vicious as to give a child AIDS?'

She shrugged her shoulders. 'It was the perfect way to gauge the pathology of the disease. This way they could monitor the kids.' Eva turned her back to Oonagh. 'I sound like a nutter, don't I?'

'Eva, I've met nutters, lots of them. Believe me, you've a long way to go.'

Eva turned and let out a slight laugh. 'Thanks. I think.'

She levelled with her. 'Eva, I'm not going to kid on, there's a lot of information here. I'm struggling to take it all in.'

Oonagh didn't want to leave it there, but she needed to gather the information and was due back at the studio. 'Can we meet again, Eva? I feel I'm just at the tip of the iceberg here.'

Eva nodded. 'Don't worry, I'm not going anywhere.'

Oonagh stood up to go. She felt awkward, not knowing quite what to say.

'Just do your best,' said Eva.

Oonagh stepped forward and hugged her. 'I promise,' she said, with no idea how much good that would do.

49

Glasgow 2002

There wasn't much that still shocked Oonagh O'Neil, but this sickened her to the core. She waited in the car at the bottom of the street. She'd had to borrow her mum's car, given that she'd wrapped her own around a lamp post. Her mum was only too glad to help, but nagged her to get a better insurance deal; one that offered her a courtesy car whilst hers was out of action. Oonagh could hardly tell her mum that her licence had been suspended and she was banned from driving until the tests were complete. She pushed the pang of guilt to one side and settled back in the seat.

The driveway was clearly visible and from here she'd be able to see any visitors coming or going. Usually a Tuesday, they'd said. Usually mornings. So she waited. She'd toyed with the idea of having a Thermos flask of coffee in the car to keep her warm and awake and to stop her getting bored, but had realised she'd be running to the loo every five minutes so she'd ditched that idea. She'd make a rubbish cop on stake-out.

Perhaps this was a bad idea. Almost two hours had passed and her legs were stiff and cramped and she was running low on petrol as she kept the engine ticking over to let her listen to the radio without draining the battery. She should have topped up on the way. Almost twelve o'clock. She was going to call it a day when the red Fiat slowed at the gates and swung left into the driveway. She wasn't 100 per cent certain it was him, but she was pretty damned sure and that was good enough. She gave him a five-minute head start, then locked the car and walked the few hundred yards to the house.

Smiley-Face opened the door again and looked disappointed to see Oonagh wasn't laden down with goodies this time. 'Is eh...?'

'She's in the garden.' Smiley-Face tipped her head towards the back. 'Loves her garden, so she does.'

Oonagh smiled and envied her being so happy in her job.

'Just go through. She's got another visitor today.' Bingo. Oonagh made her way to the back garden and saw Dorothy Malloy reclining on a lounger. She wore a large floppy hat and oversized shades with a blanket over her legs. Every inch the femme fatale of yesteryear. The man at her side sat upright, elbows resting on his knees. He had his back to Oonagh, but she recognised him immediately. Dorothy Malloy looked relaxed and happy and turned her head as Oonagh approached; in turn the man at her side twisted in his seat, his eyes followed Oonagh as she made her way to their table.

'May I?' She gestured to the empty chair but sat down before anyone had a chance to object. Dorothy looked pleased to see her and reached her hand out. Oonagh gave it a little squeeze. Her brother didn't look quite as thrilled; Graham Anderson kept his eyes down and moved a small stone along the path with his toe.

'How you getting on, Dorothy?'

'Oh, I'm much better, Oonagh.' She gestured towards the man. 'This is my brother…'

Oonagh nodded. 'We've met already,' she said.

Graham Anderson forced a thin smile.

'I'm glad you two are getting acquainted again.' Again, not much from the brother, a slight shrug of his shoulder. He rubbed his hands along both thighs, a cue to leave, and made to stand up.

'Please, Mr Anderson—' she didn't much feel like being familiar '—not leaving on my account, are you?'

'Oh, Graham.' Dorothy's mouth formed a small pout. 'You've only just got here – please stay.' He glared at Oonagh. She felt a slight pang of guilt at interrupting the family reunion but she was sure there'd be more. He glanced at his sister and reluctantly sat back down.

'Shall we have tea?' Dorothy Malloy could barely contain the excitement in her voice. Oonagh offered a tight-lipped smile and nodded, Graham Anderson gave his now characteristic shrug. Dorothy stood up and trotted off in her childlike way, excited at the prospect of a tea party.

'It was you I came to see.' Oonagh cut to the chase.

'I've told you all I know. I gave you the diary. What the hell d'you want?'

'Are your family expert shape-shifters?'

'Eh?'

'Dorothy, she seems to change her whole body with the blink of an eye. You, last time I saw you, you were at death's door.'

'Oh, I'd had chemo the day before. It gets you like that.'

'Shame.'

Graham Anderson flashed her a look; clearly the cancer card wasn't working. Oonagh couldn't be arsed any more and needed some answers.

'D'you want to start by telling me the truth?'

'The truth? Shit, I don't even know what that is any more. Where do I start?'

'How about why the hell you didn't tell me you worked with Dorothy's husband?'

'Because it's none of your fucking business!' At least that part was true. It wasn't.

'Might not be my business, Mr Anderson, but I'm making it my business. Something's very wrong here. Your poor sister's fucking gaga, your brother-in-law got his heart ripped out and your nephew was drowned in his own home by some sicko who—' He made to speak but Oonagh was having none of it. 'Don't you dare tell me Dorothy killed that wee boy. She's your sister, for God's sake, do the right thing by her.'

Dorothy waved from inside the kitchen. Oonagh wasn't sure exactly where she was going with this. 'Marjory Channing—' Graham Anderson flinched at the mention of her name '—don't even pretend you don't know her.'

'Not here.'

'OK, where? You name the time and the place.'

'It's not that black and white.'

'It is from where I'm standing.'

Dorothy sauntered down the path, the tea tray high in her hands. This strange hybrid woman-child who looked as vulnerable as a petal yet could rip out her husband's heart without so much as a backward glance. What the fuck was going on inside her head?

50

Glasgow 2002

'You know she's dead, don't you?'

He gave her a quizzical look. One that looked well rehearsed.

'Marjory Channing.' This time Oonagh couldn't read his expression. There was nothing there.

They sat outside the café at Pollok House. It was quiet enough, the schools were back after the Easter break and just a few dog walkers passed in the distance, far enough away not to hear their conversation. Graham Anderson had initially appeared reluctant to meet again, but changed his tune once Oonagh had mentioned Marjory Channing's name. Anderson's name had cropped up several times throughout Marjory's dossier. He'd been a key player in the early days. A brilliant scientist by all accounts.

'OK, start by explaining what pups are.'

'Pups?'

Oonagh sifted through the documents left to her by Marjory Channing. The word pup cropped up a lot. 'An acronym, I take it?'

'Oh.' The penny dropped. 'Previously Untreated Patients. PUPs. They were a vital component in testing the new heat-treated product.' Graham explained that heating the pooled plasma was the chosen method to rid the blood products of any virus. Oonagh sensed he was dumbing it down slightly for her. Testing the efficacy of this method had proved very difficult. Most haemophiliacs were contaminated in one way or another.

'Contaminated?'

'Yeah, don't forget they'd been exposed to so many treatments, so much contaminated blood, so many drugs, the effects of which can lie dormant in the system for years. It was almost impossible to gauge the effect of the heat-treated products on them.' He paused for a moment. 'We needed a clean batch of patients.'

He spoke as though they were lab rats. Which in effect they were.

'How could you find...?' Oonagh wasn't really sure how to pose the question. She wanted Eva Muirhead to be the nutter that everyone accused her of being. The grieving mother tipped over the edge by her son's death. 'How did you manage to find patients who weren't contaminated?'

Graham gave her a look she couldn't read. 'Kids.'

'Oh, no.'

'The younger the better, I'm afraid.'

Her worst fears were being confirmed. 'You used children as a control group for your experiments?' She caught Graham's eye; she glanced down and realised she was rubbing her tummy.

She waited but there was no response. 'Why?'

'Listen, dear, this isn't the media where we can just airbrush everything into perfection. Sometimes life's tough, OK?'

'Don't bounce this back onto me! And don't call me dear.'

Graham Anderson ran his hands through his hair. 'You just don't get it.'

'I'm beginning to. You used children, babies, as lab rats to test if your drugs were safe? Where are the fucking ethics in that?'

He traced a line through the puddle of tea that had spilled on the wooden table. His jaw set in a hard line. 'If we worried about ethics we would have no antibiotics, no organ transplants, no stem cell research. You don't understand.'

'Oh, come on, it's hardly the same thing.'

'These experiments were vital for the treatment of future generations.'

'And what about *this* generation? What about the generation you decided to inflict with a fate worse than death? Do they not deserve the same consideration as the future generation you talk about so generously?'

Oonagh got up to leave. 'Maniacs. You were all just maniacs.' She stood up, but knew she couldn't leave just yet.

'What do you think it takes for an educated man... or woman to slice into someone's flesh without a second thought? There has to be a degree of... detachment.'

'But you deliberately targeted children.' She was screaming now; a passing jogger turned to look but quickened his pace again when he saw no one was being killed.

'Dear God, are you really that naïve?'

Oonagh sat back down, shook her head; it was automatic rather than a response. He was on a roll. He looked manic. 'Where d'you think most of the medical or scientific breakthroughs come from?' He didn't wait for an answer. 'Neo-natal care. Babies who're going to die anyway. Take cooling therapy for instance. Babies born with hypoxic ischemic encephalopathy,' he waved his hand, dismissing her question before she asked it, 'Basically it's brain damage through lack of oxygen. If those kids are put into a medically induced state of hypothermia we can dramatically increase their chances of survival. But it's not without risks. And in the early days it was all trial and error.' He was on a roll; Oonagh was sickened to see a flicker of excitement in his eye. 'No-one knew for sure how it all worked but we just kept at it until we got it right. And yes, a few died along the way. Collateral damage. And now brain cooling is used not only on babies, but people with acute head injuries with remarkable results. And that's all down to the experiments in the neo-natal units.' He sat back, paused for breath. 'Dear God, if we had to ask permission for every medical experiment we'd still be using leeches.'

'Just because it's happening doesn't mean it's right!'

'No, perhaps not. But let me ask you this. You've just given birth. That child has had some... trauma during birth... brain damage, not enough to kill it, but enough to ensure you're changing nappies seven times a day and feeding it through a tube in its stomach for the rest of its life. Or, the doctors can repair the damage and the child can do all the other stuff normal kids can do. What would you want? Eh?' He held a coin on the end of his thumb. 'You're pregnant, right now. Just imagine. Your baby faces a life of misery. I can toss this coin and with your call I can make sure your baby is happy, healthy and normal. You decide the fate of your child, over the suffering of some nameless, faceless people a generation ago.' He flicked the coin in the air. 'Tell me. Would you be so high and mighty then?'

She thought of Eva Muirhead clutching her child's school shoes to her chest. The fight was leaving her. 'Stop it! This isn't about... about what you're talking about. This is about right and wrong. This is about using babies as lab rats. This is about—'

He cut right in. 'Finding a cure for an illness which kills thousands of people every year. Listen to me. Scientific breakthroughs were on the line. Careers were being forged here. Great works being put to the test. D'you think Marie Curie didn't have the odd casualty here and there? As I said, collateral damage. It happens. These boys were already diseased.'

Oonagh slumped back onto her chair. Unable to take in what he'd just said. She tried to be detached from it all. Did her best to see the bigger picture; understand the greater good, the needs of the many over the needs of the few. She couldn't.

'Fuck. Josef Mengele had nothing on you guys. At least the Nazis wore a badge.'

'Save me the bleeding heart liberal crap.'

Oonagh tucked her hands under her thighs. She didn't trust herself not to take a swing at him. 'And your sister? Where did Dorothy come into all this? Was she just another piece of collateral damage?'

She saw a chink in his armour. He slumped. 'Sometimes things just get out of control.'

She waited for him to continue. Instead he just stared out at the White Cart Water. The river was high today.

'Why did you give me Dorothy's diary?'

'You said you wanted to help.'

'You hand a journalist a diary that implicates your sister in the killing of three women, and you expect me to believe you're looking out for her. Do us a favour.' Oonagh couldn't stomach any more. She waited for him to answer.

He cleared the phlegm from his throat. 'Dorothy's served her time. I wanted you to help her. See that she'd suffered from... from something. She wasn't in her right mind when she killed Andrew.'

'No shit, Sherlock. I'd kind of guessed that when she was banged up in Cartland for the past twenty-seven years.' This was going nowhere. She needed to get him back on her side.

'Graham, you said yourself, you're dying. What difference would it make if it all came out now?'

'I've also got two grown-up kids out there somewhere. A family.' He looked scared. No one wanted to be related to a killer. Guilt by association.

'So why get me involved at all?' This wasn't making any sense.

'You've met her. She's a poor soul. I'm terrified for her. That this'll all come out. I just wanted to make sure that she had someone on her side.'

Oonagh had the distinct impression that she was being taken for a ride. She played her trump card. 'Dorothy's going to be hounded by the press from here on in anyway.'

He obviously didn't know what Oonagh was getting at.

'Dorothy's agreed to speak on camera for a programme I'm doing.' She called his bluff. 'Once it's revealed she never went to trial, was never formally charged, this is going to explode. The Home Office will be up to its knees in the brown smelly stuff and your sister's name and pictures will be plastered all over the Internet.' Oonagh needed to smoke out Graham Anderson.

'You wouldn't do this.'

She was back in the saddle. 'Graham, it's the last thing I'd want. But getting the truth out there is vital. This will ensure that no other women will be subject to the miscarriage of justice that Dorothy went through. That women will be treated properly by the mental health profession. Think of the lives of the future generation. And let's not forget careers in journalism are being forged here.'

Oonagh was sure she could see the word bitch being formed in Graham Anderson's mind. 'And once the story's out there, how long d'you think it'll take for a tabloid to track down your family for a statement?'

He worried the coin between his thumb and index finger, then flicked it in the air. 'I'll toss you for it.' The coin spun in the air. 'Call,' he yelled.

Oonagh couldn't believe she was party to this. 'Heads.'

Her heart pounded as the coin landed on the table and spun on its side for what seemed an eternity before resting with the head facing upwards.

'This is your lucky day, Oonagh O'Neil.'

51

Glasgow 2002

Alec Davies checked his phone for the third time since leaving the house. It had been over an hour since he'd dropped Oonagh a text and still no reply. She was pissed off with him. Couldn't quite grasp the enormity of the crime that Dorothy Malloy had committed and the effect it had on everyone it touched.

He made his way to Chief Constable Gordon Threadgold's home. It was the first time he'd ever been invited. Strictly speaking he wasn't quite invited this time, but what he had to say couldn't be done over the phone.

Davies straightened his tie as he stood on the doorstep and tugged down the back of his jacket. He could hear footsteps in the hall and quickly shined each shoe on the back of his trouser legs before the door was opened.

Threadgold stretched out his hand. 'Alec, good to see you, my boy,' as he gestured for him to come in. Davies tried not to look impressed as he was led through the hallway into the living room. His whole flat could have fitted in here.

'Very nice,' was all he said as he sat on the soft cream sofa.

Threadgold nodded as he made his way to the drinks cabinet. 'It's Jean who likes the nice things.' He took a decanter of red wine from the cupboard. 'I just tag along for the ride.' He grinned as he held it up to the light to examine the colour. Davies wasn't really a huge fan of red wine. He was still mortified at the memory of bringing a girl home for the first time and his mum taking a bottle from the kitchen cabinet with a raffle ticket still attached.

'D'you know there are over a thousand varieties of grapes in Italy alone?'

Davies held the document folder on his lap. 'No, I must say that's a surprise.'

'Here, try some of this, it's very—'

'No, sir.' He held one hand up in protest. 'I'm driving.'

Threadgold laughed. 'You're hardly likely to get stopped, now, are you? And it's Gordon.' He pressed the huge glass into his hand; Davies was careful to hold it by the stem. That was the full extent of his knowledge on wine. He took a sip, slightly bracing himself against the bitter taste but none came. He caught Threadgold smiling out of the side of his eye. 'Good, isn't it?'

Davies had to agree. The wine settled on his tongue for a moment then slipped down and immediately soothed its way into his body, ironing out any creases it found along the way. Davies allowed himself to relax. Slightly. He took his phone out then paused, 'D'you mind if…' Threadgold gestured for him to carry on, 'Sorry Sir, this is important', then sent McVeigh a text telling him to get a squad car to drop him off near Threadgold's house in an hour's time to drive him home. He wasn't taking any chances.

'So…' Threadgold sat opposite him in a leather armchair '… how can I help you, son?'

He looked round for somewhere to place the oversized glass and Threadgold nodded to a small nest of tables by his side. 'Well, sir, Gordon, it's ehm…' he held the folder in his right hand, preparing to unleash the contents '… Andrew Malloy?'

Threadgold tightened his jaw at the mention of his friend's name. 'There's something I need to ask about…' Davies took the charge sheet out of the envelope. He'd left the pictures of the dead boy in the office. Threadgold had been a close family friend – no point in making this any more painful than it was obviously going to be.

'Carry on.'

'Dorothy Malloy was never arrested.'

'What?'

'There's a charge sheet and no actual charge. She was taken straight to Cartland.'

The older man leaned forward in his chair. 'And?'

Davies had hoped the penny would have dropped and sparked more of a response with Threadgold. 'Well...' He wasn't sure exactly how to word this. Not only was Malloy a close family friend, but Threadgold had been a serving officer during the time of his death. In the same division. 'She should have been arrested, then taken to a police station, then...' Explaining the finer points of the arrest procedure to the Chief Constable of one of the country's largest force didn't rest easy on him. Thankfully Threadgold stepped in.

'Listen, Alec, that house was a bloodbath.' His fingers tightened around the stem of the glass. 'Malloy was slaughtered, the boy drowned, and you're coming to me to say that—' a slight beat '—that bitch hadn't been read her rights?'

Shit, this wasn't going well at all. 'No, sir, it's not that —' Davies noticed this time Threadgold didn't correct him when he called him sir '—but every such procedure would say that the accused is taken to a police station and from there a police psychiatrist is called in to assess if he or she needs to be hospitalised or sectioned.'

Threadgold put down his glass and Davies grew more uneasy. 'Don't lecture me on police procedure, son.'

'I know, I'm sorry, but...'

Threadgold swallowed and seemed to soften slightly. 'Here, let's see what you've got.'

Davies held out the charge sheet; a slight pause.

'I assume you've taken a copy?'

'Aye.' He handed it over.

Threadgold took his glasses from his top pocket. It didn't take long to read it. There were surprisingly few details.

He took a sharp intake of breath. 'You know, I've never seen this before.'

'Really?'

'Couldn't stomach it.' His eyes glanced across the page. 'We see bad things every day, Alec. We see things that no human being should ever see, but when it's a pal...'

Davies nodded. And waited. The silence filled the room. He guessed that was meant to be the answer he was looking for. It wasn't.

'I know this is difficult for you...' The words were out of his mouth before he realised how trite and manufactured they sounded. Threadgold gave him a look that said, *Don't give me that shite, sonny.* 'Sir, I'm really sorry—' and he was '—but this is a blatant failure in police procedure. Had Dorothy Malloy gone to trial this would have had the case thrown out of court.' A tiny feeling of recognition pricked the back of Davies's neck. Dorothy Malloy had never been going to court.

Threadgold stood up. 'What the hell is this?' He didn't wait for Davies to reply. 'Has that murdering...?' He paused. 'Is she trying to file some miscarriage of justice case? And what the hell does it have to do with you?'

Davies could hardly tell him he was tipped off by Oonagh O'Neil. 'I came across it when I was investigating the Raphael case.'

Threadgold raised an eyebrow. He was on shaky ground. The two files were in different parts of the building. He'd have needed to ask for it specifically. He wasn't sure if Threadgold knew this, but decided not to take the risk. 'As part of the investigation I'm looking at all murders or suspicious deaths in the city in the eighteen-month surrounding period.'

Threadgold seemed to buy this. It was a plausible enough scenario. Davies also noticed that he failed to hand him back the document.

'This was all a long time ago.'

Davies knew from experience that sentences that started like that usually went on to find some excuse as to why procedures weren't followed. Certainly in the time Davies had been in the force there had been dramatic changes in policing.

'From what I was told, there had been a lot of confusion that day. I hadn't actually been on duty, thank God, but it didn't take long for the events to spread round the station. From what I can gather Andrew's wife was like a madwoman when our guys arrived. Totally crazy. Thought the devil was in the room. She had to be sedated there and then.'

'So there was a doctor present?'

'What?'

'Who could have sedated her?'

'Oh, I see.' Threadgold had finished his wine and stood up to pour some more despite Alec's protests. 'The paramedics had arrived at the same time as our boys.'

'And the boy?'

Threadgold frowned slightly.

'Robbie Malloy.'

'What?'

'Was he dead by the time the emergency services were at the scene?'

'Presumably. Yes.'

He didn't elaborate and Alec couldn't help but think he was being fed a pile of shite.

'We struggled to keep it out of the press, as you know. We were determined that Malloy wouldn't be yesterday's fish and chip paper for anything. So, yes, Alec. Mistakes were made, and we probably didn't follow correct procedures, but it was paperwork, that's all.' He screwed the charge sheet into a ball. 'Just a lousy piece of paper.'

<u>52</u>

Glasgow 2002

She waited until she saw Alec leave. Jim had tipped her off that he was going to pick him up. Tipped off might be a bit strong; he'd dropped it into the conversation. She'd taken to giving Jim the odd call. Usually she had a reason, but this time she'd just called to say hi, and that was when he said he was off out to pick up the boss. He had no reason to think Oonagh would abuse the information. She was sailing close to the wind with this one, and wanted to keep Alec out of it. He'd go bloody mental otherwise.

Oonagh wasn't quite used to being on the back foot. But for now, she wasn't really sure what she actually knew, what she thought she knew, and whether any of it was connected at all. But she decided she'd catch more bees with honey than with vinegar so opted for the softly-softly approach.

She was nervous chapping the door. Took her back to her days as a reporter when she had to 'doorstep' people in a bid to get an interview. Didn't matter if it was a parent whose child had been killed by a dodgy batch of heroin, a drug dealer suspected of selling his wares at the local primary school, or a local councillor caught with his pants down. The pack drill was the same. Batter the door until you get a response, then don't leave until you get an interview.

That was the one thing about being a reporter she hated. It made her feel grubby, even if she got the scoop; especially if she got the scoop. One of the last doorstep interviews she ever did still made her feel sick to her stomach. A young guy, a kid really, had died in a fire at work. There had been a fatal accident inquiry, which had uncovered that the boy had died one week after his sixteenth birthday. He'd worked at the factory for almost three months, which made him slightly younger than the legal age to gain employment. But this wasn't media-land. This was the real world where kids from working-class backgrounds were regularly failed by the education system. Kids who knew they had no real prospects of gainful employment.

This kid had been proud to be offered a job in a factory and a blind eye had been turned to allow him to start just before the end of the official school term. He'd been proud, his mum had been proud, his sister had been proud; his dad had been nowhere to be seen. Less than twelve weeks later he'd been lying on a slab because the same factory that had cut corners and allowed kids to work on the shop floor had also neglected to ensure their waste was properly disposed of. Especially flammable waste. The wee boy had died when a fire had broken out and engulfed the top floor. It turned out he'd been taking his stint as a nightwatchman. The guard dog had also succumbed to the fumes. The press had made more about that dog dying than the only kid on the scheme with a job.

When Oonagh had knocked on the door after the fatal accident inquiry she'd hoped they'd slam the door in her face. Instead they'd allowed her inside. Had assumed she had a right to be there. His mum had spilled her heart out, and as she'd done so the dead boy's wee sister had been on the phone in the kitchen, telling her pals that someone from Riverside Radio was in their hoose. Excited because they'd be on the news that night.

Oonagh had taken no pleasure in getting the exclusive from that story. No professional pride in the fact the grieving family had opened up to her. Instead she'd felt a sense of shame, revulsion, call it what you liked. But she'd trampled all over a poor family who'd had so little to bank on that the two best things that had happened in their lives were that their fifteen-year-old son had got a job as a nightwatchman, and some lassie from Riverside Radio had been in their house and promised they'd be on the news.

Her heels sank into the gravel as she walked up the driveway. She'd left her car a few blocks away. Mainly to avoid being tracked down by Alec, who would surely try to find her if he knew what she was up to, but also it seemed a bit rude, even for her, to drive into someone's driveway without being invited. And if he chased her at the door she imagined leaving on foot would be a more dignified exit than trying to reverse through the narrow stone gateposts onto the street.

He recognised her immediately and if he was surprised, shocked or even pissed off to see her he didn't let on. 'Oonagh O'Neil.' He made a gesture of looking up. 'Just shows that prayers are answered after all.' He did that same thing of clasping her hand in both of his. It caught her off guard for a split second. She hadn't quite been prepared for so warm a welcome.

'Chief Constable Threadgold. What must you think of me coming here unannounced?'

'Now to what do I owe the pleasure?'

Oonagh imagined Chief Constable Gordon Threadgold spoke with forked tongue. She couldn't imagine his addressing much of Strathclyde's finest like this.

'Would you believe me if I said I was in the neighbourhood...?' This verbal dance was getting on her tits, but she had to play along.

'I'd like to, but I'm not that vain to suspect you came here for the love of me.'

'Truth is—' why did she even start sentences like that? '—I'm writing a book.' She saw his eyes flash for a moment. 'Fiction, a crime book, and, well, to be honest I just wanted a chinwag.'

'You want my deepest darkest secrets?' He was still holding her hand, but hadn't invited her in yet. He was in charge and she wasn't to forget that.

'I'll come clean.' She was horrified at how easily she lied. 'I have a character in the book who was a young PC in the seventies and I want to get it right.'

'And I'm the oldest copper you know?'

She pulled her hand away and turned slightly, as if to walk away. 'You know, I'm mortified. I should have called or dropped you a line. Please, don't give it another thought.' She was making to leave, slowly, when he called her back. She guessed he knew she was lying. You didn't get to head Strathclyde's Finest by believing shite like that.

'D'you honestly think I'd turn a beautiful woman away from my door? Come away in.' He held his hand on the door frame, allowing her to walk under his arm. He was a big guy, even by police-height standards. Although Oonagh was sure they were all getting shorter.

'What can I get you?' He'd led her into the kitchen and she sat at the pebble-blue glass island unit, wondering if it was too late to have one installed in her own kitchen. There was a wall of glass that looked onto the garden, which seemed to stretch for miles. It was impressive. She knew chief constables were well paid,

347

but guessed the added extras perhaps came from more nefarious means.

She'd laid out all the evidence the evening before. Examined it with a fresh eye. Tried to put it into some sort of order. Linking it up had been a nightmare. The facts were there. Three women are killed in Glasgow in 1975. A forensic pathologist is about to blow the whistle on a scandal that could rock the NHS. The same forensic pathologist and his son are killed. Almost thirty years later Marjory Channing comes out of the woodwork with evidence backing his claims. She too is killed in a car crash. And Dorothy Malloy is running about on tippy-toe pretending to live in cloud cuckoo land. Oonagh knew there was a link, but just not sure what. Alec was keeping things very close to his chest, and she feared her increasing paranoia was stopping her seeing things clearly.

She opted for a glass of red wine. She guessed, with this gaff, he'd have a fairly decent collection. She guessed correctly. He selected a bottle of Petrus Bordeaux. Oonagh tried not to let her mouth gape open and instinctively put her hand out to stop him. 'Gawd no! Don't open that on my account.'

He smiled, shrugged his shoulders, enjoyed the decadence. 'Mmm, you know your wines. Then you'll know I've had this open for over an hour now to let it breathe. It's my little luxury.'

It was a one hundred and fifty quid bottle of wine and Oonagh had her mum's car parked just three blocks away. She had an uneasy feeling that Threadgold would be pushing *her* for information rather than the other way around. Despite her protests he poured the blood-red liquid into her glass and waited until she'd taken a sip before pouring his own. She felt like Snow White taking a bite of the poisoned apple.

'You didn't get that at Tesco.' She allowed the smoothness to coat her tongue and ease down her throat.

'I have my own supplier. He ships it in from France.' There wasn't a hint of smugness. Just matter of fact. He picked a framed photograph from the wall. 'That's me in my early days. And my best friend.'

It was him and Andrew Malloy. So he *did* know why she was there. This was him letting her know he was onto her. He was setting the agenda. Oonagh grabbed the ball and ran with it. 'Andrew Malloy? The forensic pathologist who was murdered?'

Threadgold nodded as he placed the picture on the island unit between them.

'You know I'm in contact with his wife?' Oonagh didn't just take the ball and run with it... she was crashing through the defence and battering any remaining opposition.

'Widow,' he corrected.

'Must have been really hard to deal with.' She posed it as a fact rather than a question.

He circled the glass beneath his nose, appreciating the bouquet. The slightest nod, then he reeled his bait back in. 'But you didn't come here to talk about that. What is it I can help you with?'

Shit! He was playing with her. Oonagh stood up and looked closely at the picture. 'You haven't lost your good looks.' He gave her a wry smile. 'Andrew Malloy was a handsome man too. I bet the two of you broke your fair share of hearts back in the day.'

'You don't look like you struggle much for attention yourself, Miss O'Neil.'

She really had to rein this back in.

'How well did you know Dorothy?'

He knitted his brows together, just a tad too much. Was he claiming he didn't know who she was talking about or...?

'Clearly not as well as I thought.'

Touché.

'Had I known her better then perhaps I would have been able to...'

He looked genuinely remorseful.

Oonagh decided to not quite come clean but give him a little taste of what she knew. Or what she thought she knew.

'She must have been heartbroken about the affair.'

The faintest sign of a pulse throbbed on his neck. He couldn't mask his confusion. He pulled back in his chair. Genuinely shocked. 'What affair?'

Gordon Threadgold was not a man used to being questioned. He hoisted up one hip and half sat on the worktop. He was tall enough to still have one foot on the floor.

'You and Andrew were best friends, I can see how—'

'Give me a moment please, Miss O'Neil.' He cupped his glass in his hand. Let the wine coat the edges. 'What exactly are you saying?'

He wasn't a man to get on the wrong side of. But in for a penny. 'Was Andrew a bit of a...' she paused, choosing her words carefully '... a ladies' man?' The wine was certainly loosening her tongue.

'Listen, dear. I don't know what you know, or what you think you know. But if I ever hear you blacken Andrew Malloy's name...' He didn't finish his sentence, but she got the drift.

Oonagh had gathered enough information to see that Andrew Malloy had been playing away from home and that had driven Dorothy to kill, not only him, but any woman she'd thought was a threat. It didn't take a huge stretch of the imagination. She decided not to share this nugget of information with Strathclyde's Chief Constable. But she needed to test the water.

'Can I come clean with you? And this is off the record?'

He let out a little laugh. 'It's usually the police saying that to journalists, not the other way around, but yes, carry on.'

'No, seriously, this can't go any further.' Oonagh realised how ridiculous she sounded. Of course she couldn't give a copper of his rank information about a crime and expect him to do nothing. She doubted that his impending retirement would make him any less zealous. But she needed to get him on her side.

'You know I can hardly promise that. But—'

'I've been to see Dorothy Malloy.'

There was the briefest pause as he put the glass to his lips. This wasn't what Oonagh had planned when she rang his doorbell. 'And she says she knows who carried out the Raphael killings.'

It was only a slight choke but enough to spill some of the precious Bordeaux onto his nice clean shirt. Oonagh jumped up, dabbing the stain with a tissue. He grabbed her wrist and shoved her hand away a tad too roughly for her liking. He'd be murder in a nursing home.

53

Glasgow 2002

Oonagh needed time to clear her head. The evidence was stacking up and she didn't know what to make of it. There had to be a link, she just didn't know what it was. Marjory Channing was killed to shut her up, but that didn't make sense if the information was already in the public domain. She knew something else. Or somebody thought she knew something else.

She drove out of the city and headed north. In less than an hour she pulled into a little café along the banks of Loch Lomond, the view of Ben Lomond looming through the clouds. She'd had a jigsaw puzzle of this very scene as a kid. Trying to match the pieces together had seemed impossible; all blue sky and water's edge with masses of green in between.

'Get the corners first,' her dad had said. 'Once they're in place everything else will just slot in.' She'd looked at him with growing suspicion. 'Trust me,' he'd added.

It never really was that easy though. 'Oh, Dad, I wish you were here to help me now!' A soft breeze came in from the loch, stroked her face and caressed her back. She instinctively reached her hand to touch it and for a brief moment imagined she felt her dad's hand. She knew she'd have to tread very careful with this one. Dorothy Malloy was fragile, and any main witnesses were long dead.

Dorothy had been convinced her husband had been cheating on her. A suspicion that had fed her increasing paranoia. That was what had driven her to kill those women. What Oonagh needed now was proof. The fact that Andrew Malloy had been killed before he blew the whistle on the tainted-blood scandal was just a bit too convenient for Oonagh to stomach. Someone or something had been pushing Dorothy over the edge. The question was, did they mean to push her quite that far?

Oonagh made her way back to the car. She'd arranged to meet Davies and thought it best to do so in a public place. She was sailing close to the wind with this one, and wanted to make sure he wouldn't go off on one.

*

'Are you insane?'

She pondered the question for a moment. She couldn't guarantee that she wasn't, but for the purposes of this line of questioning she felt on safe ground.

'What on earth made you even go to his door?'

'For God's sake, Alec, he's not the Pope. I can chap on his doorstep if I like.'

'But to start quizzing him about his best friend, his wife...'

'Alec, he's hiding something. I'll bet my mortgage on it.'

Alec ran his hands through his hair. 'You told me you'd paid your mortgage off.'

Oonagh knew, despite the joke, he was furious with her. 'Yes, oh, stop splitting hairs. What we need to do now is find out what he's hiding.'

'Hold your horses, Juliet Bravo! *We* don't need to do anything. Not everything's a great big bloody conspiracy. Forget it.'

Oonagh struggled not to bite the rim of her glass. 'Forget it? Forget it. Thank you very much!'

They'd reached a stalemate. No one was taking her seriously.

'What about the DNA?'

'What about it?'

'Did it match the suspect?' Oonagh already knew the answer to that one. 'Obviously not or we wouldn't even be having this conversation.'

Davies let out a sigh. 'You're like a dog with a bone, d'you know that?'

She nodded, took it as a compliment, then slid the envelope across the table towards him.

355

'What's this?' He didn't touch it. Just looked.

Oonagh opened it and took out a clear plastic wallet containing a lock of hair. 'Can you test this for a match?'

'What the hell's that? And if you say a lock of hair I really will—'

'You can test for familial DNA, can't you?'

'Spill the beans, Oon. Whose hair is that?'

'I can't tell you.'

Alec sat back, folded his arms and raised one eyebrow.

She scratched her head, knowing he wouldn't believe a word, but she went for it anyway. 'I got it sent to me…' she swallowed hard '… anonymously, from someone who thinks they know who the killer was.'

'You'll need to give me the envelope it was sent in and any letter and—'

'I threw them away.'

'Sorry, am I meant to keep a straight face while you're talking crap?'

He picked up the lock of hair, but didn't remove it from the plastic wrapping. 'Why are you asking about familial DNA?'

'The em, the letter said their dad may have been the killer so they sent a lock of their own hair to see if…'

Alec raised an eyebrow. Let out a sigh. 'Oonagh, that line's already been used.'

'What?'

'Willie Mack's daughter said she thought her dad was the killer.'

Bugger. She hadn't thought this through and was digging herself deeper and deeper into a hole. 'I just got a tip-off, Alec, right?' She was being ridiculous and she knew it. What were the chances of getting an anonymous tip-off about a cold case that no one but the cops knew was under review? And even if that was the case, why would they send it to her?

'Please, Alec, if there's no match then fair dos. If there is a match then I'll tell you everything—' she backtracked slightly '—or as much as I know. Deal?'

She held out her hand and he took it but said nothing. She couldn't read the look in his eye. He'd been a bit funny with her ever since he'd found that sleaze ball in her bed. The one she'd thought she'd killed. He was probably judging her. Thinking she was a wreck, and he'd be right. Alec gave her hand a tiny squeeze and Oonagh swallowed hard as the butterflies fluttered in her chest. She pulled her hand away and was mortified to feel she was blushing.

'Don't look so serious, Oonagh.' He placed his hand back on top of hers.

'So you'll do it?'

Oonagh could see he looked tired. He wasn't yet fifty and kept himself fit, but today he looked every one of his years and a few besides. She noticed the smooth band of skin around his finger where his wedding ring once was. In all the years she'd known Alec he'd never spoken about his wife, or why they'd split up. In fact, despite them being friends, she actually knew very little at all about DI Alec Davies.

'You got any family?'

'Eh?' He clearly didn't get the connection.

'I was just wondering, you know?'

'Why?'

Oonagh shrugged her shoulders. 'We're pals; I thought I should probably find out a wee bit about you.'

Davies let out a laugh. 'OK, I have a brother, who I haven't seen for almost a year, no sisters, nae weans and my mum and dad live out in—'

Oonagh cut in before he finished. 'You've got a mum and dad?'

'Well, hell, yeah! D'you think I was assembled at police training college?'

'No, I mean, yes, I mean... I didn't think they were still alive.'

'I had them cryogenically frozen, they're 102. Jeez, how old d'you think I am?'

'It's just that you don't really talk about them much, so I thought...'

He looked more relaxed and seemed to be glad the conversation had steered away from the case. 'Oonagh, cops don't really talk about their mammies very often. It's not good for the tough-guy image. But if you must

358

know they live in Helensburgh, they drive me bonkers and I love them both to bits.'

She couldn't really imagine Alec being someone's wee boy.

'And before you ask, eleven.'

'Shoe size or former lovers?'

'Both! Now you know everything about me.'

She threaded the silver chain of her locket through her fingers. 'Yip, we'll be getting each other friendship bracelets next.' He let out a laugh. 'Alec, why won't you help me with this?'

'I didn't say that. It's just... unethical.'

'Unethical?'

'You know what I mean. I can't have you steering this investigation.'

'Please. At least see if there's a familial match. If there is then your case is closed.'

'If you have evidence, Oonagh, then tell me. If it's a nutter sending you weird stuff through the post, then no can do.'

Oonagh let this rest with her for a while. 'I can guarantee it's not a nutter. This is the real deal, Alec. The killer is right there. I bet my mortgage on it.'

'You told me you'd paid your mortgage off.'

'Let's not go through that again!'

She was glad to see he was smiling.

<u>54</u>

Glasgow 2002

Threadgold was waiting for him in the office. His gut burned in anticipation of the confrontation. Threadgold didn't look pleased. Davies loosened the tie around his throat; it was choking him.

'Sir.' He tried to sound upbeat, casual even, but the tightness in his throat squeezed his voice and gave him away.

Threadgold's jaw was set in a firm line; his fingers drummed out a rhythm on the desk. 'So, what've you got for me?'

Davies sat down across from him and placed the file between them. 'We have a familial match for the DNA.'

*

Oonagh ran to the front door, wiping her hands on her jeans. Whoever was there was insistent. Holding their finger on the bell; it buzzed constantly. She recognised

Alec's outline through the frosted glass. He barged through almost before she'd had time to open the door, a thunderous look on his face.

'Right, you cut the crap, Oonagh, and tell me what the fuck's going on.'

Oonagh wasn't sure if it was fear, nerves or excitement that pricked her skull, but she knew by his look that the DNA matched. She ushered him through to the kitchen; he perched one hip on the edge of the island unit.

'So, we struck gold, then?' She wasn't sure what else to say.

'Struck gold? It's not *The Sun* fucking bingo.'

Alec tipped his head; a thin band of sweat had formed on his top lip. Oonagh shook her head. 'Can't tell you.'

He walked to the hall. She thought he was leaving, but instead he opened the front door and there was a squad car outside. Two uniforms sat in the front seat. 'Then I've no choice but to arrest you, Oonagh. This isn't a game. This is a murder investigation.'

Her legs weakened and she held the banister for support. 'Oh, shit.' A wave of betrayal against Dorothy Malloy washed over her. 'It's Robbie Malloy's.'

'Fuck's sake.'

'I borrowed... OK, I stole a locket from Dorothy during one of my visits. It had the lock of hair inside.'

He closed the front door and led her through to the kitchen. 'Why? You must have had your suspicions.'

361

She told Alec of the diary and the evidence stacked against Dorothy. His jaw tightened. 'She was on all sorts of prescriptive drugs that made her crazy, Alec. Add to that post-partum psychosis.'

'But she killed three innocent women, Oonagh. For fuck's sake, you should have brought this to me as soon as you had an inkling.'

Oonagh was secretly miffed that Alec didn't ask what post-partum psychosis was. 'A clear case of diminished responsibility.'

He held up his hand. 'You're doing it again!'

'What?'

'Taking over. Can you just calm down, Oonagh? There's a lot to take in here. OK, first things first. Can I see the diary?'

She reached into her handbag, for the copies of the extract. 'I don't have the original on me.' It was on the table in front of them in a padded envelope so it wasn't quite a lie. 'But here I have copies.' She held the brown envelope lightly out of reach, knowing he could take it at any time. 'She gets treated with respect, Alec, right?'

He raised an eyebrow.

'Please. You have to give me your word.'

He nodded and once again the overwhelming sense of betrayal engulfed her. 'What happens now?'

'We'll take it from here, Oonagh.'

'Alec, she's not in a fit state to be...' Oonagh's voice cracked with emotion.

Alec softened and he reached out, holding her by the shoulders. Oonagh dropped her forehead onto his chest and let her cheek rest against the warmth of his body. He immediately jumped back.

'What is it?' he said, tugging at his sweater.

'Nothing.'

'You were sniffing my jumper. Do I smell funny?'

Shit, she hadn't meant to do that. 'I wasn't sniffing your jumper! Behave yourself.' Mortified, Oonagh busied herself around the kitchen and wiped down an already immaculate surface. 'So, you promise to take care of her, Alec.'

He nodded slightly. 'Don't worry, Oonagh, all the correct procedures will be followed this time.'

It didn't fill her with much confidence. 'She won't stand trial, will she? She'll be banged up again.' Oonagh could picture Dorothy being led back through the gates of Cartland. The place where she'd rotted for decades after the deaths of her husband and son. The place that had induced her into a medical coma for weeks and even months on end until half of her adult life had been spent in a drug-hazed stupor. That place.

Alec got up to leave and Oonagh watched him walk down the stairs. Closing the door, she couldn't help but feel she'd signed Dorothy Malloy's death warrant.

55

Glasgow 2002

Davies swirled the dregs of the milky coffee around the bottom of the cup before tipping the by now cooled liquid down his throat. He was within spitting distance of solving one of the most notorious cases in Glasgow, yet the burden weighed heavy on his shoulders. The thought of telling Threadgold that, not only had Dorothy Malloy slaughtered his best friend and his only son, but she was also responsible for slitting the throats of three innocent women in Glasgow. It was a procedural nightmare. The boss was looking to close this case before retirement and bask in the reflective glory that the press coverage would bring, but Davies had that gnawing feeling in his gut that this would be one victory that Threadgold would not want publicised.

He looked at his watch. The meeting was scheduled for 10 a.m. He was cutting it fine, but had no real desire to meet this Malloy woman.

'Y'right, boss?' McVeigh was already standing, doing that irritating thing with his left foot, dancing his heel on the ground. Davies nodded and put the coffee cup to his lip once more, but it was already empty.

The car was still warm from the morning journey, and some weak sunshine pierced through the thin clouds as they made their way to Pollokshields. He hadn't told Threadgold who the familial DNA had belonged to. At that stage he hadn't known himself, but he couldn't shake the feeling that his boss was not exactly kicking his heels at the news of a breakthrough. It might have been his imagination, but, by the look in his eye, he was sure the old boy was fucking furious. Perhaps Oonagh was right, and he knew more than he was letting on.

Davies had a few calls to make so let McVeigh drive – easier that way.

'You're driving too close to the kerb.'

'This is the correct road position.'

'Don't argue, McVeigh, and... Oh, for fu... you almost hit him.'

'No, I never, he's miles away.'

'Catch that light, catch the light, it's still green.'

McVeigh stopped at the amber light, pulled on the handbrake and eased the gear stick into neutral.

'You could easily have made that!' Davies was sure his anger issues would subside if only they'd keep other people away from him.

'Stop it. You're making me nervous.'

'Where the fuck did you pass your test? Some bloody sheep-shagging outpost somewhere with no traffic lights?'

McVeigh ignored the jibe and drove in relative silence before taking the sharp left into the driveway.

'Right, no fuck-ups this time.'

McVeigh nodded.

'Everything by the book.' Davies had no intention of having any slip-ups this time round with Dorothy Malloy.

They were led to a drawing room at the back of the house by a woman with a manic grin. Davies couldn't help but wonder had she been born with that affliction. Sunlight flooded the room and the Manic Grin Lady pulled the blind down very slightly before offering them tea.

'She'll be down in a moment.'

Davies steeled himself against meeting Dorothy Malloy, and unclenched his fist in case he was met with an overwhelming desire to punch her. He'd met people before, playing the 'I'm fucking mental' card. It didn't wash.

The door opened and in walked a small, slightly built chap, holding his hand out. 'Alec, good to see you again,' he said, and nodded to McVeigh.

Davies didn't have a clue who he was; it must have showed in his expression.

'You don't remember me, do you?'

'Just remind me, sorry – I'm hopeless with names.'

'Tom, Tom Findlay, I'm a friend of Oonagh's. We met when…'

Davies's spine tightened – the bloody wee prick of a priest that was always bleating and crying. 'Father Findlay, sorry, you've eh…' He looked completely different without his black suit, dog collar and weary expression.

Tom cut in. 'It's just Tom now.' He turned his shoulder to the door. 'I'll just go and get Dorothy. Please try and remember she's been through a lot.'

'Aye, thanks for the advice. I'll mention that the next time I speak to the families of her victims. You know, the girls whose throats she sliced open.'

Tom wandered out of the room, leaving the last part of Davies's sentence hanging in the air. He came back a few moments later with a protective arm around a woman Davies had to assume was Dorothy Malloy. He wasn't prepared for this. She was tiny, frail, and shuffled as she clung onto Tom's arm. How the hell could this scrap be responsible for so much heartache and bloodshed? Tom ushered Dorothy to a chair and she kept her head down, avoiding Davies or McVeigh.

Davies kept his voice down. 'We'll need to take her down to the station to get the DNA samples. Does she understand?'

'Is she under arrest?'

'At this stage we're detaining her under section fourteen of the Criminal Procedure (Scotland) Act. Then if necessary she'll be placed under arrest.'

'Have I been a bad girl?' The voice was no more than a whisper.

Tom leaned over and chatted to her, his voice too low for Davies to make out much of what was said.

Davies interrupted. 'She'll need to be assessed by a police psychiatrist and then it may be necessary to detain her in a secure unit. But let's just get this over with first.' Tom was getting on his tits. Shaking off his dog collar had given him a new-found confidence and whatever he was doing now was paying a helluva lot more than the church, given his gear.

Tom sat in the back of the car, his arm once more around the shoulders of Dorothy Malloy, adjusting her seat belt, telling her she'd be just fine and assuring her that she'd done nothing wrong. Davies decided to drive, wanted to get there as quickly as possible.

The police surgeon was already waiting for them when they arrived at the station. By all accounts it'd been a quiet day for him. He didn't spend too long with Dorothy Malloy.

'If you arrest her, Alec, I'll need to section her straight away. She's in no fit state to answer questions.' Davies was afraid of that. 'OK. Let's just get the DNA.'

Swabs were taken from inside Dorothy Malloy's cheek. At first she refused to open her mouth. 'Open wide, like you're in the dentist,' Tom prompted and she complied.

'What happens now?' Davies wanted to tell Tom it was none of his fucking business, but realised that getting inside Dorothy Malloy's head would be no mean feat and he needed this little prick on his side.

'This'll get fast-tracked through, then once we have the results we'll take it from there.'

'Meantime?'

'Meanwhile, take her home.' It was unlikely she'd cause any more damage.

Tom thanked Davies and let Dorothy take his arm as they walked out of the room. Even beside Tom she looked small, barely reaching his shoulder. Davies caught up with them.

'I'll get a car to take you home. And, Father Findlay —' Tom didn't correct him '—you stay with her 24–7, right?'

Tom looked as though he was about to argue back, but Davies cut in before he had a chance and pointed into his face. 'I'm telling you, if anything happens to her or if she suddenly goes walkabout you're a dead man.'

56

Glasgow 2002

Davies drummed his fingers on the desk. The DNA results were being delivered by courier and should have been here by now, but there had been a pile-up on the Kingston Bridge and most of the surrounding roads were gridlocked.

'Have you been home yet?'

Davies looked up expecting to see Bill, but it was a different desk sergeant. Clearly Bill had a life. Davies gave a non-committal nod. 'Of course I've been home.' He looked at the clock and realised he hadn't seen the inside of his flat in thirty-six hours. Not that it was much of a home anyway.

The double swing doors opened and he felt the cold wind on his back; the leather-clad courier held his helmet under his arm and Davies walked towards him to meet him halfway.

'That for me?' He gestured to the package in the courier's right hand.

The courier squinted at the name. 'DI Alec Davies?'

'Aye,' he replied as he signed the paperwork before the guy in leather handed over the package.

He didn't open it until he was inside his office. Reading the report, he scanned the pages for the important details then called the lab to make sure there was no room for error.

*

He placed the gun on the desk. The world had changed so much and he didn't want to be a part of it any more. It was customary before such an event to pour the finest whisky; it was tradition, after all. He smoothed his hand along the bottle. The glass almost felt soft as it encased the amber nectar within. The initial drink would be to steady his nerves. It took a lot to shake him, but today he allowed himself the tiniest flutter of nerves.

Everything was prepared. He couldn't allow Jean to find him; she'd never get over that. And had to make it look like an accident; guns were always going off when they were being cleaned. He'd bought theatre tickets that morning for him and Jean. Slipped them under the magnet on the fridge door with a note, telling her to dress up for date night. Made a few phone calls too. Arranged to meet the boys for a round of golf on Saturday. A dental appointment as well; that was three months down the line. It was fucking murder getting an appointment there, but that didn't matter. The important thing was that everything would look as though suicide were the last thing on his mind. An accident. It had to be, why he'd made so many plans, not the actions of a man on the edge of taking his own life.

The cleaner was due round in an hour. It was a shame she'd be the one to find him. She was a nice young girl. Pleasant enough, but it was either that or Jean, and he couldn't risk putting Jean through any of this. It would be bad enough, but at least this way she'd have his pension and he'd get the honour of a full funeral with all the top brass. And his record would be unblemished. It was important to keep up appearances.

He tipped the whisky into his mouth and held it there for just a second before allowing it to slip down his throat. He immediately felt the surge of warmth in his chest, radiating outwards. Gripping the bottle, he wished he could down it all, but that would put everything at risk. Downing a bottle of whisky would raise its own suspicions. Or worse, he might botch the job and end up injured and permanently disfigured. The thought sickened him slightly.

His finger traced the rim of the glass and the doorbell rang. Shit. He could do without visitors right now. But again, if he didn't answer then that might arouse suspicions later.

*

Davies pressed his finger hard against the bell then ran his hand through his hair. He wished he'd rehearsed what he was going to say; a bit late for that now. There was no car in the drive, and he was secretly hoping he'd be out when he heard the telltale noise behind the door of someone padding down the hallway.

'Sir, can I come in?' He'd already stepped over the threshold before Threadgold had a chance to answer. 'It's important,' he added, knowing he'd overstepped the mark.

'Well, you'd better come in, then.' Threadgold walked into the living room as Davies followed. He sat down on the armchair, Davies remained standing. A thin band of sweat lined the older man's lip; he seemed to have aged since the last time they'd met.

'OK, what is it?' Threadgold made no attempt this time at pleasantries. No drinks offered, no tea, not even a friendly word.

'We have a DNA match for the killer, sir.'

Threadgold nodded slowly as he breathed in deeply through his nostrils.

'You already told me that.'

No, we had a familial DNA that matched the crime scene, but we've now managed to match it to a suspect.'

'I see.'

This wasn't quite going to plan. He looked pissed off before Davies had even had the chance to tell him the bad bit!

'And there's something else.'

The older man said nothing; gestured for Davies to sit down. He perched on the edge of the settee. Had no idea how he was going to broach this. 'The day Andrew Malloy was killed, sir.' Threadgold said nothing.

Davies opened the file, slid out the photographs and passed one to Threadgold. He didn't look at it, just held it in his hand. 'Sir, I hate to ask but...' he let it rest in the air for just a moment '... why did you say you weren't at the house that night?'

Threadgold's eye dropped to the photograph in his hand. The crime scene had been cropped and enhanced, but instead of the fatal wounds of Andrew Malloy the grainy picture showed a copper's hat, with the name clearly visible on the inside: *G Threadgold*. And there was no mistaking his reflection in the mirror as he walked up the stairs. Almost thirty years had passed but his solid frame and strong features were the same.

'Who else has seen this?'

Davies dropped his head in his hands. Shit, he'd hoped he'd just open up. 'Me and McVeigh. But that's not the point—'

The older man cut in. 'You're a smart copper, Alec, and I know you're one of the good guys, but what else could I do?'

This was lost on Davies; he didn't have a clue what Threadgold was alluding to. 'What *did* you do, sir?'

'Don't tell me you wouldn't have done the same in my shoes.'

Davies rested back on the settee, let him continue.

'I let them down, Alec, I let them both down and because of that my best friend and his son were killed. I should have stepped in sooner.'

Once he started talking he was surprisingly frank. 'I'd always liked Dorothy, used to tease Andrew that he was punching above his weight with her. She came to me in the beginning, you know. When it was all kicking off. I could see her unravelling right in front of me. I didn't believe her, of course.'

'Believe what, sir?'

'She told me Andrew had killed that girl. But that was just absurd. She was paranoid, delusional. As the weeks went on her ranting and accusations got worse. But I had no idea she'd snap and kill him, and the boy too.'

For the first time Davies noticed a glimpse of emotion in Threadgold's eyes. A tear caught the back of his throat and he swallowed hard. This wasn't quite stacking up the way Davies had expected. He kept quiet for the moment.

'I did nothing to save Andrew, or the boy for that matter, but I was sure as hell going to make sure he'd be remembered for the good he'd done and not as a crazed killer.'

'But you said yourself that was absurd.'

'And it was, but if the press had got a hold of that. And who knows who else she spoke to, or what she'd come out with?'

Threadgold sank his head until his chin touched his chest. 'Fancy a drink?' This time he poured two whiskies from the decanter on the sideboard. Davies left his where it was. Threadgold downed his in one.

'We got smashed one night. Me and Andrew. He started saying all sorts of stuff about how Janet Channing wasn't supposed to die.' He poured himself another drink. A larger one this time. 'He was with her the night she was killed, you know.'

Davies stood up, took a few deep breaths before he trusted himself to speak. 'Why the hell didn't you tell me? And why was that never in the original case notes? Andrew Malloy was at best a key witness, if not a prime suspect.'

'Och, calm down, son.'

Davies paced the floor. Didn't have a clue how to play this.

'It wasn't him. He was with me at the time of her death. He'd seen her on the bus then came to meet me.' This seemed to be Threadgold's meagre attempt at excusing the whole thing.

Davies knew estimating an exact time of death was never an exact science. In 1975 it was practically a guessing game. 'But he carried out her post-mortem.' He

376

was shouting, but couldn't care less. The whole case was rotten.

'Aye well, that was a mistake.' Threadgold jabbed his index finger in the air to make his point, 'But I never knew that at the time. He never told me he was with her till weeks, maybe a month later.'

'You didn't believe him, did you?'

Threadgold looked back at the picture, the memory of that day washed across his face. 'I don't know what I believed.'

'You suspected he might have killed those girls, didn't you?' Davies guessed Threadgold had done everything he could to keep his best friend's name out of the picture.

'I'll never forget that phone call. *I've killed him,* was all she said. I wake up some nights hearing that. In the wee small hours.'

'You knew the shit was about to hit the fan, didn't you?'

Threadgold didn't answer.

'That's why you reopened the case and trumped up this shite about Willie Mack. Tried to bury this forever.'

The enormity of it all appeared lost on Threadgold, who suddenly looked from a bygone era. 'I couldn't do it alone obviously, but a few of us rallied round, pulled strings, made sure the case would never get to court. It was surprisingly easy, if truth be told. I felt sorry for

Dorothy. Truly I did, but she was so far gone by this time that there was nothing we could do for her.'

'It wasn't him.' Davies kept his voice low.

Threadgold looked up. 'What d'you mean?'

'The DNA evidence – it wasn't Andrew Malloy who killed those girls.'

Threadgold slumped back in his chair and a single tear threatened to spill out from his eye. 'Thank you, son...'

It was obvious that he'd had his doubts all along. For the first time in his career Davies almost pitied Threadgold. He'd been played by the system in the same way the rest of them were. Offered a big promotion for keeping everything under wraps and turning a blind eye when the investigation into The Raphael killings hadn't always followed procedure. Hadn't taken long to rise up the ranks. His success had been almost meteoric.

There were too many loose ends and Davies wasn't entirely sure he was getting the whole truth. 'You weren't altogether surprised when I told you Willie Mack's remains had been mutilated.' It wasn't a question but he expected an answer.

Threadgold shook his head, 'That fucking idiot McClemand.' He didn't even try to pretend to be in the dark with this one.

'He wasn't an idiot sir.' Davies thought back to George's widow, 'he was a decent, hardworking man who'd done his best for his family.'

'Aye, well he couldn't hack it.'

'Why the hell did he try to preserve his heart?'

'Fuck knows and who cares.'

Davies stood up, 'Well, I fucking care, right!'

'Listen, I tried to look out for that prick. Felt sorry for him. Bailed him out several times when he was caught tampering with bodies. He was fucking mental, had lost the plot and I guarantee if you dig up 10 graves in Glasgow you'll find George McClemand's calling card on at least half of them.' He thought for a moment, 'Maybe seeing Mack's body brought back memories about Andrew, and he just went a bit too far.'

Davies guessed McClemand's breakdown was down to more than being a bit on the flaky side. That man had been shit scared; not just grieving for Andrew Malloy.

'Who was behind all this?' He'd been mister nice guy here for long enough. The corruption was leaving a bitter taste in his mouth and he needed answers. As good as Threadgold was, he couldn't do all this as a rank and file copper.

'You need to understand how big things like this are. It's never just one person.'

It was sinking home fast that, despite the fact Davies had done well as a cop, he'd never reach the dizzy heights that Threadgold had. He felt like a right tit for believing in hard work and determination. What it actually took was street smart, animal cunning and a fucking great big wad of cash to bribe any poor bastard that stood in your way.

The information started to percolate through his brain. He thought of Oonagh claiming that Marjory Channing was killed because she'd uncovered some information. 'What d'you know about Marjory Channing?' He didn't bother calling him sir, couldn't be arsed any more.

Threadgold let out a sigh. 'Leave it, OK?'

'No, sir. I won't fucking leave it, and if you ask me again I'll arrest you for withholding evidence.'

Threadgold raised his eyebrow and let out a laugh. 'Took you long enough to get your balls out.' He held up a glass, pointing it in Davies's direction. He declined.

'I really don't know too much about Marjory Channing. But occasionally one is asked for a favour. I was told she knew who killed her sister and—'

'So you had her killed and made it look like she was a hopeless drunk?'

Threadgold slammed the glass down on the sideboard. 'I had no one killed. Let's get that straight. But making someone look like a drunk driver isn't the hardest trick in the book. For God's sake, if they can do it with Princess Diana, d'you not think we can pull a few strings with Marjory fucking Channing? I killed no one, just made sure that her death wasn't investigated as requested.'

'You must have been shittin' yourself that it would all come out about Malloy.' He was yelling now. 'A key witness in one of the biggest murder investigations this city has ever known, not only withheld vital information, but carried out the fucking autopsy on one of the victims. All under the watchful eye of Strathclyde's finest.'

'It was more the Pandora's box it would unleash.' Threadgold looked tired; the fight had gone from his eyes. 'You going to put me out of my misery, then?'

'Believe me, if I had a gun I would.' Davies's phone rang; it was McVeigh. 'You got an address for us yet?'

'Aye, he's living just outside Edinburgh.'

'Right, I'll meet you at the station in ten.'

He stood up to leave, didn't shake the old man's hand. 'I'll need a full statement at some stage.' Threadgold nodded and walked him to the door.

'Don't do anything...' he chose his words carefully '... irrational, eh?'

'You're a good cop, Davies. You should have gone further than you did.'

He walked down the driveway without looking back. Settling into his car, he pulled the seat belt across his chest and jumped slightly as a passing car backfired. It was funny how that noise sounded exactly like gunfire.

57

Glasgow 2002

Oonagh had no desire to meet Graham Anderson again, but felt she had no choice. His compliance seemed guaranteed after she assured him Dorothy's identity would be kept under wraps – as long as he played ball.

The M8 seemed to stretch on forever, taking an hour to get from Glasgow to Edinburgh. She slipped the car back up to fifth gear just beyond junction five; the rush-hour traffic was behind her now, and for that she was grateful.

She did her best to see the bigger picture; understand the greater good, the needs of the many over the needs of the few. She couldn't.

Slipping down a gear, she left the motorway onto the A road to the quiet Lothian suburb. Leading her to the leafy avenue where residents lived next door to a man who felt no remorse at experimenting on kids as young as five. It was all getting too much for her to stomach.

It took him longer than the last time to open the door. He'd been reluctant for her to visit his home again, but Oonagh knew he'd be even less likely to open up in a public place.

She sat down without being asked and placed the recorder on the table between them. He walked slowly, leaning on a stick Oonagh had never see him use before. She wasn't sure if he was using it as a prop for sympathy. But after what he'd told her he'd need to be in an iron lung to illicit any sympathy from her. He stumbled slightly as he sat down on the armchair opposite. Oonagh instinctively lurched forward to help him, but he shrugged her off and tightened his cardigan across his chest.

'I've just put the heating on. Takes a few minutes to kick in.'

Oonagh fanned her face. The room was like an oven and the wood-burning stove glowed red-hot embers. There was a small radiator in the room and she hoped to God it was as useless as it looked. Any more heat and she'd collapse.

'None of it was planned, you know.' He crossed his legs slowly, revealing an emaciated ankle. His blue eyes clouded over. She struggled to feel any sympathy for him, but instinctively thought he was telling the truth.

'People have died, Graham, people are still dying and there's no justice for them. You need to come forward.'

He gave a phlegmy cough that made Oonagh feel sick, and cleared his throat. 'We were all bright young things, straight out of med school, ready to show the world what we were made of. Desperate to make a name for ourselves. Haematology wasn't the sexiest of departments.' He allowed himself a very slight laugh. 'Andrew, as you know, went into forensics. He was bloody good too, and—'

Oonagh feared he was just going to give a recap of what he'd already told her. She needed to steer him back.

'So you introduced Dorothy and Andrew?' She already knew the answer. She was about to ask if they seemed happy, but decided against such a stupid question. No one cut their husband's throat because they were a bit pissed off with him leaving the toilet seat up. No one, male or female, could commit such an act on their spouse without some sort of psychosis being present.

'It's difficult to make any sense of it all now.'

'Well, you need to try, Graham. That's just not good enough.'

'It's hard to know what order things happened in. But before we knew it we were in deep. All of us. But it didn't seem to matter. The end goal was the prize. Nothing or no one mattered along the way. Andrew just didn't get that. He didn't understand.'

'He was going to blow the whistle on the contaminated blood, wasn't he? Marjory Channing told me as much.'

'Andrew was a fucking idiot.'

'A moment ago, you said he was a good surgeon!'

'D'you think all it takes is being a bit nifty with the scalpel? It takes breeding and strength of character to become a surgeon. Jesus Christ, he was a fucking butcher's boy. He had no idea what was at stake.'

Oonagh felt chilled by his change in manner. The coldness in his eyes.

'OK, sometimes we bent the rules, but, as I told you before, we were in this for the long game.'

'If you were all so brilliant why didn't you guess the risks of the blood products? You must have known there was a huge risk of cross-contamination. You were using skid-row donors, for God's sake!'

'Aye, hindsight's a wonderful thing. There was so little known about the treatment of haemophilia. At the time we knew the clotting agent was working. That was good enough for us. Not to mention to advance into the treatment of hep C. I'm sorry, if there were casualties as we perfected the treatment then so be it.'

'Did it really all come down to money?' Oonagh felt sick and it wasn't down to the heat.

'Who d'you think pays for all this research?' He pointed to her handbag. The corner of her cigarette packet was visible through the open zip. 'When you're diagnosed with lung cancer, or worse, you'll be the first one crying for treatment. D'you think that comes ready made from the lab? Years, decades, lifetimes of research go into perfecting each and every treatment. Despite what you may think, it's painfully slow to have a drug approved for use. The drug companies are king when it comes to this. They pay for everything, so they call the shots. That's why the States have Blood Shield Statutes which effectively gives outright immunity to the pharmaceutical industry.'

'How?'

'It's a bit long winded, but basically all treatment with blood products is regarded as a service and not a product, therefore hospitals, blood banks and the likes are safe from sales based liability.'

'So they can peddle a pile of poison and nothing can be done?' Oonagh could barely believe what she was hearing.

'Well they can't be sued in the strictest sense of the word. But what d'you think would happen if the pharmaceutical giants pulled their funding? There would be no drugs, no treatments. Nothing. Just tea and sympathy from the NHS and see where that gets you when you're screaming in pain with bone cancer.'

It sounded like a well-rehearsed speech. Oonagh stood up; once again Graham Anderson was trying to excuse the inexcusable. 'That doesn't give them carte blanche to trample over human beings, destroy lives and use innocent patients as guinea pigs.'

'Well, guess what? It does!'

'It's all profit margins, then, eh? The pharmaceutical giants dangle a big carrot in front of the NHS and you all roll over?'

He sat back, gave a smile. His teeth were small and perfectly even. His lips slightly slack. 'That's about the size of it. How many senior MPs d'you think have links to these drugs companies?' He didn't wait for her to answer. 'MP's that can actually shape NHS policy, and everyone turns a blind eye.' Graham Anderson didn't need to spell out the corruption to Oonagh, but he did. 'I won't even mention paedophile rings in Westminster, ones that go right to the top. But, you know, everyone's so busy covering their own tracks they've no time to blow the whistle on anyone else. And at the end of the day, why rock the status quo? For the most part it works.'

'You're a monster. You actually make me sick.'

'Listen, I'm on your side here. I'm giving you the information you want. But I won't be judged. Not by you or anyone else.'

It slowly dawned on Oonagh that Graham Anderson did indeed have a God complex. It wasn't his sister who was the ill one; this man was insane.

'You used the blood drained from corpses in Russian morgues. What's that to do with forging ahead with new

387

treatments? That's about profit. Blood money. Simple as that.'

Graham Anderson licked his lips slightly then wiped his mouth with the back of his hand. His voice was little more than a whisper. 'I know how that must sound. But you have to believe me when I say we didn't know where the blood was sourced from. OK, we knew there was a prison programme and the likes, but that was all within the legal framework. We had no idea how contaminated it was.'

He was right to a point. They hadn't. Not right away. But it had soon become apparent, yet continued for decades.

Oonagh fished around in her briefcase; she held the notes in front of her face. 'A certain children's unit in Glasgow using infected products two years after they knew it was infected. Two years.'

Graham held his hands up. 'OK, I'll admit that was wrong. There'd been a suggestion that one of the medical reps was either shagging or bribing the sister who signed off the order for the products and they just kept using it.'

'Now I really am going to be sick.' She thought for a moment. 'So who killed Andrew, then?'

Graham looked at her, clearly confused. 'Dorothy. I thought you knew that.'

'Oh, come on. That's a bit convenient. And where does Dorothy fit into all of this?'

He didn't answer, instead stared out of the window. She was totally pissed off with this.

'Right, you won't talk? I'm going to the police.'

He let out a snort. 'For almost thirty years thousands of people have been campaigning for a public inquiry. For almost thirty years victims have begged for justice. For almost thirty years people have died from medical negligence and not one person has lifted a finger to help. And you. You? You think you can change that with one phone call. Grow up! Get your ego in check, you stupid cow, and realise this is bigger than anything you can imagine.'

She wasn't prepared for that and didn't like being on the back foot. Then it slowly dawned on her.

'This has nothing to do with keeping your kids away from press intrusion, has it?'

For the first time he looked genuinely scared.

'You're terrified. Those kids are the insurance policy against you blabbing.'

He shot her a look.

'I'm right, aren't I? Listen to me, Graham, you tell me what I came here for or I guarantee I'll find your family, and I can find them, you're darn tootin the guys that found Marjory Channing'll find them too. The press'll be the least of your worries.'

The by now familiar sense of panic was rising in her chest, but she swallowed it down. The buzz from her phone snapped her back on track. A text from Davies.

She didn't read it. She'd get it later. Whatever he wanted, it could wait. She sat back and crossed her legs.

'I've got all the time in the world, Graham. And if you don't play ball I guarantee when you croak it, I'll be screaming from the rooftops about how much information you gave me – and what you don't tell me, I'll make up. We'll see how safe your family is then.' She was aware there were tears in her eyes, but she needed to keep this in check.

'You can't do that.'

'Well, you'll hardly be in a position to stop me.'

'Bitch.'

'Is that how you refer to strong women on the east coast? You need to visit Glasgow more often.' The sadness for Dorothy Malloy and Eva Muirhead now formed a solid ball of anger in the pit of her stomach. Moments passed. The clock on the wall the only thing to break the silence. Then he spoke.

'Andrew was never meant to die.'

Oonagh gave the slightest nod, telling him to continue.

'Things just got out of hand. He'd been keeping his own set of notes from each autopsy. When he could see that young kids were presenting with chronic liver failure he was convinced they were contracting it from the blood products. He was going to blow this thing wide open.'

His voice was low and calm but Oonagh could see a thin band of sweat form on his top lip. Globules of saliva gathered in the corners of his mouth.

'But as you already said, a lot of this was in the public domain—'

He cut in before she could finish. 'Not at that stage. We were still at the very early days. We had everything to go for with this.'

'What was your cut?' Oonagh guessed Graham Anderson wasn't just complying with this for the greater good of mankind.

'My what?'

'You must have got something out of this.'

'We *needed* the contaminated victims.'

'Sorry?'

'I need you to know it wasn't about the money. We needed to know the pathology of the diseases. We were getting patients under near perfect conditions.' He became more animated, almost looked excited. 'D'you realise how rare that is in medical research?'

She didn't bother answering him. She'd heard about as much as she could take. But was still no closer to the truth about who killed Andrew Malloy, and this old man in front of her knew the answer. He looked tired, grew increasingly frail, but she wasn't leaving until she had what she was looking for. She let him continue.

'Then, when a completely new viral strain started to appear, well, let's just say that's not something which happens in medical science every day. This was a chance to be part of history. Be up there with Lister, Louis Pasteur, Alexander Fleming.'

Oonagh knew he was talking about AIDS, HIV. She'd been a teenager in the eighties. Grown up with the threat of AIDs. More terrifying than any unwanted pregnancy. She was scared to ask. But knew she had to. 'Was there ever an occasion…? Did you ever…?'

He nodded; she didn't even have to finish. 'Did we ever knowingly infect someone with HIV? Yes. Yes, we did. I'm not proud. But I'm not ashamed either.'

Both Marjory and Eva had already told Oonagh that it was primarily children, boys as young as five, who were infected with the AIDs virus. The best way to understand the pathology of a disease was to examine it for as long a time as possible. The best way to do that was to experiment on children. Oonagh felt a sense of shame when she recalled her first conversation with Marjory. She'd thought she was a nutter. A fantasist. Bigging up her part and getting lost along the way. But everything she'd said was true. And lots more besides.

'Miss O'Neil,' Graham cut in on her thoughts, 'we now live in a world where people live *with* HIV, rather than die from it. It's no longer the death sentence it once was. Can you honestly tell me you're not pleased about that?'

'But your kids are safe.'

'I beg your—'

'Your kids. You've spent all this time in exile terrified that they'll come to harm. Let them die for the greater good. If you knew that five thousand people would live if they had to die would that be OK?'

'This is not personal.'

'It's personal to the mother whose seven-year-old son died from AIDs. It's fucking personal to her husband, who topped himself because the doctors accused him of having a homosexual affair and infecting his son in the womb. It's fucking personal when it haunts her dreams each night and each day is a living nightmare for her!'

She stared into his eyes and he didn't falter for a moment. His rheumy gaze was fixed on her.

'As I say, Andrew was never meant to die.'

Suddenly the murder of Andrew Malloy was more palatable than talking about the deliberate genocide of the innocents.

'We knew Andrew was keeping his own research notes, which could put half of us in prison. It's one thing having a nurse or a legal secretary squawking away, but when it comes from a top surgeon who works closely with the Home Office, then...' he shook his head '... that's just not on. I need you to know I wanted to protect Dorothy from all this. I was trying to make sure she was OK.'

'Have you any idea what happened to her in Cartland? More fucking medical experiments by posh boys with their medical degrees playing God again. Well done.'

'I'd had no idea she was suffering from post-partum psychosis. Well, what I mean is I had no idea how damaging that could be. We drip-fed her information. Made calls suggesting that Andrew was having an affair.'

'What for? How could that stop him being a whistle-blower?'

'At first it was as a distraction. A warning to him. Then we needed to discredit him.'

Oonagh's phone buzzed once more. Alec again. Once more she ignored it. This wasn't the time to break for a chat. She wasn't liking what she was hearing. Judging by Dorothy Malloy's diary, it hadn't taken much to tip her over the edge.

'Dorothy became more and more unstable. Her paranoia being fed by the belief that Andrew was cheating on her.'

'Was he?'

Anderson shrugged. 'I doubt it.'

Oonagh wasn't getting this. The leap from suspicious wife to vicious killer.

'Even with the erratic behaviour, did she have enough reason to kill Andrew?'

'As I said, things just got out of hand. That stupid bastard just wouldn't listen. He was ruining it for the

394

rest of us. He wouldn't get off his fucking moral high horse.'

Oonagh could picture the scene. The young Andrew Malloy not being grateful enough to be part of the gang.

'Did he really have to die?'

Anderson sank his head into his hands. 'I wanted out by this time. After the first girl was killed.'

Oonagh's heart raced in her chest. Her throat grew dry. She needed to tread carefully with this one. 'Janet Channing?'

He nodded. 'She was feeding Andrew information from her sister in the States. Giving him the backup, the proof if you like, that the blood came from "skid-row donors", as you put it. And that it was most likely so contaminated as to be deadly.'

'Who signed off that one?'

'I have no idea.'

'Cut the bullshit.'

'I've got no reason to lie to you now, have I?' He faltered for a few seconds. 'The truth is I just don't know. All I know is that she was passing Andrew the information from her sister, then she was killed.'

'And the others. Why were they killed? What did they have to do with it?'

'Would you like some tea?'

'No, I wouldn't like some tea. I would like some answers please.'

Despite this he slowly rose to his feet and padded out of the room. Oonagh wasn't getting any of this on tape. She grabbed a notebook from her bag and scribbled down as many notes as she could. Cursing the fact she'd missed so many shorthand classes and preferred to spend her days in the pub. She opened the text messages from Alec. There were three in total. The first:

Where are you Oons?

The second slightly more urgent:

Oonagh are you safe. Call me as soon as you get this.

She was just about to open the third when Anderson came back in with a steaming mug cupped in his hands and she slipped the phone back into her bag.

She was anxious to get the story back on track. 'Are you saying, then, Janet Channing was deliberately targeted to shut her and her sister up?'

'Happens more often than you'd think.'

Oonagh tried not to think. Not of that anyway. 'But you've no idea who did it?'

He did that shrug thing, which was now starting to annoy her.

'So it wasn't Dorothy, then?'

He looked genuinely shocked at this. 'Dear God! Is that what you think? That Dorothy was the killer?'

A slight pang of embarrassment came from nowhere and pierced her chest. 'I thought perhaps...' Then she remembered the diaries once more and galvanised herself. 'I had good reason to think that – after all, Dorothy's diaries suggested she had prior knowledge as to when the killings would take place. You must have read it yourself. You gave it to me.'

'There were a lot of people involved. It was very complicated.'

'Too right it was complicated. D'you want to just stop skirting round this and tell me what happened?'

'As I say, we fed her paranoia that Andrew was involved. It was all to discredit him. Shut him up. If he decided to blow the whistle then we'd have Dorothy's accusations and it wouldn't take much to drum up some evidence.'

Oonagh wasn't prepared for what came next. Perhaps it would have been better to believe that Dorothy Malloy, suffering from post-partum psychosis and fearing her husband was cheating on her, had killed three innocent women in Glasgow.

'It wasn't too hard to botch the investigation into Janet Channing's murder. It happens all the time.'

'What about the others?'

'You need to believe me that I had nothing to do with any of this. I wasn't party to this.'

Oonagh reassured him; she was desperate for him to get on.

'It's funny how once a boundary is crossed it's easier to do it again.'

She wasn't sure where this was going.

'I'm afraid the other two were collateral damage.'

'What d'you mean?'

'You've heard that the best way to cover a crime is to commit another crime?'

Oonagh had never heard of that logic but sort of pretended she had.

'We had to make Janet Channing's murder seem like a random act.'

'Please don't tell me another two innocent women were killed to make it seem like a serial killer was on the loose.'

'The police are fucking morons, you know.'

The enormity of what he was saying slowly sank in. The countless people whose lives were ruined, families who'd lost loved ones, years of heartache and for what? The profit of a multinational conglomerate? The ego of a few maniac doctors who thought they'd play God?

'So, this was all one big giant cover-up? You make me sick.'

He let out a laugh. 'Oh, the irony, Miss O'Neil, when I'd set out to stop sickness.'

'I'm sorry, I don't get the joke. It's just not funny.'

Graham Anderson went on to explain that Dorothy was led to believe that Andrew was the killer. In her psychotic state she was open to even the most fantastic of suggestions. Apparently she'd followed Andrew and saw him meet Janet Channing and believed they were having an affair. Then, when Janet was killed, the phone calls had made Dorothy believe that Andrew was in fact the killer.

'It wasn't too hard to frame Andrew. That way we had him back where we wanted him and could force him to keep his mouth shut.' For a split second Oonagh saw what she thought was a glimpse of remorse. 'I had no idea Dorothy would kill him.'

'And Robbie?'

Once again his rheumy eyes threatened tears. 'That was a mistake.'

'A mistake? My home perm when I was sixteen was a mistake. This was more than a fucking mistake.'

He could no longer look her in the eye. 'So who killed him?'

'He was a great kid. Masses of curls, always laughing.' He drew the back of his hand across his nose. 'Something went wrong. Our guys got there and thought...'

She palmed the mobile phone in her pocket. Set it to record. She hoped it was strong enough to pick up at least some of this. When she was confident it was recording she slipped it out of her pocket onto her lap.

'You telling me they drowned a five year old boy without a thought? But why?'

'Sometimes things get lost in the chain of command.'

Oonagh struggled not to thump this piece of shit. 'Apparently by the time Threadgold got there the boy was already dead. Nothing could be done.'

Oonagh had assumed Dorothy had been carted off to Cartland to keep the lid on the fact she thought her husband was a serial killer. But clearly this put it into a whole new ball-park. One whiff from her that her son was torn from her arms and drowned would have been impossible to cover up. 'Give me a name.'

'There are no names. There are forces at work here bigger than you can imagine—'

Oonagh thought for a moment, 'It's the Masons, isn't it?'

'Ha ha, is that what you think?' Anderson didn't even try to keep the mocking tone from his voice, 'D'you think this would be left to a bunch of tossers meeting in a crumby scout hall every week with their trousers at half mast? That lot are the best smoke screen we have. Useless pricks.'

'Well, whoever it was enjoyed their work.' Oonagh cut him off.

He shot her a look. He clearly didn't understand.

'The police have looked again at the evidence.' She wasn't sure how much to tell him, but reckoned she had nothing to lose. 'Whoever you're protecting? They held Robbie in the bath face up so your sister could watch as her son was drowned before her eyes.'

'Bastards.'

'Save us the tears, Graham.'

Graham Anderson began to gag as he retched. His face distorted as his chin dissolved into his chest. His right hand began to shake uncontrollably as he slumped to one side. His tongue hung from his mouth as the spittle gathered and dripped down his chin. Oonagh lunged forward to catch him before he fell from the chair. One look at his face and she knew. It was the very same when her dad had taken a stroke. That grotesque mask. She pushed his shoulders, leaning him back on his armchair. 'Graham, I'm going to get you help.'

Her hands trembled as she fished her mobile from her bag. She was about to dial 999 when it rang. Alec Davies. 'Oh, Gawd, Alec, I need a blue-light ambulance. Fast.' She gave him the details knowing he'd get one quicker than she could.

'Oonagh, I need you to get out of that house.'

'Alec, he needs help. Can you please just hurry up?'

'Oonagh,' he was shouting now, 'for once in your life listen to me. The familial DNA. It's Graham Anderson. He's the killer. Get out of that house.'

'Oh, shit. Just get the fucking ambulance.'

She cut him off, knowing that every second they talked meant a second wasted getting the paramedics. Oonagh had no idea if she genuinely wanted to save Graham Anderson, or if she needed him alive to get the truth out about this story. She rested her hand on his forehead. 'You'll be fine,' she said, but struggled to find any real sympathy for him. She dabbed his slack mouth with a tissue and felt sick.

He tried to speak, but the words wouldn't form in his mouth. Oonagh leaned forward to hear but couldn't make anything of the misshapen vowels. He was limp down one side. He reached his other hand and grabbed at her sweater. His grip was surprisingly strong. The smell was odd. It had a shape. It was sharp in her nostrils and caught the back of her throat. She tried to prise his hand away from her chest but he'd clawed his way up towards her throat and wouldn't let go. She took both hands and tried to prise open his fingers. He pulled her closer. Roughly enough for her to lose her footing and stumble on top of him.

'Graham, please let go.' His face was unshaven and rough against her cheek. His breath held stale coffee and mucus. She began to gag as she tried once more to loosen his grip. Then that smell. The sharp one again. It cut through the stench of his breath. Gas. No mistake. A slight flurry of panic gripped her chest. She pulled herself back but he refused to let go.

'Graham, I can smell gas. I need to get you out of here.' She glanced in the mirror at the back of his chair and froze. His oxygen cylinders, six in all, were lined up in the adjoining room. Her heart skipped a beat. 'Graham, please listen to me. Have you left the gas on? We need to get you out of here.' The heat from the stove was on her back. Fuck. The stove. She twisted her head;

there were glowing embers of coal. Enough to ignite a gas leak, that was for sure.

This time she screamed at him, but he just seemed to grimace. He tightened his grip and gave her a lopsided grin then snorted a laugh. The mucus ran down one nostril. Once more he tried to form a word. 'Fffuu... ffuu...' She didn't think she'd be able to carry him out. She shoved her arms around his back and tried to hoist him off the chair, but he was a dead weight. And still he tried to speak, not letting go of her sweater. 'Fffuu... ffuu...'

'Graham, please, you need to help me here.' The smell was growing stronger and Oonagh had no idea how long they had before the cylinders would ignite. She pulled at him once more and finally he managed to utter something which she understood.

'Fffuuck ooo, bitch.' He gripped tighter then wrapped his right leg around her knees, pinning her against him once more. 'Fffuucken bi-itch.'

It suddenly hit her what was going on. He was refusing to let go. He was going and he was taking her with him. Oonagh pulled one knee up, but she was too close to knee him in the balls, so she forced her knee between his legs and knelt on him as hard as she could, at the same time she dipped her head down and wriggled out of her sweater, leaving her free to slam the heel of her hand up against his chin. His head whipped back and instinctively his leg loosed around her. She jumped

403

up and faltered for just a second. Clenching her fist, she punched him full on the face.

'That's for Dorothy, you bastard.' Another swipe, harder this time. 'And that's for killing my bloody cat.' Then she grabbed her bag and ran for the front door. She could hear sirens in the distance. She turned the key in the mortice lock then glanced back. Instead of leaving she ran back inside towards the kitchen. Every gas tap on the cooker was on. The gas sucked the oxygen from the room. She struggled to breathe and buried her face in the crook of her elbow. Quickly she turned the taps off, picked up a stool and smashed it through the window, sending shards of glass into the garden. She ran from room to room, smashing the windows she couldn't open. She felt her lungs grow tight as she struggled for oxygen. Her legs trembled as she stumbled her way once more to the front door and ran down the driveway onto the street.

58

Glasgow 2002

'You ready, Dorothy?'

Dorothy nodded and held onto Tom's arm as he helped her into the back of the car. Oonagh got behind the wheel and checked them both in the rear-view mirror as she fastened her seat belt.

'He's dead, isn't he?'

Both Tom and Oonagh looked at Dorothy. She was more lucid than either of them had seen her.

'Robbie. He's dead.' This time she posed it as a statement rather than a question.

Oonagh paused before starting the engine. She shot Tom a look, didn't have a clue how to respond. Tom picked up Dorothy's hand. 'Yes, Dorothy, I'm so sorry.'

She looked at Oonagh. 'Some nights I thought I'd dreamt the whole thing. Others I thought I'd imagined having a son at all.' Oonagh reached round; this time Dorothy didn't flinch away but took her hand. 'D'you have children?'

Oonagh shook her head. Her throat had tightened; she didn't trust herself to speak.

'Can I try your watch on?'

This time Oonagh smiled and slipped the silver bracelet from her wrist. 'Of course you can.' She handed it to Dorothy. It slid over her tiny hand and hung loose on her emaciated wrist.

'You can keep it, if you like.'

'May I?' Dorothy smiled, thoughts of her dead son apparently blotted out once more.

Tom gave Oonagh the nod and she started the engine.

She drove through the Clyde Tunnel towards the south side. Graham Anderson had been transferred to Glasgow's Southern General Hospital - at Alec Davies' insistence Oonagh guessed. She glanced every so often in the rear-view mirror at Dorothy in the back seat, who was admiring her new watch.

Graham Anderson had thrown his wee sister to the wolves in order to save his own skin. Oonagh was no longer a believer but prayed there was a special place in hell for such people.

The car park sprawled the length of the hospital grounds and she parked up and let Tom and Dorothy go on ahead whilst she popped the change in the meter. She watched as Tom guided Dorothy by the elbow. To the outside world she could be his mum, an aunt, an elderly neighbour and he the good Samaritan escorting during visiting hours. Nothing belied the tortured soul within.

Neither Oonagh nor Tom could fathom if Dorothy knew about her brother's involvement. She'd never let on.

Despite the sunshine, there was a biting wind coming from the Clyde. Oonagh broke into a run and hurried to catch up with Tom and Dorothy, who were waiting in the warmth behind the sliding doors. As soon as she got in the smell hit her. Hospitals. They smelt the same the world over.

'I don't get it.' Tom sniffed the air. Oonagh told him it was because he'd spent so long in the priesthood and chapel houses. Cabbage-smelling hospitals were a welcome relief.

People thronged towards them; official visiting hour had apparently just finished.

Tom held Dorothy's hand as they got into the lift. Her collarbones protruded and she kept her eyes down, hardly meeting their glance. Her eyes gave nothing away. As they got into the lift, Oonagh saw a face she recognised. She was about to nod a brief hello, but instead dipped her head and avoided eye contact. The last thing she could be bothered with right now was small talk.

'D'you two want some time alone together?' Oonagh directed the question at Dorothy as she watched light on the wall flash the numbers for each floor. The lift moved slowly, but without stopping and smelled of sour milk.

Graham Anderson's prognosis following the stroke was surprisingly good. His speech was impaired, he'd lost the use of the left side of his body, but the doctors said with the correct therapy he could regain a lot of movement, and even his speech. And his prostate cancer was treatable. Oonagh had been terrified his body was so eaten up with cancer that he'd croak before the trial. No-one asked about the bruises on his face.

Oonagh struggled to find any sympathy for Graham Anderson. 'Life can turn on a sixpence, Oonagh.' That was what her dad used to tell her: 'a sixpence'. Her dad had died at sixty from a stroke. He'd lingered for the best part of a month. No one had given them the glimmer of hope that this shitty bastard was getting.

Oonagh's own prognosis was decidedly better. No stroke, no signs of epilepsy, no indications of anything more sinister. Nothing at all in fact. It was put down to the panic attacks; she'd told no one about topping up her prescription with drugs from the online pharmacy. At first when she'd been given the all-clear the relief had engulfed her and she had sobbed with gratitude. Then she'd burned with shame imagining everyone could see into her soul and know that her condition was self-inflicted.

'You ready, Dorothy?' Tom had already briefed Dorothy that her brother might look different on account of the stroke.

As they got out of the lift a nurse squeezed past them, coat on, rucksack over his shoulder, that look of contented relief that his shift had ended. Dorothy smiled and waved, the way a child would. Despite the look of exhaustion, he waved back and smiled as the doors closed. A uniformed officer walked towards them from the direction of the coffee machine, wiping his mouth with the back of his hand. He was still chewing. As soon as Dorothy saw him she cowered.

'Come on, Dorothy, you're OK.' Oonagh gestured to the plod. 'Is it OK if...?'

He nodded. Mortified at being caught off guard, but Graham Anderson was going nowhere. Despite his condition Alec had insisted on a police guard.

Tom pushed through the double doors leading to the corridor, they heard the mayhem before they could see it and the uniformed cop shoved them aside as he broke into a run.

A cacophony of voices and screams came from the single ward, a team of doctors and nurses yelling instructions, panic rising in their tone. The policeman ran then stopped dead at the door, 'Fuck me.' He turned and herded Oonagh, Tom and Dorothy against the wall as a crash team wheeled the bed past them at speed. Tom wrapped his arm around Dorothy, holding her head close to hide her view, but Oonagh caught a glimpse of Graham Anderson on the blood soaked bed and the sight of his mutilated face. From the sounds of it he was still alive. Gurgling, choking noises could be heard above the panic. Then they were gone.

A young nurse ushered them all into a family room, she was visibly shaking as she sat them down, her chin trembled as she offered them tea and assured them someone would speak to them soon. Oonagh held Dorothy's hand and prayed this was another image she would be able to blot from her mind. Dorothy reached out with her free hand and Oonagh flinched slightly as Dorothy tucked a strand of her hair behind her ear.

'It's ok silly, I won't hurt you.'

Oonagh nodded. Her nerves were shot to hell. She hated feeling scared all the time and needed a drink.

'He was a bad man,'

Oonagh nodded, she didn't know how much Dorothy knew of Graham's involvement, she looked to Tom, he held out his palms. He was as much in the dark as she was.

'Even when we were little he was bad.' Dorothy toyed with her new watch, rolled it around on her wrist. 'Mummy got me a kitten once. Graham used to hold it under water to see how long it could hold its breath for.' Her lip trembled, 'Said he'd do the same to me if I told.'

'Bastard.' Oonagh was glad she'd punched him in the face.

'He used to visit me you know. I told him about the bad men. The ones that didn't like the noisy ones. He didn't care.'

The door opened, a doctor eased her way into the room, carefully closing the door with both hands. She touched Dorothy's shoulder, said her name quietly, and sat down to break the news. It took all of her bedside manner to tell Dorothy that someone had sliced off her brother's tongue and stuffed it back into his mouth. Oonagh could hear the young cop in the corridor pleading his case, '*I was only gone a minute. I only grabbed a coffee.*'

The team had managed to stabilise Mr Anderson, but he was critical. He'd been choking on his own blood and they had to perform an emergency tracheotomy. It was only when the doctor confirmed that yes he was in a lot of pain and suffering from severe shock, that Oonagh allowed herself the briefest of smiles.

<u>59</u>

Glasgow 2002

Late April brought an unexpected stream of sunny days. Oonagh shrugged her jacket from her shoulders and stretched her arms, enjoying the heat on her back. The waiter placed the coffee on the table as Alec sat down opposite her.

'Can't believe we're sitting outside. Feels like summer eh?'

'When have you ever known summer in Glasgow to be this warm?'

She noticed the tan line around his hairline. 'You had a haircut?'

He rubbed his hand across his head. 'Yeah, is it crap?'

She laughed. 'No, it's nice. Very dapper.' He looked a bit embarrassed that she'd noticed. 'Say something nice about me now!'

'Oonagh, you're terrible.'

'Is that the nicest thing you can think of? Bloody hell, I must be losing my touch.'

He smiled as he sipped his coffee, leaving a foam moustache across his top lip. Oonagh instinctively leaned across and wiped it off with her thumb. 'Oh, God, I'm sorry. You must think I'm like your mother doing that.'

He raised an eyebrow. 'No, believe me, the last thing I was thinking at that moment was that you were like my mother.'

She stirred her coffee and moved the ashtray onto the table opposite.

'Have you really given up?'

'Twenty-six days, four hours and—' she glanced at her watch '—twenty-three minutes.'

'I'm impressed.'

'So what happens now?' She needed to steer the conversation away from smoking.

'With regards to?'

'Alec!'

He softened slightly, relaxed back into his chair. 'Well, as soon as Graham Anderson is well enough we'll charge him with Janet Channing's murder.' They both knew that could take a long time and he could well croak it before any formal charges were made. Oonagh tried to shake off the guilty pleasure that at least he'd live long enough to experience some of the pain and torment he inflicted on others.

'Has he managed to say who attacked him?'

Alec shook his head. 'Nightmare. We're going through CCTV, everything, but it's just a blank. He's under twenty-four-hour guard.' He caught him looking at her. 'A proper guard this time.'

Oonagh felt a pang of sympathy for the officer who'd nipped off for a fly coffee and left Graham Anderson alone. She imagined Alec had had him shipped off to some godforsaken outpost cleaning toilets with a toothbrush for the next year.

'What about the bigger picture?' She was talking about Robbie Malloy, she was talking about Mark Muirhead, she was talking about the whole sorry mess and everyone who'd suffered at the hands of those who were meant to save them.

'Oonagh. It's not a simple cut and dried case.'

'No one will ever be put away for any of this really, will they?' She knew the answer before she even posed the question.

Alec sucked a breath in through his teeth. 'Well, the Raphael killings, that case is closed.' He offered it as a crumb of comfort.

Threadgold had already been buried with the full honours reserved for a serving police officer. Official line was that he was cleaning his gun, nothing more than a tragic accident. Oonagh hadn't gone to the funeral, but, given his status, parts of it had been televised and she'd seen his widow walk the steps of the cathedral with obvious pride at her dead husband's achievements. Alec seemed to read her mind.

'Threadgold did the decent thing in the end.'

Oonagh raised an eyebrow.

'For what it's worth, I genuinely believe he knew nothing about Robbie's drowning. He thought Dorothy did it.'

Oonagh wasn't convinced. 'So what about Marjory Channing?'

'Oonagh, I told you, I'll do whatever it takes to find out if her post-mortem results were doctored. But she's been cremated – what the hell can we do now?'

'I just can't believe it, Alec. I just can't believe the criminal activities of, of...' She struggled to find the words. There had been so many lives ruined, so many poor people living every day with this legacy of tainted blood, yet not one person had ever been brought to justice.

'Your lot can do more about this than we can.'

'Yip, I'll make a programme, people will be shocked, then they'll switch over and be shocked by something else. That's how it works.'

She felt like throwing the towel in. Buggering off somewhere and making a fresh start. Alec cut through her thoughts. 'Life's not fair, Oon. That's just how it goes sometimes.'

She was surprised to feel tears welling up in her eyes and, despite the sun on her back, she shivered. 'Dorothy

Malloy will probably die in an old folk's home, Alec.'

He nodded but couldn't meet her gaze. She'd served her time, but Dorothy would never have the luxury of a normal life afforded to other people.

'She's the only one who's faced justice.'

He let out a sigh. 'C'mon, why don't we go get plastered?'

'That's it? That's your answer?'

'You've done your best, Oonagh, now it's time to move on.'

He stood over her and reached for her hand to help her up. 'So, you seeing anyone, Oons?'

She shook her head. 'I thought I wanted a boyfriend, but managed to work out how to set the timer on the central heating myself so thought, naaah.'

He laughed out loud. She bounced the question back at him.

'Hardly, who'd have me?'

Clearly a rhetorical question but she couldn't resist. 'I know; especially with that bloody haircut!'

'So, where d'you fancy?'

She thought for a moment. 'You choose.' They walked down Byres Road with the sun on their backs. She caught Alec eyeing his reflection in the shop windows. Maybe her mum was right, maybe she could do worse.

Epilogue

There was an angry sky as he arranged the flowers, taking the faded ones from their holder and putting them in a poly bag to discard later. St Kentigern's was set on top of a hill, the Western Necropolis to its left, with Possil Marsh to the right. In the distance beyond the city boundaries the Campsie Fells were just visible through the smirring rain. They'd spent many happy days there as a family. It was their special place. Sometimes Louise would stay at home, allowing them their *boys'* day out. Then jokingly chastise them for not wanting their tea when they came home, stuffed from the fish supper he'd buy them at the café on the corner.

He breathed deeply, allowed his lungs to expand. The air felt cold and clean with none of the grime from the streets below.

The grass had been freshly cut that morning by the looks of it, and he dropped a cushion down to save his knees as he took out a trowel from his rucksack to tend the small area of earth around the headstone. The weekly ritual kept everything neat and tidy. The headstone was clean, but habit forced him to dampen the cloth with the bottle of water from the car and gently wipe away any dust that had settled in the engraving:

Tread softly as you pass by here... for underneath our boy lies sleeping.

The last twenty-three years had done little to dull the pain. The morning Michael died still burned red hot in his chest. His Mikey, his brave boy. Just six years old. They'd fought tooth and nail to have him buried. The hospital had pushed for cremation, said it was policy with HIV patients, but he'd dug his heels in. Louise was gone now too. Cancer was a bastard.

He checked his watch, for time had no meaning here and he often found an hour or two could pass in just moments. He was due back on shift shortly; night shifts were a killer for most, but for him they blotted out the days and afforded him the luxury of not having to communicate too much with others.

The lights were in his favour for much of the short journey, and he drew into the car park a good fifteen minutes earlier than usual; he might even have time to grab a coffee in the staff room first. The heavy weight on his chest felt slightly lighter this evening. Perhaps tonight would be a good night.

He nodded a few pleasantries to the others, who were only too glad to see him, desperate to get home. As usual the handover was quick. After a ten-hour shift most of the staff were on the brink of exhaustion, especially here. Especially in ITU.

He paused at the door of the single ward, pulling on the blue, plastic apron and protective gloves before stepping inside.

The patient's eyes widened as the charge nurse approached the bed. Tried to call out but the tube from his neck swallowed any sound, impotent limbs jerked and twitched, but he was going nowhere. He leaned over the bed and grabbed his face. 'Shh, come on, calm down,' then forced open his mouth to check his handiwork. 'Not bad.' The wound had been cauterised; the short stump of what was left of Graham Anderson's tongue was swollen and bruised. 'Not bad at all.'

The door opened and the uniformed copper on guard popped his head round. 'Fancy a coffee, Frank?'

'Lovely stuff.'

'He all right?' He tipped his head at the bed where Graham Anderson lay wild-eyed, paralysed limbs trembling.

'Och, he's fine. Hard to kill a bad thing, eh?'

The young cop laughed as he closed the door and Frank sat down, rested his back against the chair. Graham Anderson didn't take his eyes off him. The room was warm with only the soothing beep from the heart monitor to break the silence. He relaxed and crossed his arms, his tattoo visible through the thick curly hair on his arms. The fox looked as though it was smiling.

Acknowledgements

Oh where to start! As always, I owe a massive thanks and big hugs to a whole team of people who helped make this happen. Everyone at Aria publishing, especially Lucy Gilmour, Sue & Melanie. Their hard work, attention to detail and all round loveliness are a joy.

My fabulous agent Nicola Barr, who works tirelessly in the background.

My every growing family, especially my niece and brain-twin Toria Law who allowed me to use her name – and quirks – in this book. Follow your dream Toria – to the grave!

Early readers, William George & Brian Hannan who laughed and cried at all the right places. Also, fellow crime writers Douglas Skelton and Michael Malone; they're bloody fussy eaters but they mean well! A special thanks to Chief Superintendent Stewart Carle from Police Scotland, who I'm sure rolled his eyes at my constant questions, but never let on.

Two fellow writers really pulled out the stops for me; Shari Lowe, whose generosity of spirit never ceases to amaze me, and Denzil Meryick who pushed me in the right direction.

Johnny Green, hairdresser extraordinaire – he comes out with some cracking one-liners and lets me use them.

It's hard to find the right words for someone who has brought such meaning into my life but I'll try. Dr Jeremy Fellick, AKA, *Bloke With Beard* – who is patient, makes great porridge and manages to cope with being woken at 3am with such questions like, 'how does brain cooling *actually* work?' and 'how tall *is* tall?' Jez you keep me calm without quelling the craziness. Thank you, Sweetheart.

Dr Margaret Balsitis, for her help with post mortem proceedures.

A shout out to every reader, blogger and reviewer who breathes life into characters and give writers a reason to go.

My biggest thanks is saved for Bruce Norval, without him I doubt this book would ever have been written. His courage and candour is humbling to say the least. Bruce and the many thousands affected by the Tainted Blood Scandal do not need our prayers or sympathies, they need justice.

Author's Notes

In the 1970s and 80s, almost five thousand haemophiliacs in the U.K were given Factor VIII – a new blood-clotting product contaminated with HIV, Hepatitis or both. Thousands more people became infected after routine blood transfusions in what Lord Robert Winston described as '...the worse treatment disaster in the history of the NHS.'

Much of the blood-product had been imported from the U.S. which used 'skid-row donors' – namely prisoners, drug addicts and sex-workers – all from high risk groups who were paid for each donation. The vast profits to be made seemed to incite manufacturers to seek out donors from the most dubious sources. One Canadian drug company has since admitted importing blood from cadavers in the Soviet Block, and re-labelling it as coming from Scandinavian donors. This was a multi-million dollar industry for both the drug companies and the prison authorities alike.

The dangers of contaminated blood-products had been apparent from very early on. In 1975 *World In Action*[1] screened 'Blood Money', a documentary which showed that there had been an *'unprecedented outbreak of hepatitis among Haemophiliacs'* – an outbreak which one consultant linked to a blood-clotting product.[2]

Donor screening, HIV testing and heat treatment had been recommended by scientists worldwide; despite this, precautions were not adopted quickly enough, and tragically many doctors unwittingly administered the contaminated product believing it to be safe. Others simply used up the 'old batch' of Factor VIII on the shelf before ordering a new consignment – one that would more likely have undergone a more rigorous screening process.

British victims and their families have campaigned for decades for answers – demanding to know how such a catastrophic failure could have gone unchecked for so long. Incredibly there have been no criminal prosecutions, unlike in France, where two senior officials were jailed when more than thirty doctors, blood centre officials and ministers were prosecuted for criminal offences.

People have died, lives ruined, families torn apart. Victims were offered ex gratia payments if they signed a waiver agreeing to drop any further claims. Many had no choice but to accept the money – their crippling illness had left them unable to work.

As a journalist I had of course heard of the 'tainted blood scandal', but like many, regarded it as a tragic consequence of a new breakthrough treatment. I believed the arguments that suggested most haemophiliacs would have died without the treatment, so at least Factor VIII had given them a fighting chance. Sadly it was killing them; those with the power to stop it did nothing. Instead they sat back and put profit before lives.

Keep Her Silent is set in 2002, before the Penrose Inquiry – ordered by the Scottish Government – published its findings in 2015. The much awaited report which failed to apportion blame was dismissed by campaigners as a whitewash. In July 2017 the Prime Minister Theresa May announced that there would be a full U.K inquiry into the scandal. At time of writing, seventy more people have died from infection since she made her announcement... but now almost one year on, the Inquiry has still not started and there are still no Terms of Reference.

The characters in Keep Her Silent are fictional - but based upon interviews with those who have had their lives ruined by contaminated blood. One person in particular put his trust in me, and I hope that through this work of fiction I can tell at least part of his story. Thank you Bruce.

---

[1] World In Action was a current affairs programmed made by Granada Television.

[2] Dr John Craske, a consultant virologist spoke on the programme, a transcript of which was used as part of the evidence submitted to The Penrose Inquiry.

HELLO FROM ARIA

We hope you enjoyed this book! Let us know, we'd love to hear from you.

We are Aria, a dynamic digital-first fiction imprint from award-winning independent publishers Head of Zeus. At heart, we're avid readers committed to publishing exactly the kind of books we love to read — from romance and sagas to crime, thrillers and historical adventures. Visit us online and discover a community of like-minded fiction fans!

We're also on the look out for tomorrow's superstar authors. So, if you're a budding writer looking for a publisher, we'd love to hear from you. You can submit your book online at ariafiction.com/we-want-read-your-book

You can find us at:
Email: aria@headofzeus.com
Website: www.ariafiction.com
Submissions: www.ariafiction.com/we-want-read-your-book
Facebook: @ariafiction
Twitter: @Aria_Fiction
Instagram: @ariafiction

954180R00242

Printed in Poland
by Amazon Fulfillment
Poland Sp. z o.o., Wrocław